A DEADLY SEVEN NOVEL

LUST

LANA PECHERCZYK

Prism Press, Perth Australia.
Copyright © 2020 Lana Pecherczyk
All rights reserved.
ISBN: 978-0-6454994-3-8

Text copyright © Lana Pecherczyk 2020
Cover design © Lana Pecherczyk 2022
Editor: Ann Harth

www.lanapecherczyk.com

CARDINAL CITY MAP

← - - - - - -
MISHA'S HOUSE

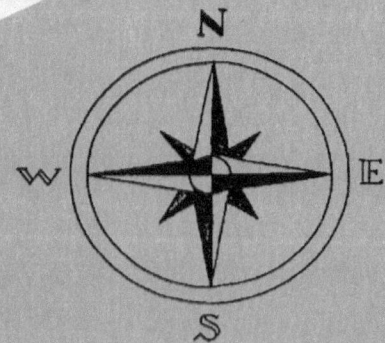

AIRPORT

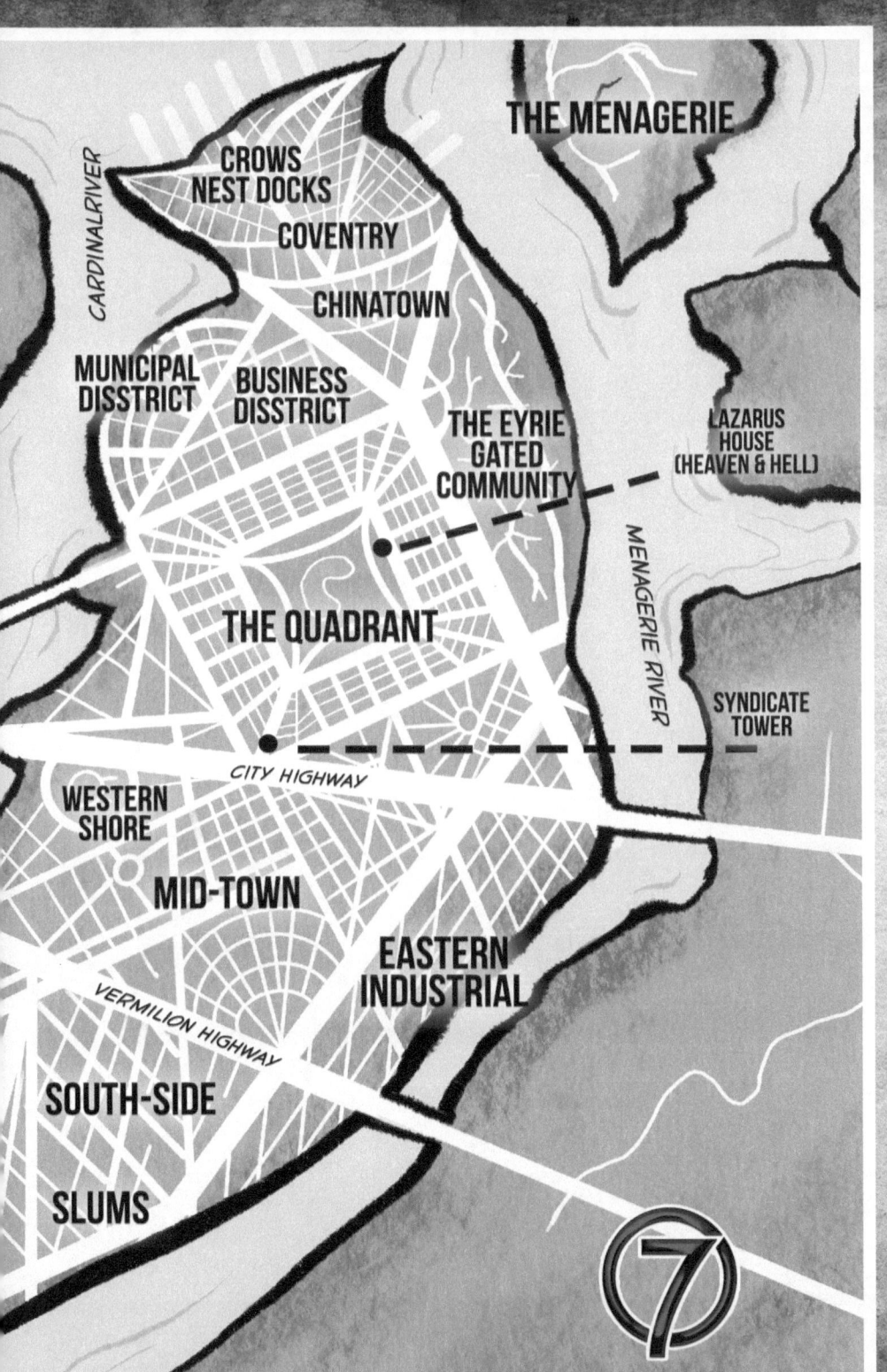

"Lust rushes
But love waits"

—BRIDGETT DEVOUE

THIS WAS GOING to be torture.

Liza Lazarus stood outside Ringo's Bar, hugging her brown leather jacket against the cold Cardinal City afternoon, wishing she could just go home.

This will be fun, they'd said.

You work too much, they'd said.

"They can all shove it up their wazoos," Liza mumbled to herself. This was not her idea of fun, but to admit it would be to admit weakness. Admitting weakness of any kind, anywhere, made her vulnerable. In this case, it was the threat of a crowd of drunken fools, which sounded innocent enough, but being distracted by a pretty man could get her killed. She had to put on an impenetrable front. Never show weakness. Somehow, Liza didn't think the *onna-bugeisha* who'd trained her in the Art of War had this sweaty bar in mind when dispensing that piece of advice.

Condensation trickled down the glass door in rivulets. A knot formed in Liza's lower belly, signaling the sin of lust emanating from slobbering and desperate patrons as they prowled for potential sexual partners.

"Let's get this over with," she growled and yanked open the door.

The bell dinged overhead, announcing her entry. Conversation, heat, and the sour smell of spilled beer assaulted her senses. She forced a breath. To anyone else, she took stock of the room, maybe searched for friends, but her gut roiled in turmoil. The closer she was to lust, the stronger the pain and sickness. The deadlier the lust, the more pain.

Sin.

Everywhere.

Oozing from that jock-type as he took a swig of beer and leered at the strawberry blond with big tits at the end of the long wooden bar. Lust hemorrhaging from the beefcake as he rubbed against a curvy woman whilst on his way to the bar. Lust bouncing off three businessmen, ties loosened, Rolex watches glistening, as they ogled Liza with predatory intent.

She casually opened her jacket and placed her hand on the CCPD badge still clipped to her belt. It glinted under the halogen lights. The same lights revealed sweat-stained armpits on one man, shiny scalp showing through the balding hair on the second, and remarkable cheekbones on the third. The businessmen resumed their conversation, avoiding Liza's direction. She relaxed. Being a detective had its perks.

She stroked her badge fondly and shouldered her way through the eddying crowd, at least a hundred thick. It didn't seem like the kind of place her family would gather for drinks, so she assumed a less claustrophobic area was somewhere. True to her assumption, she found a beer garden where the crowd had thinned dramatically. Gas patio heaters kept the area warm. Less crowd meant less sin to sense.

Decades of combat training snapped to attention when she spotted the most dangerous people in the room—her siblings.

Dark and foreboding, Wyatt, Tony, and Griffin crowded into a booth near the entrance. A burst of feminine laughter drew Liza's attention to where her brothers' life-mates sat in another booth at the back of the room near the jukebox. She shifted her attention to the brooding men. All three were tall, built, and held a grace that may have seemed casual, but sent alarm licking up her spine. They weren't three men lounging in a booth, they were three panthers lying in wait for the next poor unsuspecting buffoon to make a wrong move. Wyatt glared at anything coming through the door. Griffin sat tall and alert, watching the rear exit. Tony hid behind a baseball cap, but already noticed Liza's entrance and tipped his chiseled jaw her way.

She approached and raised a brow.

"You all in the doghouse again?" She smirked, knowing full well why they were separated from their women.

Wyatt's jaw flexed stubbornly. He glanced in the direction of the women, and then took another sip of his artisan draft. Right. *He's being an overprotective dickwad, then.* His mate was heavily pregnant, and they were all understandably nervous. Misha had lost her mother during childbirth, and if the Syndicate ever discovered the bun in her oven, they'd do everything in their power to get their hands on the genetically special baby. As reformed lab-rats themselves, each Lazarus sibling would give their life before allowing that.

But Misha couldn't live cooped up. She was an independent woman.

Liza turned her gaze to Tony. His baseball cap was a disguise to hide his celebrity, but his handsome mug was still well known. She would bet he'd already been approached for selfies with fans. Good thing his mate was ex-CIA. Bailey obsessively watched him from the back booth as much as he watched her.

The only one with any restraint was Griffin, who adjusted the fake black-rimmed spectacles on his nose and nodded in greeting.

"They're a few booths that way." He pointed to where Liza had already seen them. "And we're not in the doghouse. We're just giving them some space. They want a girl's night."

"Right," Liza scoffed. "So where's the rest of the Scooby gang?"

Tony flashed his Hollywood smile. "I'm Fred in this analogy."

"I got dibs on Daphne." She waved down her toned and curvy body.

"Ew," Tony grimaced. "But we're siblings. Everyone knows Daphne has the hots for Fred."

"No, Fred has the hots for Daphne. So that's you being gross."

Wyatt sighed heavily. "You're both dickheads."

He flagged down a server and ordered a double serving of fries.

Both Tony and Liza pointed at Wyatt. "Shaggy!"

Griffin frowned with his best death stare. "You shouldn't draw so much attention. We're supposed to be keeping a low profile."

"The music is loud enough," Tony said. "No one can hear us, anyway. And if they did, they'd just think we had excellent pop culture taste. Who doesn't love Scooby-Doo? Besides, we've marked our escape routes. Relax, Velma."

He tossed a soggy beer-coaster at Griffin.

Tony locked eyes with Liza and they burst out in hysterics. Velma. Perfect! She dashed tears of laughter away, realizing the sense of lust had dimmed enough that she felt more at ease.

"So, the others?" Liza asked.

"Evan's closing up at Deadly Ink. Grace is in surgery. Parker is working. Max and Sloan are finishing their wedding preparations. They have a meeting with a priest," Griffin replied.

Tony simpered. "I'm ready to party, but these turd-burgers won't let me leave the booth."

"The girls wanted a night out with Liza," Griffin reminded them. "And since Wyatt doesn't want Misha out without powered protection, we're here keeping a respectful but close distance. That is all."

Ouch. It was unlikely Liza would ever manifest her powers.

She let Griffin's words simmer a little, but the more they stewed, the more bitter she became. Each of the Lazarus siblings was genetically modified to sense sin, but without a mate to balance them out, they were in danger of having too much, or too little, sin in their bodies. An imbalance caused blackouts and berserker sin-chasing rages. That's why their special abilities didn't manifest until they met a partner who embodied their sin's opposing virtue. And that's why Liza was royally screwed ten times until Sunday. She was yet to meet someone who embodied chastity at the same time as having a healthy sex life. It just wasn't possible. Her balanced mate was probably a priest, or worse, someone who didn't feel lust at all!

She'd given up on love a long time ago.

Still, *powered protection*? No need to rub it in. Liza was a detective and had seven years of training in the Art of War from masters around the world—including Akari, the deadliest female samurai alive.

Liza wasn't the only strong woman at the table. Bailey worked at Nightingale Securities, the firm on retainer as bodyguards for the partners of the Lazarus brood. Not all three "powered protectors" needed to be there, but Liza did not understand what it felt like to be in love, let alone mated to someone who not only dimmed the sense of sin within but unleashed her full, dark, and dangerous potential. If she had a mate, she might be obsessively protective too, and after the Syndicate kept throwing things like plant monsters their way, who knew how she'd feel?

Thinking about the plant-monster brought Liza's mind to her ex-partner, Joey Luciano. He'd been the lead FBI agent on the task force investigating the mutated monster's aftermath. National law enforcement now knew that something wasn't quite right in Cardinal City. Their leads had gone cold, but Liza knew Joey. He wasn't one to give up so easily.

That's why it cut deep when he'd left Cardinal City for no reason or explanation. Twice. The first time was years ago when they'd worked together as detectives. One minute, he'd worked alongside her at the CCPD. The next, he was recruited into the FBI and never looked back. But that was almost half a decade ago. He'd also left town suddenly two months ago after their investigation on the disturbance at the zoo closed. She pursed her lips. It was common for an FBI agent to shift around the country. She should stop stewing over it.

Wyatt said something.

"Sorry, what?" she asked, angling in to hear over another burst of laughter from revelers.

He jerked his head toward the girls. "I said, they just want you to get laid so they don't feel so guilty. So—" He shooed her toward the girls' booth. "If you could just hurry and pick up some poor fuck, then we can all go home."

The air left Liza's lungs, and a crushing weight replaced it. None of her family knew how pitiful her love life truly was. She kept plenty of things a secret from them. The truth was, that although her love life used to be the stuff of legend, the intensity of her sin-sensing had grown over the past few years. She used to ignore the sickness, but not anymore. Her skin crawled at the possibility of sex now. For the sake of her sanity, her dry spell had turned into the new normal.

But if they'd all been talking about her, they'd have gossiped about Parker too. No wonder he wasn't there. As one of the only two unmated Lazarus siblings without powers, the prideful son-of-a-bitch would eat his own shit before admitting he was at a disadvantage.

That wasn't what sent hot, prickly rage coursing through her veins.

They all pitied her.

She narrowed her eyes at Wyatt. She didn't give a shit if her fist would break against his skin. "You're cruisin' for a bruisin', brother."

Before he could engage, a feminine shout from across the room caught Liza's attention. Misha's blond ringlets bounced, and while the heavily pregnant woman couldn't get out of her seat, she waved emphatically at Liza. Damn her and her perpetual Polish sunniness.

Liza shot her brothers a dirty look and ruffled Griffin's perfectly styled hair before she swaggered to the girls' booth.

Misha's warm smile brought a blush to her freckled cheeks. Lilo sat next to her, and Bailey sat on the opposite bench alone. Eight shot glasses were lined up on the table. Only six looked like alcohol. The last two were probably Kool-Aid.

"What's up, ladies?" Liza said casually, trying not to think about Wyatt's comments, but she swore to God, if one of these women mentioned Liza's recent love-life slump, she'd have to do something drastic to keep them off her case. The last thing she wanted was to be the sole focus of a pity parade.

"These all for me?" she joked, pointing at the drinks.

"Well, mostly," Lilo laughed, then burped softly. "I've had a few already. And to be honest, I probably shouldn't have any more."

Lilo was Griffin's wife. She worked at the Cardinal Copy News Network. This made her the Deadly Seven's eyes, ears, and finger on the pulse of the city's news. With wavy brown hair, the mixed Polynesian-Italian heritage woman looked like she'd just stepped out of a wind-blown tunnel. But perhaps the blush in her cheeks was from the two empty cocktail glasses.

Bailey's outfit was unassuming, a black jacket and white shirt, but

Liza would bet Bailey was carrying a concealed firearm, ready for the first sign of trouble.

So, a pregnant woman, a half-hammered news reporter, and a security agent pretending to be off duty… all so Liza could get laid. Bitterness swarmed in her stomach before a hit of resignation made her go cold.

They had good intentions, but maybe she should have kept up the charade of an active love-life for longer. This was going to be a long night if Liza didn't make it easy for them. She shot back two tequilas, steeled herself, and then slid onto the bench seat next to Bailey.

"Nos-fucking-trovia, right?" she said to Misha. "Did I say that right?"

Misha laughed. "Yeah, except the f-word part."

"That part was my favorite," Lilo exclaimed.

Liza high-fived her across the table.

"Right," Liza added. "So who have you picked out for me?"

"Um," Misha giggled. "What do you mean?"

They all looked nervously at each other.

"I mean," Liza continued. "You think we're here to find me a date, right? So who have you picked out?"

Lilo blinked. "No one."

Bailey held up her finger. "Yet."

Liza slammed her palm on the table with a smirk. "I knew it. All right, then, let me save you some trouble."

She shrugged off her scarf and jacket, popped the buttons on her blouse until her lace-covered cleavage showed, and then stowed her CCPD badge inside her jeans pocket. Her city-issued firearm was back at the precinct, so there was nothing else on her that identified her as a detective. She pulled the tie out of her long brown hair, fluffed the length, and swept a predatory glance across the room.

Within seconds she zeroed in on the tall, handsome businessman who'd been eyeing her when she'd entered. He'd inched his way closer and was now near the entrance to the beer garden. Blond hair, aristocratic nose, square jaw. He looked like he loved his mirror and talked about seizing the day. Baby blue eyes watched her like he imagined her naked.

Huh. So her badge hadn't scared him off. He might be a holster sniffer. Some dudes loved a confident woman with a badge. Good. This made it all the easier. Liza slid out of the booth.

"Where are you going?" Bailey asked.

Without taking her eyes from Baby Blue, she replied, "I'm going to ask the hottest guy in the room if he wants to buy me a drink."

Bailey snorted. "That would be your brother, and gross."

"You mean Wyatt," Misha corrected.

Lilo laughed and sent her husband a fond smile. "Clearly, you're both wrong."

Liza rolled her eyes. "You ladies are all whipped. Watch and learn."

Resigned to the task, she felt herself remove a little from her body, and strode into the front room with a forced sashay in her step. Lust intensified the closer she got. She'd picked the right mark.

Her lips curved on one side and she gave the man an approving once-over. Unlike his two friends, he filled out that suit like he benched weight. Screw the drink.

"Alley or bathroom," she said to him.

He blinked. "I'm sorry?"

His friends shared a confused, but earnest look. She checked them out, dismissed them, and returned to Baby Blue. His fingers clenched tight around his beer. Lust virtually climbed out of him and down her throat.

She widened her smile. "I assumed since you were eye-fucking me across the room, you wanted a private moment. So where do you want to do this? The bathroom, or the back alley?"

Another gobsmacked blink.

For Christ's sake. She took his drink from his fingers, handed it to his friend, and then curled her fingers around the back of his neck. Nice. Warm. Sweat-free. She brought his mouth down to hers and licked along his bottom lip until he opened and then she gave him the French kiss of his life. When she was sure all the blood from his brain had turned south, she licked his earlobe and whispered huskily, "Alley or bathroom."

"Alley," he croaked.

Perfect. The path to the back door would take her right by her nosey family and she could collect her jacket and scarf. It was cold outside. She licked her lips, shot him a grin full of sensual promises, and then hooked his finger into her back pocket before walking away.

Since the weight of his finger stayed there, she knew he'd taken the hint.

She passed her brothers, gave them a mock salute, collected her items, and then stage whispered to the girls, "Don't wait up."

The last thing Liza heard before leaving through the back exit was Misha's loud congratulatory whoop.

THE ALLEY WAS COLD, dank, and disgusting. The small buzz Liza received from expensive male aftershave dulled when it mingled with the smell of garbage and urine, but she needed to do this. It wasn't just for show. She needed to prove she wasn't pitiful. That she could take a man and screw his brains out whenever, and wherever she wanted. That she wasn't faulty. That she had options.

She checked the alley exits. Down one side was nothing but overflowing dumpsters and a dead-end. Down the other, a busy city street. The sun hid behind an overcast sky and dimmed with the looming night. Anyone walking down their little corner of hell would see them. Liza focused on the thrill skipping up her spine, not the queasiness in her gut.

No problems.

She zeroed in on a space between two dumpsters. Perfect.

"There." She pointed.

"But it's broad daylight," he sputtered.

Stupid man. He was the one who suggested coming out here instead of the bathroom.

"That a problem?"

His eyes flared. "Nope. I just thought…"

She unearthed her CCPD badge and clipped it to the gaping middle of her blouse so her bra showed. "If anyone asks, I got it covered."

And just like that, his lust flared. *Holster sniffer.*

Liza swallowed down the tequila rising in her gullet. Her head swirled, and her eyes fluttered with her attempt to keep control. Blue Eyes took her hips.

"God, that's so hot." He licked his lips. "Fuck, *you're* so hot. You going to arrest me, baby?"

"This works better the less you talk." She urged him to their spot and dumped her jacket and scarf. She rested against the grimy brick wall, and then yanked at his trousers, trying to work his fly with trembling, stiff fingers. "We doing this?"

He nodded. "Fuck, yeah. I mean. Yeah. We're doing."

She unzipped him, quirked a brow at his package, and then met his gaze. "It will do."

He blinked for a moment. Probably used to ladies drooling over it. Or himself in the mirror.

Taking a deep breath of stale air into her lungs, Liza swallowed more nausea and readied herself. The lust was about to get worse.

She dipped her hand into his pants, wrapped her fingers around his arousal, and started jerking him off. His groans of pleasure echoed against the brick wall. He dropped his face to the valley between her breasts, nuzzled around the badge as he licked and kissed the flesh. A desperate mumble of disbelief punctuated his every move.

"I can't believe I'm doing this," he said into her chest. "I can't believe I'm touching your sweet tits." Kissing. More licking. More grinding. "Can't believe I'm about to fuck a cop."

"Detective."

"Right. Detective."

He pawed her bottom and murmured more exaltations.

Liza was going to puke just from his words. She grabbed his hair, yanked his head up so he faced her.

"Shut up," she demanded.

He nodded. "Whatever you say."

"You're still talking."

Alright. I can do this.

He pushed down the cup of her lace bra and then that mouth fell blessedly silent because it busied itself on her breast. It should have felt good. But his lust flared brighter, dug deeper. Her grip on him tightened. He ground into her and that sick sensation curdled in her gut.

She tasted tequila, shoved him away, and vomited on the pavement before she realized what had happened.

"What the fuck?" the man gasped. "Are you... are you okay?"

This isn't going to work.

"Go," Liza said, then retched again.

"Should I call someone?"

Wrong thing to say.

She shot him daggers. He zipped his fly and backed away. He mumbled insanities and then must have left because, when Liza hurled another mouthful of tequila, the only sound was misery pounding in her ears.

Tears burned her eyes.

Fuck this.

Fuck all of this.

Her throat tightened. Her chest wracked, and the undeniable urge to sob almost got out, but she pushed it down. Deep. Not today. Not ever, would she feel sorry for herself. She squeezed her eyes shut and reminded herself of all the good things she had in her life. Sure, she'd developed a disposition to puke every time she scored, but so what? She had an honest job where she could make a difference in the real world and not fuck about in the shadows like her siblings. She had a roof over her head. She had money. She had good looks. Health. Strength. And a family who supported her, as misguided as they were sometimes, it all came from a good place.

Daisy had none of that.

Daisy was the eldest of the Lazarus siblings, but not a Lazarus. She'd been separated from them during the escape from the Syndicate laboratory that created them thirty or so years ago. As the eldest, Daisy, or Despair as she was called back then, led the way in keeping morale positive. Liza had only been four or five yet she remembered with crystal clarity how Daisy would insist each sibling cuddled her first thing in the morning. She would even chase them about the small living quarters if they denied her.

"Lu-ust," Despair's sweet, melodious voice sang. *"Come here and give me my morning cuddle!"*

"You have to catch me first, 'Spair." Liza's four-year-old legs jumped onto a table, slipped, and toppled to the side. She screamed.

Strong childish arms caught her. "Don't worry, Lust. I'll always catch you when you fall."

Liza doubled over, grimacing. A sharp stab of pain pierced her gut. So much agony. So strong. As if... Her internal alarm sounded. It wasn't the sense of lust from inside the bar. This was different. *Deadly.*

When most people heard the word lust, they associated it with sex. But the worst kind, the most deadly kind, was the kind of lust that made you crave something so bad you would do anything to claim it.

That was the kind she sensed now.

The distinct sound of a woman's raised, tight voice sent Liza stretching beyond the shadow of the dumpster to peek. A tall man wearing an army jacket followed a skinny blond teenager into the alley. He looked about twenty or so, was decent looking enough to make him appear less threatening. The scar on his face only garnered sympathy. The words coming out of his mouth were smooth and sweet, but Liza recognized the girl's armor, the way she carried herself, her false bravado. She was a runaway.

That deadly sense of lust *pinged* in her gut, growing in intensity, and Liza knew she had to get closer to hear more. She creeped around the dumpster's wall and darted to the next, accidentally tipping over an empty bottle before sheltering herself behind the metal bin. With a wince, she hid herself and held her breath, hoping that she wasn't found.

The conversation continued, and this time, she could hear the words.

"Come on," the guy crooned. "You don't look old enough to be out on your own in this neighborhood. It's dangerous. You want me to call someone for you?"

She lifted her stubborn chin. "I'm older than you think."

"Like what, twelve?" he scoffed.

"I'm sixteen. Had my birthday last week."

"Oh yeah? I bet a pretty girl like you has lots of friends to throw you a party. Was it fun?"

Her expression dropped. "I didn't have a party."

His face turned all compassionate. "Ah, shit. I'm sorry. I shouldn't have brought it up."

She looked away, but he ducked to stay in her view.

"How about I take you somewhere warm and give you a party? I got sweets, cake, soda. Whatever you want."

Her eyes lifted, hesitant. "Cake? I ain't never had no birthday cake."

Lust flared so hard it blurred Liza's vision. Every instinct said this fucktard was a spotter for trafficking or a pimp. If that girl went with him, she'd never be free again.

Blind rage trembled through Liza. And then she blacked out.

two

LIZA LAZARUS

LIZA SURFACED FROM HER BLACKOUT, surrounded by the devastation of a hurricane. Pain flooded her hands. A woman screamed. The man in the army jacket writhed on the alley floor, clutching his groin. Blood was everywhere. She couldn't tell if it was from *there*, or the other swollen parts on his face.

The teenage girl cowered in fear, head hiding beneath her arms and hands.

Something restrained Liza's wrist. Frowning, she glanced down. A big male hand held her. She followed the hand, to the arm, to the face. Black hair and scowling blue eyes.

"Wyatt?" She yanked her hand back. "What the fuck?"

"I sensed wrath," he explained quietly, and then gave a pointed look at the man on the floor. "Good thing I came straight out, *Detective.*"

Liza's gaze ping-ponged to the man on the floor and back to Wyatt. He was saying... she did that?

Holy fuck, she'd blacked out. Her first time.

Wyatt leaned close to whisper, "You want to take it that far, perhaps it's time to finally join us dressed in your battle gear at night."

He flicked the CCPD badge still hanging from her gaping blouse.

Shit.

Fuck.

She'd blown it.

The army jacket man cursed and scrambled to his feet. He bared his bloody teeth at Liza. "You're going to pay for that, bitch."

"Yeah, tell it to someone who cares!" she shot back, despite the stutter in her pulse.

Wyatt's cell phone rang and he answered. "I'm coming back." His eyes flicked to Liza. "Nope. Nothing to worry about."

Then he cut the call and gave Liza one last glare. "You need to decide what world you're living in, Liza. You can't straddle both."

She swallowed the lump in her throat, nodded, and watched him leave. He was right. It was getting harder to pretend she was normal. This may have been her first blackout, but it wouldn't be her last. It was harder for her to stay in balance these days. She wasn't sure a quick trip to the cathedral was going to cut it, and she was out of alternative ways to keep her internal sin equilibrium in balance.

She glanced at the teenager, now quietly sobbing. But at least she wasn't screaming anymore. Liza extended her hand.

"I'm so sorry about that. He was a spotter for a sex-trafficker. If you had gone with him, you'd have been hooked on drugs, made to work as a prostitute, and would never see the light of day again." She sighed. God, she sounded like an awful callous bitch. "There was no way you could know that, though. I've been putting these assholes away for years. That's the only way I can tell. Don't... don't beat your-self up about it."

The girl's bottom lip trembled.

She needed to say something to take her mind off it, so added, "It's your birthday, right?"

The girl nodded.

"Happy birthday. It can only get better from here. What's your name?"

"Mirabelle," she mumbled.

"Nice to meet you, Mirabelle. I'm Detective Liza Lazarus. Come on. I won't hurt you. My job is to protect you. Let's take you somewhere you'll be safe. I know a good shelter that gives coupons and cake to anyone who's having a birthday."

LIZA SANK into her office chair, mentally exhausted. It wasn't the cold outside, or the journey she'd taken across town to drop Mirabelle at a domestic violence shelter, or her bloody knuckles. It was the fact the station was virtually empty, and she'd come back to it after taking the afternoon off.

She glanced around the bullpen where the detectives sat. Her "office" consisted of a small desk laden with case files. No walls separated her from her coworkers. Only one detective remained.

Briggs was a forty-something ex-patrol cop built like a linebacker. These days the muscle had turned to pudge, but he still cut an imposing figure. The rest of the dayshift had vanished early. That was the sad state of the detectives at the CCPD. No one cared to do the actual work, and the captain also skipped out early, so he failed to care to reprimand them. Only, while they'd left because they had a social life, Liza had been pretending. What was the excuse for the rest of them?

When Briggs stood, loosened his tie, and closed the drawers on his desk, Liza glanced at the clock.

Five p.m.

She wanted to punch something.

Briggs gathered his coat and hat from the rack before striding toward the door. When he passed Liza's desk, she jumped up and blocked him.

"Hey, Briggs," she greeted.

"Liza." His heavy brows drew together. "You good?"

"Yeah, I'm good, except... where is everyone?"

Briggs's eyes dropped, and he suddenly became interested in the pattern on the tiled floor. "Don't know. Knocked off early, like you, I suppose. I gotta go."

He tried to shove past, but Liza never cowered around big guys. She'd spent her life growing up around them. She sidestepped and blocked him again.

"You're keeping something from me," she said.

"Don't know what you're talking about."

"Come on, Briggs. It's me. I'll figure it out, eventually."

He stared at her.

She could sense he was about to make up an excuse, so spoke first. "This many detectives leaving early isn't right. Must either be one helluva homicide, or a special occasion."

His body language betrayed him. Sweat on the upper lip. Pupils contracting when she'd said the latter. "So it's a special occasion." She frowned as the truth dawned on her. "And if you're all going, and I know nothing about it, then I wasn't invited. What the fuck?"

He winced. "Don't take it personally, Liza."

She grabbed his tie and yanked. "What the actual fuck, Briggs?"

"Joe Luciano is back in town."

Liza's hand went lax. The tie slipped through her fingers. "What?"

Briggs sighed. "He asked us all to keep it quiet. He's back in his old place and has invited us dudes for a poker night. I'm sure he'll catch up with you soon. Look, I'm late. I gotta go. Poker night starts in an hour and like most bastards who were invited, I still need to get across town to see the wife before heading out."

She stepped aside and muttered, "Yeah, sure."

It took a full two minutes after Briggs had left before she regained her senses.

Joey Luciano, her friend since middle school, had flat out asked that she not be told about his return to Cardinal City. And if he'd moved back into his old place, then it might be for good. Had he transferred out of Violent Crimes? Hell, had he left the FBI?

Aw, fuck no.

Screw Joey. He couldn't just leave Cardinal City without a word, then come back and ignore her. They had a history. And if she'd done something wrong, she needed to know about it. Enough bad shit had happened today, she didn't need more.

It was time she had a quiet word to Joey, and she knew the exact thing to bring with her. Crossing to her desk, she opened the bottom drawer of the filing cabinet and fished around until her fingers landed on a velvety rough surface. *Bingo*.

She pulled out an old baseball covered in childish signatures, all either Liza's or Joey's. She rotated the ball in her hand, smiling. Over the years, the signatures had become less legible with their age. The ink bled into the leather. All the signatures had a line through them, except the latest: L.Lazarus, clear and unimpeded.

The first wobbly signature was made when she was twelve. She still remembered seeing the white ball rolling across the green grass and then hitting her sandal covered toes as she sat on the batters' bench. The sun had been warm, and the rough wood had given her splinters where her shorts failed to protect. She'd been relegated to the "cheer squad" by her jerk-face brothers. They'd kept saying it would

be her turn soon, but failed to call her up to bat. That's when a young Joey Luciano had waved at her from across the field.

"Hey!" he'd said. "Over here."

Liza picked up the ball and turned it in her hands, testing the weight. She looked at it with such longing. She didn't want to be sitting on the bench. She wanted to be out there, playing the game with her brothers. All of them were playing, even baby Evan who was only eight. If Sloan hadn't stayed home with Mama to cook pizza, Liza would have another girl on her side to stand up to her brothers.

Especially that jerk-face Parker. He was such a know-it-all.

Liza stood and threw the ball back to the tall, lanky boy. It sailed straight through the air and landed in his glove with a resounding smack. He'd dropped the ball almost immediately, removed his hand from the glove, and shook it out like it hurt. When his eyes had met Liza's, they'd widened.

She grinned. She liked surprising boys.

The scowl from Parker at the home plate made her sit with a pout.

It wasn't fair.

But she didn't want to cause trouble. Mama had lectured them about trying to appear normal in front of the locals. If anyone found out she was stronger than most boys, she'd get in trouble. So she stared at the ground.

The white ball rolled and hit her toes again.

This time, the boy came trotting over. They both reached for the ball at the same time and knocked heads. She got the ball first and handed it to him.

He grinned. He had a nice smile and a dimple on his chin.

"How come you don't play?" he asked, tossing and catching the ball like he was clever.

"Um. My brothers won't let me join their team."

"Oh. Well, you can join mine if you like." He puffed his chest out. "I'm the captain."

She glanced over at her family. All of them were either on the diamond in the coach's box, at the home plate, or standing behind a chain-link fence, waiting for the pitch.

"*You got a good arm,*" *the boy continued.*

"*I know,*" *she replied.*

His lips curved in a way that captured Liza's attention, and she wasn't sure why.

"*My name's Joey. What's yours?*"

"*Liza.*"

Someone shouted from the diamond. "*We gonna play, or what?*"

"*Sorry,*" *Liza murmured.* "*That's my stupid brother, Wyatt. He gets a bit angry.*"

Joey shrugged. "*My dad gets angry all the time. Angry doesn't scare me. So, you wanna play?*"

Joey's childhood voice echoed in her memory and she smiled. She'd played on his neighborhood baseball team the entire summer. Her younger brothers hadn't cared, but the older ones? They'd been mad as hell about her betrayal. But Liza knew they wouldn't tattle on her. Mama would just put them in their place and say a girl could do whatever a boy could do... as long as they were being careful with their strength.

And Liza did. She'd become the team's official pitcher, despite the game being heavily male-orientated. The sad part was, once summer was over, baseball was too. Joey had turned up at the last game with a split lip and said he wouldn't be able to play for a while. He'd been distant and quiet, but in the end, he'd handed her the baseball and wrote her name on it.

"*If you ever need someone on your team, throw that into my yard, and no matter what, I'll come. Codename: Baseball. Right?*"

She hadn't understood what he'd meant at the time, but as the years went on, Liza had signed her name and thrown the baseball a few times. Joey had returned it too. If one of them needed help, no questions asked, the ball came out. Sometimes in lockers at school, a lunch box, or pockets. It was a secret code.

Even after Liza's years abroad, and they'd reconnected at the police academy, the baseball was still in play. That's why it still mattered now.

If Joey thought she'd forgotten all that, he had better get his affairs in order.

She put on her jacket and scarf and then was across town at Joey's apartment within thirty minutes. The super let her in with a flash of her CCPD badge, and then she made her way up three floors. She pounded on Joe's door and stood back to wait with the baseball turning in her hand.

Joey was her friend. The only person she'd ever felt at ease around. The only person she'd never sensed lust from, and that included her family. Every time a pretty girl walked past one of her brothers, she'd get a cramp. But never around Joey. She used to think he was broken, then she thought he was gay, but she knew deep down that was a lie too. She still would have sensed lust from him. But the last time she saw him, he claimed to have been in a relationship for the past two years. He was a mystery she needed to solve.

He certainly wasn't her mate, she knew that for sure.

The mating bond triggered upon touch. Liza and Joey had touched numerous times throughout their lives, so it had to be something else, or she'd have powers by now.

She pounded on his door again.

It swung open.

A tall and dripping wet FBI Special Agent scowled down at her, dimple in chin pronounced. He wore only a small white towel wrapped around his hips. A *tiny* white towel. Very narrow hips. Her eyes dragged upward over his naked torso to take in sculptured muscles, broad shoulders, and smooth Mediterranean skin she hadn't seen since the police academy locker room.

A droplet of water fell from his short, dark hair to run down his five o'clock shadow and then plopped onto one very defined pec that twitched under the weight of her attention. The dark hair on his chest had been clipped close to the skin. He manscaped.

Heat surged up her neck to hit her cheeks.

Liza blinked.

Since when had he gotten so... not like Joey?

three

JOE LUCIANO

LIZA LAZARUS WAS the last person Joe Luciano expected to see outside his apartment, but there she was, staring up at him with big, perfect eyes. The sight of her was a hit to the sternum and, for a moment, his brain stopped communicating with the rest of his body. If he'd thought the impact of her beauty and presence would dim over time, he was wrong.

"What do you want, Liza?" he growled, one hand gripping the doorknob, the other clutching the wet towel around his waist. "I'm kind of in the middle of something."

"What the hell, Joey?" Her brows slammed together. The sass that had chased him his entire life resurrected. She threw something at his chest. He caught it with one hand.

Every excuse vaporized.

Painful memories of hot summers, secret laughs, and unrequited love opened a gaping hole in his chest.

Codename: Baseball. She remembered.

Liza pushed through the door.

Dazed, he pulled the door closed so his neighbors wouldn't hear the argument he knew was coming. Then he crossed the small one-bedroom apartment, bypassed unpacked boxes, and went to the open sliding door facing the balcony. He closed that too, but remained and stared through the glass panes to the opposite building. They were three levels up, yet he felt the pull of gravity like he was falling.

His fingers trembled around the ball.

"It's not Joey anymore. It's Joe." His voice was like gravel. "I told you that the last time we saw each other."

"The last time we saw each other? I've left you gazillions of messages since then. It's been two months."

"Two months since you last insulted me."

Yeah, sure, Joe. That's why you're staying away from her. Keep telling yourself that, maybe one day it will stick.

He strode to the kitchen and placed the ball on the counter. It glared back at him, so he turned his back.

Liza's eyes seemed to soften, and Joe could have sworn guilt flashed in those whiskey caramel depths. But as usual, she brushed off his pain as though he was an afterthought. He mentally shook his head. She hadn't changed a bit.

"What insults?" she scoffed.

Every muscle in his body went rigid, and a familiar wash of pathetic capitulation urged him to ignore her until he squashed it down. Not this time. Never again.

He didn't know why he'd assumed she'd see him differently the last time they'd met. He'd spent years with the FBI, training to be... what was it her brothers had said all those years ago?

"You'll never be good enough for her."

He'd spent the past half-decade learning to match the high standards her family had set, to be *good enough*. But that was the thing. He'd never wanted to be *good enough*. He'd wanted to be *better*. And

better was a fool's dream, for the line was always shifting, and sometimes it was he who shifted it.

"What insults?" he repeated incredulously and began a slow prowl toward her doubting, beautiful face. Maybe she saw the steely determination in his eyes, or maybe his new bulkier frame dwarfed her athletic physique, but she backed up until her rear hit the wall next to the door.

Well, I'll be damned. Liza-fucking-Lazarus, the woman who made her own rules and bowed to no one, backed up. Because of him.

Maybe this was the kind of man she'd needed all along. Forget the nice guy, she wanted an alpha-asshole, just like her dickhead brothers. Learning this may have filled the old Joey with naïve hopes, but Joe Luciano, FBI Special Agent in Violent Crimes, had no fucks to give.

His lip curled as he placed a palm on the wall next to her face.

"Let me refresh your memory. One. Last. Time." He changed the tone of his voice to high-pitched, so it was clear who'd said the next words. "*What does your boyfriend think of my dress? Joey's saving himself for marriage. The only date Joey goes on is with his right hand.*" He relaxed his tone. "You want me to go on?"

She stared blankly for a moment before rallying with a sarcastic pout. "Aw. Poor baby Joey. I hurt your feelings. You want me to fetch your diary so you can write about it?"

He slammed his other palm on the wall, caging her in. She didn't startle. She never did. It was as though she lived in a constant state of awareness, that she was prepared for this kind of intimidation at every turn. Did the woman ever relax?

She gave a small laugh. "Fuck off, Joey. I was only kidding. Jeez."

"Kidding?" He leaned in until his nose was an inch from hers. "Your jokes had the entire precinct thinking I was some pansy asexual robot."

She tried to laugh it off. "You know what the guys are like there.

You have to be crude or you don't fit in, especially for a woman. Besides, it was kind of true. You never went on dates. You never felt an iota of lust for anyone, and do you know what? I accept you no matter what sexual orientation. Don't blame me for stating the truth."

His eyes narrowed. "And how, exactly, would you know what the truth is?"

She blinked. "I mean. It was clear. Obviously."

His gaze dipped to her lips, to the soft, sensual pillow of her generous mouth. How he'd dreamed of those lips. How they'd kept him company for nights on end. How they'd given him wood, just from watching her take a sip from her Starbucks coffee using a straw so her teeth wouldn't stain.

He met her gaze with a challenge on his own. "*Obviously*, you never looked down."

The air between them crackled with tension. It snapped at his skin, skittered down his stomach, and wrapped its hot little fingers around his cock. The towel tightened around his hips. And through it all, he held her gaze, daring her to look down.

For once in your fucking life, notice me, Liza.

Her lashes lowered. Stopped at his crotch. A hissed intake of breath and then—

Knock-knock-knock.

"Come on, G-Man. We're here!" someone shouted through the door. Sounded like Houlahan.

He checked the clock on the kitchen wall and cursed. They must have flashed their badges to get into the building, much like Liza probably had.

"They're early," he muttered.

And he wasn't dressed. The place wasn't ready. Unopened boxes from storage still littered the room and stacked against the wall. As usual, Liza had waltzed into his life and turned his plans upside down. He'd wanted the night with just the old boys so he could drill them for information on his new case. This would ruin everything.

He scrubbed a hand down his face and slid Liza a resigned look. "Make yourself useful for once and leave."

Her eyes were still glued to his crotch. The blood had drained from her face and it looked like she'd seen a ghost. He snapped his fingers. "Liza, I know it's impressive, but you need to go. *Capeesh?*"

"I'm not going anywhere, you turd. You can't invite half the precinct to a poker night and not me." The tremble in her voice betrayed the anger in her eyes. "So march yourself back to the shower, finish... what I obviously interrupted, and I'll set everything up."

He stifled a smile as she blustered to his kitchen. He'd ruffled her feathers. Good. Wait—what was she doing? She opened the fridge and pulled out the antipasto plate he'd purchased. Sensing his attention, her shoulders tensed. Without looking up, she said, "*Codename: Baseball.*"

Well, shit.

He had to follow the rules. If he didn't, then he was shitting all over their history, over what those simple two words had meant. And they had meant the world to a thirteen-year-old boy with a stinky arm cast who'd secretly left the signed baseball in a twelve-year-old girl's lunch box so she'd sit with him when no one else would.

With no other option, he returned to his bedroom, slid on some jeans, and slipped on a t-shirt. A quick check in the mirror saw to his hair. With it messy, he looked too much like his father, and that wouldn't do.

Joe flexed his fist, watching his fingers curl and then open, wanting to dispel the feeling of violence that always seemed beneath the surface. He'd only ever let it slip once.

"You're just like your father," his mother shouted at him in their car,

parked before his school. "You think you're so different, but you're not. You're exactly the same."

"I am nothing like him," Joe shot back, ignoring the way his heart crumbled inside. "I raised my fist in defense, not from some sick desire to dominate."

He'd started a fight, which resulted in suspension from high school. Three days was his penalty. But it was worth it. Those assholes had called Liza a slut behind her back.

His mother had only laughed as she turned the ignition on and put the car into gear. "You keep telling yourself that, Joey, but you Luciano men are all the same. Any excuse to beat someone senseless will do. Today it's a boy in the yard, but eventually, you'll bruise the people closest to you, too."

Joe cracked his knuckles, then shook his hands out.

He'd been proving his mother wrong his whole life. And he owed Liza, at least one last time before he pulled her life apart. He covered up the case files on his bed and hid them beneath the mattress. Then he covered the crime scene pictures on the wall with a large city map poster. The last thing he needed was for Liza to barge in and see what he was investigating. She'd blow the case.

four

LIZA LAZARUS

LIZA HALF EXPECTED Joe to boot her out of his apartment. There wasn't room for her at the small round table with only two chairs. Houlahan and Briggs brought fold-up camping chairs. Tom from administration took the second chair.

"Liza," Houlahan said with a frown at the lack of table space. "I didn't know you were invited. I would have brought another chair."

She cracked the cap off a beer and handed it to him with a wink. "My invite got lost in the mail."

With no television in the apartment, the couch faced the balcony's sliding door windows. She studied the layout and, for a moment, almost turned tail and left, but decided she would not cave that easily. She wanted answers from Joey—ahem, *Joe*—and he was being a jerk about it. He was either going to give them to her now, or she would wait until the end of the night. Besides, she liked poker and was pissed she hadn't been invited. She would not let this go.

"Shift the table near the couch. I'll lean against the back of it," she said and gestured with her hand.

The three detectives helped her move the furniture, and before they knew it, they were all settled down for their first round of poker, much to Joe's chagrin and sideways glare as he finished setting up refreshments on the kitchen counter.

He returned to the table without a drink for her, but made sure the guys were served.

Ooh. So that's how it's going to be, huh? The old cold shoulder standoff.

"You're showing your colors, Luciano," she murmured with a hint of tease in her voice.

He raised a brow as he picked up his cards and sorted them. "How so, Lazarus?"

As if he didn't know.

"Forgetting to serve the lady? If that's how you screw, then no wonder you're living alone in this one bedroom."

"Lady?" Joe snorted. "I don't see a lady."

The men chuckled cheekily behind their cards. She stared coldly at her hand, letting her anger simmer beneath the surface. She'd received shit her entire life at the precinct for being a little more masculine than feminine. It wasn't her body, she had curves in all the right places. It was the lack of makeup and girly fashion. Her potty mouth. Her practical, nail-polish free hands. If only they knew how deadly those hands could be. Bitterness lanced her tongue. *Not a lady, huh?*

She placed her cards down, stretched her arms out wide, and removed her jacket, pushing out her chest seductively. Then she untwined her scarf and found a tie in her jeans pocket to secure her long brown hair in a top knot. With every movement she made, she took special care to play into her femininity. It was there... she usually preferred to ignore it. And admittedly, she ignored it more often than not since she'd started puking after sex.

"Bit stifling in here with all these hot-headed assholes," she joked,

and fanned her face, and then trailed a lingering finger along her décolletage as she shifted an errant strand of escaped hair.

The men snorted sarcastically. Except Joe. His expression remained stoic, as though he did his best to hold in any reaction. But she caught the flick of his gaze to her neck and then the slow drag to her breasts before he busied himself with sorting his cards again.

It should have made her feel triumphant, but it didn't. It made her unsettled, squirming, and a little flushed.

She needed a drink. While the men started the round, she went to the kitchen and helped herself. It was a typical male spread, antipasto mixed with random things like nuts and raspberry licorice. A few cold beers sat unopened. She took one, popped the cap, and hesitated. She preferred to use a straw when drinking from a bottle. She might not be a prissy girl, but her teeth were the one thing she liked to keep nice. The acid in beer, coffee, and wine would eventually stain.

Liza checked cupboards to see if she could find something else to drink, or even better, straws. She bent low and opened doors, but found nothing but plates and utensils.

She felt him before she saw him—a lick of heat along her spine as she straightened.

"Here," Joe said. He reached past her to open an overhead cupboard. For a moment, all she could see was his broad chest. All she could feel was his body heat. And his scent—deep, masculine, and freshly showered. He pulled out a small cardboard box of paper straws and dumped them on the counter. "These what you looking for?"

Someone cracked a joke at the table, and a burst of laughter filled the room. She picked up the packet and faced Joe.

"Thanks," she murmured.

He gave a half shrug, made to return to the table, but she stopped him by blurting out the first thing she could think of.

"You've changed, Luciano," she commented with a wry look at his physique.

God damn, Lazarus. What's with the pervy comment?

His lips pursed, he folded his arms, and then gave her ass a pointed look. "You haven't."

"What's that supposed to mean?"

He dodged the straw she ditched at him, barely containing the grin twitching on his lips. "You know what it means." His expression shifted to a concerned pout. "Maybe you should cut down on the raspberry licorice. Don't want to cause a split like last time."

"That was one time only, and it was because my jeans were old!"

She huffed, folded her arms, and gave him daggers. Maybe he hadn't changed. He was *still* giving her shit about embarrassing moments.

"My ass is all muscle, thank you very much," she said, turned her rear, and flexed her perfect globes fitting snugly into her denim. "Go on, squeeze it. Punch it, even."

Silence. She looked up to find his expression had gone lax, except for the simmering heat in his eyes as he held her gaze.

A moment of silent awareness passed between them.

"I'm good," he said, still holding her gaze.

"That's what I thought. You're afraid you'll break your fist on it."

His blazing eyes tracked down her body and settled on the curve of her rear in a way that made her heart thump in her chest. Confident Joey was a little hot. It sent her stomach flipping. She tried to laugh off the tension.

"Next time you mention my ass, Luciano, it better be because you think it's amazing, or I'll clock you like that time in gym class."

Did she just say she *wanted* him to say her ass was amazing? Adrenaline surged in her system, leaving her skin feeling itchy and hot. What was she doing? Flirting? She hastily grabbed her straw and returned to the poker table. This new Joe was throwing off every instinct she had about him. The old Joe would never have stared at her ass like that. He'd have laughed off the joke, too. *Jesus Christ*, she was in turmoil.

She'd barely picked up her cards when a knock came at the door.

"You fucking kidding me?" Joe muttered. "Does the super in this building let everyone up?"

Liza hid her smile behind her hand, but it died when a female voice shouted through the door.

"Pumpkin, you home?"

Every person at the table stilled. Brigg's widened his eyes, then held up his palms. "It's not my wife."

Houlahan, for some reason, patted down his front, as though searching for his wife in his shirt pockets. "Not mine."

Tom raised a brow at Joe. "That your missus outside?"

Mrs?

Liza scowled at the door.

"Shit," Joe mumbled. "Sorry, guys. I didn't know she was coming."

He scraped his hand through his hair before going to the door.

Liza caught more than one shared stare among the men at the table. They were as surprised as she at this development. She shouldn't be. Joe had told her he had a girlfriend, a serious one, but somehow, she'd never really pictured the reality of it.

From the way Joe dragged his feet to the door, she would almost say he wasn't ready for it either.

The players at the table tried to continue the game, but no one could miss the bright, bubbly whirlwind blond who pushed into the room carrying a crock-pot. She wore a vintage style flared skirt, a tight top that pushed her ample breasts up, and a ponytail that curled at the end. Bright red lipstick accentuated her thin-lipped pout. Liza looked down at her plain blouse and brushed a fallen piece of rasp-berry licorice to the floor.

"Oh, hello," the newcomer said breathily to the boys at the table. Without skipping a beat, her eyes skated over Liza as though she was part of the furniture. "I didn't realize Joe would have company."

Joe walked stiffly beside her. "That's because..." He thought better of what he was going to say and shook his head. "Tanya, you should have called."

"Nonsense, sweetie. I just wanted to bring some nutritious food for you to eat. God knows you don't feed yourself properly. I mean, look at this junk. Raspberry licorice for dinner?" She rolled her eyes, then helped herself to the cupboard where the plates were kept. "But there's plenty for everyone."

Liza slowly dropped the stick of red that had made its way to her mouth with an "Oh-my-God" face shared with the boys. When she looked up, Joe glared at her.

She jumped up to cover her bad manners. "Joe, aren't you going to introduce us?"

"Tanya," he said through gritted teeth. "This is the crew I used to work with at the CCPD. Guys, this is Tanya."

What kind of introduction was that?

Tanya smiled at them all, a little too sweetly. Liza wiped her palms on her thighs and then strode into the kitchen where she could better assess the new arrival. Tanya's jaw was tense, her nails were pointed, and her hair smelled like hairspray.

"Liza," Joe warned under his breath, but she just shot him a tight smile.

"You've been dating this woman for two years, and that's the introduction you give?"

"Two years?" Tanya's laugh tinkled as her fond gaze landed on Joe. "That's so sweet, honey, that you're thinking of us long term." She leveled a more serious expression on Liza. "It's only been two months, but I feel like it's been forever too. Next stop, marriage, right?"

She patted Joe sweetly on the jaw. He refused to meet Liza's gaze.

Two months?

"What did you say your name was again?" Tanya asked, blinking innocently.

She'd heard Joe speak before, surely. He was never good at whispering.

"Liza," she replied sharply.

"Oh." Tanya stilled. Her posture shifted from bubbly to vixen. Liza wouldn't be surprised if those pointed nails distended into claws. "You're *the* Liza."

It took all of her resolve not to slap the woman and Joe with a tone and comment like that. She straightened her shoulders and lifted her chin.

"Can't stop talking about me, hey, Luciano?" she smirked.

His eyes turned to slits.

Briggs shouted from behind, "I think that's our cue to leave."

Poker chips tinkled as they were rounded up, signaling Liza should probably leave too, but this was all too weird. Why would Joe lie about how long he'd been dating someone? If this was true, then when he'd told her two months ago that he was in a serious relationship, he might not have been dating at all. What did he do, go out and find a girlfriend, just to prove Liza wrong?

An icky feeling rolled in her gut, and she tried not to think it was related to guilt, but the feeling wouldn't go away.

After packing up the poker, the boys shuffled toward the door, all with their gazes downcast. Houlahan lifted a palm as he exited, saying over his shoulder, "Catch you at work, G-Man. Then we'll answer those questions you need for that case."

He shut the door, leaving just the three of them left.

"What case?" Liza looked at Joe.

Anger flared in his expression. Tension sizzled in the air as his gaze darted around the kitchen before landing on the baseball. He picked it up and then collected her jacket before walking back to the door, yanking it open, and shoving her into the hallway.

five

LIZA LAZARUS

LIZA STOOD IN THE HALL, gaping as Joe handed over her jacket.

"You know what?" he said. "I'm glad you brought the baseball. Now you can take it back and know that we're done with it." His brow furrowed at the ball between them. "It was supposed to mean something else. It was supposed to mean we were on the same team, but that hasn't been the case for years. You forgot, Liza, that you were the first one to stop taking calls from me. The past two months of playing phone-tag are nothing compared to the years you avoided me while I was with the Feds."

He shoved the ball at her chest. She had no choice but to take it.

"I'm done playing games with you, Liza. We're done being friends."

"Joey!" she protested. "You don't mean that. I've been busy, that's all."

"Yeah, well, while you were busy, I grew up," he said. "But you got jaded. You got mean. And it's Joe, not Joey. Don't make me fucking say it again."

Pain cut straight down her middle, from her heart to her stomach, like she'd ripped in two. He turned away. She seized his wrist. An intense electric shock cracked between them, searing from her hand down to her elbow. She gasped, let go, and stepped back, shaking her hand to dispel the sensation.

Joe pushed Liza gently into the hall and closed the door with a resounding *click*. The last thing she saw before it closed was Tanya's smug smirk over his shoulder.

Liza's breath became ragged. Her heart pounded like a jackhammer. Her skin went sweaty, prickly, and hot in waves.

This isn't happening.

"No," she mumbled. She refused to believe Joe had kicked her out, just because… of what? Some offhand insults she'd thrown his way. Absolutely not. He'd always given snark as good as he got.

There was something else going on. He was lying. He had to be.

She pulled on her hair. This was too much to comprehend. Joe was her *friend*.

A woman's voice filtered through the closed door and a sick feeling unfurled in her stomach—lust. Tanya's. A snarl curled Liza's lips. Heat zipped up her neck. Every instinct wanted to kick down the door, shove her Glock in Tanya's face and squeeze the trigger. If she'd actually had it in her hands, she almost thought she'd have done it.

She shook her head—this wasn't like the potential trafficker in the alley, this was run-of-the-mill sexy-time lust. There was no threat, so why was she acting all irritated?

Only one way to find out. A self-imposed stakeout.

Liza shoved the baseball into her pocket and exited the building. At ground level, she crossed the street, hugged the shadows along the sidewalk, and shimmied up the fire escape ladder on the building opposite Joe's.

Screw that bitch. Screw Joe.

Liza needed closure. None of this made sense.

Taking two ladder rungs at a time, Liza was on a third level fire escape before anyone had noticed. The night was dark, giving the perfect cover for a stakeout. Liza checked the window of the apartment attached to the fire escape. Both curtains and windows were closed. It didn't look like anyone was home. Perfect.

She squatted and kept her body hidden in the darkness between a tall planter and the building. She settled her gaze squarely across the way—at Joe's. He'd kept the curtains open and the lights on, so she had a clear view inside.

She wished she hadn't.

Tanya had her paws all over him. A hot and prickly sensation down Liza's spine grew stronger. It spread to the tips of her fingers, and despite the cold temperature of a Cardinal City winter evening, she felt as though she were on a balmy beach in the Caribbean. Sweat itched her skin. She tugged at her blouse and fanned the fabric.

Joe broke away from Tanya. He ran a hand through his hair and walked to the kitchen. Tanya was locked in place, hands fretting. When Joe turned back to her, he gestured erratically.

"Oh, here we go," Liza murmured, suddenly wishing for an audio surveillance kit. "Trouble in paradise."

Something squeaked at her feet. A brown rat leaped onto the platform and scampered over Liza's boots.

"Shoo." She shoved it away with her hand. Gross.

Joe's argument was getting heated.

He paced across the floor behind the couch. Tanya was doing that thing where you look at the ceiling and shake your head. Disbelief. That's what it was. She wasn't accepting what Joe had to say.

Squeak.

Another rat scampered onto the fire escape.

"Piss off, rats."

The next time Liza looked up, Joe and Tanya were kissing.

"You see that?" Liza snapped at the rats. "He's not supposed to act like that. I can't sense his lust."

Liza concentrated. The closer she looked, the more it seemed like the kiss was one-sided. Joe's posture was stiff and unwelcoming. Liza bit her lip, frowning as Tanya coaxed Joe to the couch facing the window. He reluctantly sat down. Tanya unzipped his pants.

"Whoa." Liza stepped back, blinking. "TMI, bro. Too much information."

This was getting a little cozy for her liking... she should go... but... she slid her gaze back. She couldn't tear herself away.

It was Joe—*Joey Luciano*. The one friend she'd never felt lust from. The one person who'd been on her team for most of her life. The same friend who'd just told her to *look down* at his impressive, very hard package. And then he told her to fuck off.

As Tanya settled in to give Joe the best time of his life, Liza couldn't stop staring. This was... impossible.

There were only two explanations. One, Liza was broken. Her sin-sensing was off.

Two...

Joe was her mate.

But he couldn't be. It wasn't possible. Yes, she couldn't sense his lust. That was clear. But if they were bonded, she'd also have powers. Supernatural powers like her siblings. There was more: her sin equilibrium and tattoo would reset every time she was in his proximity; her hormones would rage and set off pheromones around him so he couldn't resist her lure. It was a biological response programmed into all the siblings, a safeguard to ensure that when they finally found their mate, they kept them.

None of that had happened.

Grinding her teeth, Liza flexed her fists as everything she'd known to be true turned upside down. Joe was getting some... and... Liza's brow lifted in surprise. Joe *wasn't* enjoying it.

Some sort of sick satisfaction rose in her.

He'd reclined on the couch, an arm splayed on each side of the backrest, but his bored gaze had focused outside his apartment and to the right. Even from across the street, Liza could tell his attention was elsewhere than the thin lips wrapped around his erection. He looked wearied. Then Joe frowned. His hand pulled something out of the gap between the pillow and the couch. He brought it to his nose, lashes fluttering, and lids turning heavy.

Was that... was that Liza's scarf? Her hand fluttered to her neck and found it bare. Yes, she'd left her scarf in his apartment. On the couch.

Something scampered over her foot. She squeaked and jumped to the side. God damn, it was another *rat*. She swatted it away with her sweaty hand.

Ugh. This building was overrun with stray rodents and God-knew-what else. Disgusting. Maybe the rat was a sign for her to leave. This was too bizarre. But when she glanced one last time at Joe through his window, she found him staring back.

She couldn't breathe, couldn't move, couldn't think.

The expanse across the street disappeared. The woman at his lap faded away. It was just Liza and Joe, locked in a battle of wills. He refused to break eye-contact.

She should have felt shocked. She should have felt pissed. Angry. Furious. Even numb, indifferent. Why did she care? Why did *he* care? But seeing Joe in a hedonistic act she'd never thought him capable of stoked a long-denied desire within her. Hot, sweaty, prickly lust curled around her every nerve ending. Her nipples pebbled. Heat rushed between her legs. She plucked her blouse from her damp skin.

At her movement, a half wicked smile grew on Joe's face.

Who was he?

She scrambled to the side, knocked the plant, and cursed. Her boot hit something soft. She looked down and gaped. The rats. They were both dead. Pale yellow smoke curled from her palms like mist in a forest. It smelled funny. Poison?

"What the fuck is going on?" she gasped.

Then she saw the state of her yin-yang tattoo. Only a few hours ago she'd been so full of her sin that she'd blacked out and beaten a man in a berserker rage. Her tattoo should have been closer to fully black, but it wasn't. It was perfectly balanced.

Mate.

He's your mate.

There was no denying it. She wasn't broken. This yellow substance was her power. She stumbled back, hit the rail of the fire escape, and glanced across at Joe.

He knew something was wrong, and Liza had the sudden sense of being caught in a trap. As if knowing his prey would flee, Joe pushed Tanya from his lap, and lurched to his feet, eyes luminous and locked on Liza.

Get out of here. Now.

She hurdled over the railing and raced down the ladder. Her heart thudded so hard it almost jumped out of her chest. But she kept going. She didn't look back. She took one fire escape landing after the other, vaulting over rails, landing, launching, and repeating.

When her boots hit the sidewalk, she dared. She looked up.

Joe stood with his palm on his window, watching her.

Liza ran.

LIZA PUSHED through the big heavy doors of the one place she knew she'd feel at peace—the Cardinal City Cathedral. It was almost closing time, but it was her favorite time. Fewer people. Less sin. More innocence. This was her process to balance the turmoil in her system and, despite her tattoo saying she was fine, she needed to settle her nerves. A few minutes in the cathedral after having too much lust in her system was like taking a cold shower.

She walked down the aisle and headed toward the front. The only person in the cavernous room was a dark-haired figure kneeling by the prayer candles through an archway on the side. Good. Liza didn't want to be disturbed. When she got to the front, she slid onto a wooden pew and sat with her fists on her knees, staring up at the crucifix hanging sadly on the wall behind the altar.

Liza took a deep breath through her nose, letting the incense in, but try as she might, she couldn't relax. Her mind whirled. Her body buzzed. It felt like a million ants were in her veins, itching and skittering. Her shirt stuck to her sweaty skin. Was it sweat? She wasn't sure. *That yellow mist.*

Forcing herself to be brave, she looked down at her balled hands. Trembling, she opened them. *Oh, God. That's not normal.* Ochre yellow residue coated her palms, sinking darkly into the cracks of skin like nicotine stains. She rubbed her palms on her jeans.

Dead rats.

She gulped air. Then gulped again.

Sanity dangled on a thread. One push and it would fall.

She squeezed her eyes shut and forced herself to think logically.

Go through the scenario one step at a time. Starting with Joe.

He hated her.

Stop. Go back.

He didn't want her there. He'd been avoiding her because he'd said she'd gotten mean. Jaded. There was more to it, there had to be.

He had a girlfriend. Maybe that was why. But they didn't seem to act like a couple who'd been together for two years. Liza got the impression Tanya was unwelcome at the poker night.

So was she.

Visions of the scene she'd glimpsed through his window slammed into her mind. Joe and Tanya kissing. Joe backing off. Them arguing. Then her trying again. Him capitulating. He was so bored... until he'd found Liza's scarf. He'd inhaled as though Liza's scent was a lifeline. And when he'd caught Liza watching, he didn't freak out. He didn't act in any way like he had when he'd pushed Liza out of his apartment. No, he *got off* on her watching him.

Joe was a sexual man, just as much as any of them. She'd been so wrong about him.

That alone boggled her mind because, if Liza hadn't sensed lust in Joe since they were children, it could only mean one thing. Their mating bond had triggered during the innocence of their youth.

Half-triggered.

She glanced at her stained palms. Her power had manifested. Now, when it was too late. Now, when Joe hated her guts.

"You got jaded. You got mean."

He was right. She was jaded, and she had been mean to him because if she wasn't, then he'd eventually end up just another man trying to get in her pants, another man who she'd eventually end up vomiting on at the most intimate moment, and then he'd see the real Liza. The coward so desperate to get close to someone, she allowed herself to get sick over it.

Because of this, love was never in the cards for her. It had been easier to put walls up and protect her heart.

"Mija."

Liza's eyes snapped open. Mary, her adoptive mother, stood before her with a frown. The petite, Mexican-heritage woman was in her fifties but was as fit and deadly as one of her children. Probably more. The woman did nothing but hone her ex Hildegard Sisterhood assassin skills. Trained as a *Sinner*, Mary had been tasked with executing the Lazarus children to avoid them being tools of mass destruction. Only, Mary had chosen to defect and rescue the children. All but Daisy had been saved.

Mary must have been the person Liza had seen praying by the candles, which was weird. Despite Mary working for a religious organization once, she didn't believe in God. Liza didn't blame her. If Liza had been plucked from everything she knew, trained as a seductress and an assassin, and then told she was going to hell for it, she'd do everything in her power to *not* believe in hell. Or heaven.

The concern on Mary's face made Liza's heart stutter. Air plundered her lungs. Her vision blurred and darkened. She couldn't face the scrutiny. The judgment.

Liza made to stand, but Mary pushed her back down. She sat next to her daughter and faced the front. Liza continued to make shuddering, sobbing motions without the sound.

Mary said calmly, "Remember your training."

Instantly, the visuals hit Liza's mind's eye. Hours and days of fighting and meditation, calming her chi, washing it clean. She closed her eyes, pushed the soles of her feet into the ground, and placed a palm on her belly. With every inhale, her abdomen pushed her hand out. With every exhale, her hand moved in. She imagined her busy thoughts moving from her brain to her abdomen, then to her feet.

When the last breath left Liza's body and took with it her panic, she opened her eyes and calmly met her mother's perceptive stare. Mary gave a small nod of approval.

Liza wiped the remnant dampness from her eyes. "What are you doing here, Mama?"

"Do you have a monopoly on churches?"

"No, I just—" The panic rose in Liza. She forced another steady breath. *Exhale.* "Sorry. I just wanted to know."

"I was lighting a candle for Daisy."

She glanced at the tiny gold crucifix around Mary's neck. "So it's true. You've taken up the religion that took away your life."

"The Sisterhood led me to all of you," she replied, and then her eyes went to the front and stared long and hard. "I don't know what I believe anymore," she admitted. "They've left us alone all these years. Who knows if they're evil?"

"They made you kill for them."

Mary shifted uncomfortably.

Moments of silence passed, then Liza asked, "Do you believe in Heaven and Hell?"

Mary shrugged. "I never used to. But there's... something. There has to be. Without it, life feels..."

"Hopeless?"

Mary winced.

On the fateful day of their escape from the Syndicate lab, it was Mary's choice to leave Daisy when she'd run back into the burning building to comfort their biological mother and creator, Gloria. It was Mary's choice to hit the elevator button that sent them down to the basement. And it was Mary's choice to get into the escape van and drive away.

That choice had saved seven of the Lazarus children.

It had doomed one.

Liza knew her mother felt the pinch of that guilt daily. She also knew that it was a fool's errand to feel regret over it. If Mary hadn't made that choice, there would be eight doomed Lazarus souls, not one. Because of that choice, Liza had lived a fairly normal childhood. She'd met Joe. She knew what hope was.

"If there is no hope," Liza continued, "then how will we save Daisy?"

Mary took Liza's hand in silence and gripped hard. Together, they stared at Christ on the cross. Catholicism said he'd hung there for three days. Did he have hope? Apparently so. But it also said he rose from the dead three days later and ascended into Heaven. That was bullshit if she'd ever heard it.

Liza's throat closed up. "You know, Daisy used to make me hug her every morning."

Mary nodded with a half-smile. "I remember she made everyone hug her. Even grumpy Sister Josephine."

Liza let go of Mary's hand and shoved it away. "She started every day with hope, and yet it was hope that led to her downfall. And the worst part is I want to blame someone—Gloria, the Syndicate, God —but I can't. It is what it is. Hope, despair. Lust, love, fucking chastity, or indifference—whichever it is. Eventually, I'll succumb, just like Daisy." She slid bitter eyes toward her mother. "How can you come here and *pray* for that?"

A hardness came over Mary. "You're mixing love and lust. They're not the same thing."

"I know that," Liza scoffed. "But they're two roads leading to the same end."

"One road is shorter. Lust is a sprint. Love is a marathon." Mary sighed. "We're all going to die one day, Liza. Wouldn't you rather take the long road? The one that made you happy? There's not a day that goes by that I don't thank God I chose the right path."

All the fight left Liza's body. Her next words came out a trembled mess. "What kind of god would do this to someone? I'm hideous. I finally find my mate, and I find out that it's someone I've known half my life. Someone who may have loved me once, but years of rejection and snide insults have turned him away from me. He's disgusted by me at the same time as being attracted to me."

"I'm sure that's not true."

"It is."

"Liza, you've always been hard on the outside, but soft in the middle. Once you show him some of that gooey center, he'll come round."

"He's FBI, Mama. He will never agree with what we do."

"Joey?" Mary's eyes widened.

Liza nodded. "You know what they drill into them at Quantico. They don't condone the actions of those who use dishonest or unethical means, no matter what. It's in their damn motto. Fidelity, bravery, and integrity. There's no way he'll approve of my true self."

Mary's gaze turned thoughtful. "I wish I could take your pain away, *mija*. All I can say is that Gloria hasn't gone wrong yet. Five of your siblings have found love. You just need to have a little—"

"Hope?" Liza laughed bitterly.

"I was going to say, faith. In yourself. In Joe."

Liza's hand went to the baseball in her pocket.

Mary checked over her shoulder, and then asked, "What's your power?"

Liza shrugged. "All I know is that yellow mist came out of my hands. I swiped at a rat, and the next minute, it was dead."

More than one rat.

Mary scrutinized Liza's face. Her gaze snagged on the corner of Liza's mouth. "You have yellow stains on your lips too."

The room spun. Liza leaned forward, elbows on knees. If her gut instinct was right, then the yellow mist was poison. If she could kill people with a touch, or a kiss, who knew how destructive she could be if unbalanced. That blackout with the trafficker was nothing compared to her full unlocked potential.

Mary stood and held out her hand, then saw the yellow, and drew her hand back. "We need to speak with Parker."

She was probably right. Even if he knew it, and was an arrogant asshat, Parker was as much a genius as the woman who'd created them —their biological mother. He'd been sitting on Gloria's original encrypted laptop for years, claiming to almost have it unlocked. All of them had long suspected he'd actually done it, but kept it from them. There must be a good reason. It was time to go and see what that reason was.

Half the lights switched off and the cathedral turned an eery dark.

"Closing time," Liza noted.

Together, they went down the aisle and headed toward the exit. Just before Liza reached for the big door, it opened. Both Mary and Liza tensed, senses coming alert. Liza's hand hovered over her hip but realized her gun was back at the station.

In came an average height, slim woman wearing a shapeless business suit. The masculine jacket draped over her frame, and the pencil skirt came down to the woman's knees. No makeup, a few freckles, and spun golden-red hair tied at her nape in a bun. The Harry Potter spectacles resting on her nose were smudged.

She also stopped.

She didn't jolt. She didn't flinch. Her eyes narrowed coolly.

Then Liza recognized her.

"Oh, shit. Alice, right?" Liza pointed at her.

Alice's brown gaze darted between Mary and Liza, and then she transformed. A smile illuminated her face and she nodded.

"Do I know you?"

"Liza Lazarus. Parker's sister."

Alice used her pointer finger to adjust her spectacles at the bridge. "Oh! Of course. I'm so stupid. I should have recognized you both. I mean, it's not like I've not seen you before. I only run errands to your place like every other day, am I right?"

She giggle-snorted.

Mary cleared her throat.

"Oh, sorry, Mama," Liza added. "Have you met Alice? She's Parker's assistant."

Alice adjusted a package. Her spectacles almost fell, but she recovered nicely and held out a hand to Mary. "Nice to meet you, Mrs. Lazarus."

To anyone who knew Mary, the blank look she gave Alice wasn't as benign as it appeared. A million thoughts calculated behind Mary's eyes as she worked out whether Alice was a threat, friend, or a pawn they could use to their advantage. Then Mary suddenly animated, much like Alice had done earlier, and she became a new person.

"Lovely to meet you," Mary said and shook Alice's hand. "I'm afraid the cathedral is closing. They've just shut off the lights."

"Oh, I know the Mother Superior." Alice tapped her package—something book-shaped but wrapped in a plastic bag. "I promised her I'd give her this before the end of the day, but you know Parker. He likes things to be perfect before he leaves. And sometimes he never leaves."

"If you need me to show my bro who's boss, just let me know." Liza tipped her chin down.

Alice blushed and looked away. "Oh, no. It's all good. It's my job."

A sound behind them had them all turning. A nun restocked the tabernacle with loud, precise movements. Her habit hid her face, and the shadows gave nothing away. Alice gave them a small smile and nodded as she sidestepped.

"Well, nice seeing you," Alice said.

"Likewise."

Liza opened the big double doors and stepped outside. When she turned, she realized Mary still stood on the threshold, eyes boring into Alice's back as she walked toward the nun, a slight limp in her step.

"Everything okay?" Liza asked.

Mary snapped out of her daze and then joined Liza on the landing of the steps. The door closed heavily behind her.

"It's nothing," Mary replied.

"Didn't look like nothing."

"There was something familiar about her. That's all."

"She's Parker's assistant. I'm sure you've seen her before."

"You're probably right."

7

six

JOE LUCIANO

JOE SPENT the morning doing laps in his gym's swimming pool, trying to get the events of the previous night out of his head, but even on his fiftieth lap, he couldn't avoid thinking life had a way of coming full circle for him. He'd tried to leave Cardinal City but was right back where he started. He'd joined law enforcement to get away from his abusive father and a mother who saw nothing wrong with it—yet now he worked in Violent Crimes where violence was his bread and butter. At least he wasn't the one dishing it out—or receiving it.

And then there was Liza Lazarus... he'd tried to get her out of his head, but she'd managed to edge her way back in, even deeper than before. Even deeper than when she'd made him smile, while waiting with him for x-rays of his broken arm. Even deeper than sharing her hotdog when he'd turned up to the ballgame without a dime to his name. And even deeper than when she'd tossed the signed baseball to him after years of silence between them.

She was all he could think about, and by the time he'd showered and made his way into the Cardinal City Police Department, her citrus-berry scent was an ever-living fragrance in his mind.

When Tanya had turned up last night, and his stomach had dropped instead of filling with excitement, he knew instantly that it was over between them. But he'd tried to protect his heart from Liza, ignored the disappointment, and pretended he was okay with what Tanya wanted—a life together. Damn it, he'd tried. But he'd never been good at being something he wasn't.

One inhale of Liza's sweet scent on her scarf and he'd gone harder than steel. And when he saw Liza outside, watching him with a mix of curiosity and, dare he think it, arousal… *Christ.*

His insides had combusted. Suddenly, it hadn't been Tanya's lips on him, but Liza's. Like a desperate addict, he hadn't been able to stop, even though he knew it was wrong. Even though he was an asshole for doing it. But then Liza had panicked. Something happened to her on that fire escape, and the moment she'd fled, Joe's mood had died.

Neither he nor Tanya could argue with their failing chemistry, despite his lies to the contrary.

That's when he ended his casual relationship with Tanya. He'd been using her to get over Liza and that wasn't fair to anyone. How could he explain to Tanya that the entire time they'd dated, he'd been wearing a mask so clever that he'd fooled himself into believing it was real?

There was only one thing left for him to do. Take the mask off and go all-in with Liza.

Fate had brought him back to Cardinal City, back to *her*—his sweet poison, killing him softly. All he knew for certain was that he wouldn't go to his death without a proper taste. A banquet.

With his duffel bag slung over his shoulder, he located the office Captain Morais had assigned him for the duration of his stay at the CCPD. It was smaller than his bedroom, but bigger than the open office he'd shared with the other detectives years ago. He would get teased for this when they arrived for the day.

A small smile played on his lips. He truly missed the camaraderie he shared with those guys. Last night was over too soon.

He dumped his bag on the floor next to the empty desk and unloaded his case files. There were two sets. One was filled with the reason he was here today—a new task force and interdepartmental investigation. The other set belonged to a classified FBI investigation and the reason he'd wanted to drill the CCPD detectives without Liza present. He opened the top classified file to view the dossier on Sloan Lazarus. Her profile was squeaky clean, not even a parking ticket or two. But Joe knew the Lazarus family—had known them since they were all kids. They weren't saints.

He turned the page and handled two pictures, both were taken from security footage at a private school a few months prior. Sloan and her fiancé Max were pictured walking in and out of the academy with a student. The next page detailed eyewitness reports of two white-robed and Halloween masked attackers who'd allegedly fought with Sloan on campus. One witness described Sloan kicking her way out of a car and "going ape-shit" on the gasoline doused attacker.

It wasn't the first time these white-robed terrorists had been seen in Cardinal City. More pictures of them had been taken near the Kremlin Nightclub just under a year ago, and earlier near a warehouse in the South-Side slums. The last time they'd been seen was in the Quadrant Central Park and Zoo only two months ago, along with trace evidence of some sort of plant biological matter that couldn't be explained.

Each time, a Lazarus, or one of their partners, had been captured on CCTV nearby. Joe knew because he was the one to look up security records after linking the events. His gut feeling said the Lazarus

family was the vigilante group known as the Deadly Seven, but it wasn't enough for a conviction. Not even close. Yet.

He had to first prove who they were, then prove they were responsible for a list of felonies a mile long, including, but not limited to, reckless endangerment, aggravated assault, and manslaughter. Maybe even murder.

Liza needed to emancipate herself from that family. He'd counted six different Deadly Seven costumes captured in shady newspaper clippings and hand-held home video footage on YouTube. There were meant to be seven of them, but he'd only counted six. Joe's gut also said Liza wasn't getting dressed up in Halloween digs like the rest of her family. She was too busy saving lives the right way.

Pride swelled in his chest. She'd always been a stickler for the rules, and she'd always hated being told what to do by her family. As soon as he'd made the mental leap to connect the family to the vigilante group, so many things in their history made sense. Liza's and her siblings' seven years "studying abroad" for one. All of them had come back changed. There had been a hardness to them, yet a creeping silence, a violent calm. Anyone with military training could see they were power coiled and veiled beneath feigned mundane appearances. They worked hard at shifting the conversation to their public identities, but Joe had known them before.

Before they were killers.

That was why he had to be the one to bring them down.

Liza didn't deserve to go down for her family's vigilante ways. He would help her see that. Maybe he could save her from suffering their fate. One day she would thank him for it.

Before he'd left for the gym that morning, he'd checked the balcony she was on the night before. He'd found dead rats. Had she seen them, and that's why she'd fled? But he didn't think she was the kind to be afraid of rats. Nothing seemed to scare Liza Lazarus.

A quiet knock came at his door. A small female detective stood in his doorway.

"Captain is ready to give the briefing," she said. "Five minutes."

Joe nodded, packed his classified files back into his small filing cabinet, and locked it with a key. Then he straightened his suit and tie and smoothed his hair. One check in the small mirror behind the door, and he was ready to go. Walking down the hall, he tried to remove the image of his reflection from his mind.

His eyes were bleak, cold, and empty. They still belonged to the mask he wore. Maybe he'd been wrong, and it wasn't so easy to take off. Perhaps he'd worn it for so long it was now a part of him. Worse, maybe the man he'd been before joining the FBI had been the mask and this was the real Joe.

Hard. Unforgiving. Dead.

THE BRIEFING ROOM consisted of a display board at the front and several lecture desks and chairs. Already there were a few faces he recognized. Houlahan. Briggs. Bugsy. Tom. Debbie from Accounts. Joe scanned the room and failed to see Liza.

She should be here.

Had that incident on the fire escape been more serious than he gave credit? Thinking back, he tried to pinpoint any evidence that indicated a problem. It wasn't the rats. She'd stared at her hands, then she'd fled. Remarkably, Liza had descended the fire escape with the dexterity and speed that had stunned him, but only cemented his suspicions about her training.

Conversation in the room picked up in decibel as more detectives and officers entered. Geoff, Joe's colleague from the bureau, arrived late, tucking his shirt into his pants and straightening his hair. Joe frowned at him. How the rookie had passed through Quantico, he'd never know. Geoff was constantly late, always in a disarray, and his sandy brown hair was never neat. The twenty-two-year-old looked like a ring-in. But the ex-high-school quarterback was good with the grunt work and great in a fight.

Geoff jogged up to Joe and flashed him a cocky grin. "Sorry, I'm late."

Joe stifled an eye-roll and handed over the case files pertinent to the briefing. "Stick those to the board once the official task force meeting starts."

"Rogee."

"You mean Roger."

"Nope." Geoff smiled again. "Rogee."

Joe blew air through his teeth. Geoff was always making up his own words. As if he couldn't look more incompetent, the petite detective who'd alerted Joe to the briefing arrived looking more disheveled than Joe remembered. He slid his gaze to Geoff who only cleared his throat and glanced away.

"Seriously?" Joe mumbled. "Couldn't keep it in your pants for five minutes?"

Geoff replied, "It was a good five minutes."

"Is that all it takes millennials these days?" Joe shot back wryly.

The portly Captain Morais entered the room and conversation shuttered. Joe doubted the man had ever been fit in his life. Burst blood vessels around his nose, neck, and face were a testament to his waning health. But being unfit hadn't stopped the man from becoming Captain. He had a personality like a shark and was no one's friend. Didn't matter to Joe anymore. He wasn't Joe's boss, after all.

Without pausing to greet Joe, Morais took the podium at the front and cleared his throat. He opened his mouth—

"Sorry, I'm late." Liza burst through the door.

Joe's heart stopped at the sight of her.

Every. Damn. Time.

Long, sun-kissed brown hair. The body of an Amazon warrior. The smile of a seductress. Dark, amused eyes belonging in the bedroom. She wore tight jeans, a soft white shirt that clung to her shape with static and pulled under her arm from her holster. The CCPD badge pinned on her belt drew his eye to her swaying hips before she sat down near the back and placed her hands on the lecture desk. Black leather gloves covered her hands.

Odd.

When his gaze lifted to hers, he found she watched him. More specifically, the area below his belt too. She lifted her gaze and blushed.

One side of his lips curved upward.

"Day-um," Geoff murmured, eyes on Liza. "She's hot."

"Act professional."

"Rogee."

Joe tuned into Morais' brief.

"... As you all know, a slew of missing persons and homicides have been reported in the city over the past few months. Some homicides are linked to a killer known as the Ripper. To say the nickname is cliché is an understatement, but when the press runs with something, we're stuck." A laborious sigh. "So, we're taking a multi-agency approach to catch this killer. A special task force based out of the CCPD will take advantage of a collaborative team effort and shared information from local and federal agencies." Morais paused and looked at Joe. "Some of you remember Joe Luciano from his CCPD days. He's now Special Agent Joe Luciano, and his colleague is Agent Geoff Slinksi. Our budget for team contribution will include Detective Lazarus and Detective Briggs. Please report to Special Agent Luciano for your briefing. Anyone gathering intel about the Ripper in

Cardinal City, please forward it to the task force. That will be all. Dismissed."

Captain Morais moved to leave the room. The crowd stood. Liza shot out of her seat and tried to head him off.

"Sir," she protested. "I can't be on the task force."

Morais raised his brows. "Why?"

"The Ripper is a sex-related crime. I specifically requested to stay away from them." She winced. "I don't want to go back."

"He's also removing internal organs. Eighty percent of homicides involve sexually related motivations. And then there's the trafficking component. Not all are sex related. I'm afraid you're going to have to deal with it. You're in law enforcement. Sex-related crimes are unavoidable."

"B-but…" Liza's wide eyes shot to Joe. "I have cases."

"Miss Lazarus," Morais said. "You're our best closer in sex crimes and Special Agent Luciano asked for the best. That's all there is to it. You can hand your cases over to Houlahan. Now, unless there is a valid reason you want to go against orders?"

She pressed her lips together and shook her head.

The captain turned to Joe. "If you need any more resources, please let me know."

"That's generous."

"I just want your director off my ass." Morais strode out of the room.

Most of the crowd went with him until it was just Geoff, Joe, Briggs, and Liza. The latter of which gave Joe daggers sharpened with suspicion.

Joe clicked his fingers at Geoff. "Pin those pictures to the board. Briggs, you can help. Liza, a word."

He walked out of the briefing room and down the hall to his office. The scent of berries stayed with him, so he assumed she followed. He stood inside the door and waited for Liza to enter, shut the door behind her, and closed the venetian blinds on the window. Once satisfied they had privacy, he faced her.

Their eyes clashed and electricity zipped up his spine, in the air, in the world. Every time they were in the same room, his body sang with awareness. It almost hurt to look away. How could this be one-sided? How had she spent their entire friendship ignoring this charge between them?

She put her hands on her hips and flared her nostrils. Each time she inhaled, her chest inflated, and the press of white lace pushed against her blouse. An indignant eyebrow raised. That's all she did and, yet, he felt like she'd razed him to the ground. He'd intended to have a quiet word with her, to insist that their collaboration would remain professional, but words came out from a dark, hungry place.

"Did you enjoy watching me last night?" His voice was thick, rough.

Rosy lips parted, surprised. Joe caught a tantalizing glimpse of wet, pink tongue as it darted out to moisten. Then her lips mashed together.

She scowled. "Did you enjoy *me* watching *you*?"

"Yes."

It was the honest answer neither of them expected.

He stepped closer. The pulse point in her neck rabbited. Her berry scent turned heady and drunk, doused with champagne. Desire clouded his mind. This was inappropriate. But...

She inched closer.

"Tanya?" she murmured.

He took a step. "Broke up."

"Her loss."

"Mm-hmm."

"Joe," she whispered. *Pleaded.*

Her body heat licked his skin. Painful pleasure sensations. He was a moth. She was the flame. She would consume him. He knew it was bad. But it didn't stop him from claiming the final inch between them. His mouth hovered near hers.

Both froze. Neither willing to make the final concession.

She exhaled. He inhaled. Their breaths mingled, heated, and buzzed with anticipation.

Will she?

Will he?

This wasn't normal. He was losing himself. Without Liza, Joe was a man who crossed his t's and dotted his i's. With her, he couldn't recite the alphabet.

She's not pulling away.

Pupils were blown. Color painted her freckle-dusted cheeks. Her gaze darted to his lips every few moments. She squirmed, as though unable to contain the sensations in her body.

She's into it. Into him.

The realization surged through him with triumph.

This was what he wanted. Kissing her was all he'd damn well wanted for the past twenty years. That's why he pulled away.

She chased his lips with her own. A hard warmth bloomed in his chest. Amusement hit his eyes. Yes. He liked this better.

It was Liza's turn to wait.

He opened the door. "We have a strategy to prepare."

She blinked at him.

"After you," he prompted.

"Who *are* you?" she breathed, squinting at him.

"The same guy I've always been."

When she walked past him, her body brushed his front, and thank Christ she didn't look down. His gig would have been up.

seven

DESPAIR

DESPAIR DESCENDED creaky wooden steps into the basement level of a laundromat that doubled for a Faithful headquarters. There were nine such establishments around Cardinal City. This one was special.

She paused at the foot of the stairs and scanned the large room. In it, twenty or so Faithful in white robes reclined and gathered in leisure, their usual white Halloween masks discarded or pulled back on their heads. Billiard tables, gaming stations, and large flat-screen televisions depicting the latest streaming entertainment were scattered about the room. Help-yourself bars filled with all you could eat food and drink were at either side of the room. But at the front, directly ahead of Despair, was the pièce de résistance on the podium next to a lectern—a replicate tank.

The Syndicate rarely revealed their prized intellectual property, but this replicate tank was special. Inside grew a clone of the leader of the Faithful—Quarry. Not just a clone, but a new and improved clone. A replicate. Floating in viscous water was a blemish-free, younger version of the man standing at the lectern, giving a speech.

The real Quarry had scars down one side of his body. He'd been in a devastating car accident when he was younger and was left disfigured and partly disabled. The Syndicate had promised him eternal life as a powerful, superhuman being. The evidence of which floated in the tank in full view.

Faithful numbers had been dwindling as the Deadly Seven had grown in power. The deal with the Syndicate was the Faithful had to give their life to the cause and, in return, the Syndicate would resurrect them as a perfect, immortal replicate. Except the Deadly Seven had made it a point to keep captured Faithful alive for as long as possible, having them sent to prison instead of killing them outright.

If they weren't dead, then they wouldn't be regrown as replicates. It was a firm rule of the Syndicate, only one copy of each human being alive at one time. Multiple clones of oneself existing would draw too much attention.

It was getting hard to entice loyalty when the promise of a quick resurrection was taken from the Faithful. Nobody was a fan of prolonged suffering.

Something had to be done to inspire devotion again. Despair's gaze washed down the replicate tank. The virile specimen neared maturity and already sparked with electrical surges. Occasionally his limbs jolted with spasms, eager for life.

She slid her gaze to Quarry and sneered. That was the name he'd given himself when he'd joined the Faithful, and he encouraged all others to pick new names too. It was all part of the experience. Shed your lowly human life and pick a god's name, because that's how people will see you when you're reborn.

His old name was Gareth Smith.

Pity he didn't know the truth. Unless she retrieved stem cells from Wrath's unborn child's umbilical cord, they wouldn't be able to halt the expiration problem with the replicates. As it stood, replicates died at a few months of age. If any of them knew that, this place would be empty.

Quarry gave her a small nod of acknowledgment and then finished up his speech. The five people listening at his feet nodded emphatically like star-struck groupies. From their lack of robes, they were new recruits. When Quarry stepped down from the podium and approached Despair, he first stopped and graciously shook the hands of the newly converted cannon fodder.

Despair had plans for them.

"Enforcer," Quarry said. His lip was split, and he had bruising down one side of his face.

Enforcer, or Falcon, was the name these cretins knew for Despair. Her father Julius, one of the leaders of the Syndicate, knew her as "my darling" or Despair. And her family—her brow flinched—*the Lazaruses*—knew her as Daisy. Identity was becoming a fluid thing for Despair. She hardly knew which name to go by.

"What happened to you?" she asked.

"As it happens, one of the Seven struck me."

"Which one?"

"Lust."

She mulled that over. "Tell me more later. We could use this. For now, do you have enough Faithful for our plan?"

His cold eyes searched the room and nodded. "It's not ideal, but I think it will do."

"And they're aware of expectations?"

Another nod.

"Good," she continued. "I'll need them to be ready at a moment's notice. You have your strength-inducing serum supply."

Despair's cell phone rang.

"Yes," she answered.

Her father's voice echoed down the line. "Are you there?"

"Yes."

"Good. Hand the cell to Quarry."

Frowning, Despair passed the handset to the Faithful leader. Since when did Julius go around Despair to talk to Quarry?

Since you started blacking out, said a little voice in her head. *Since he's already written you off.*

No. Julius had Despair's hair in his locket. If she was done for, then he would bring her back—perfect this time. Without the sickness in her gut every time someone felt despair. He promised.

Quarry handed the cell back to Despair. "He wants to talk to you."

She pressed the handset to her ear. "Yes."

"You have one chance, my darling. Use it well. If this doesn't work, well, then we will have to resort to more drastic measures of obtaining the stem cells we need."

"The pregnant whores aren't enough?" she asked.

Julius's silence betrayed his irritation. He didn't think she knew Quarry had been tasked to catch prostitutes and send them to the Syndicate lab. And if it wasn't hookers, it was teenage runaways. But he was getting sloppy, leaving evidence and a trail of dead bodies across multiple states. He already thought he was invincible.

The Syndicate didn't care where their backup stem cells came from. These hookers were just for practice. The real deal would come from Wrath's child.

And that important job was for Despair. It was why she'd waited so long to put it into action. She had to be sure everything went according to plan.

eight

LIZA LAZARUS

LIZA WAS in Joe's car, patrolling the streets, looking for familiar people to question about the trafficking. But it was the middle of the day, and she was still worked up from the almost kiss they'd shared that morning. Joe hadn't mentioned it once, but it was all she could think of.

This was Joe. *Joey*—the friend who used to sit next to her at baseball games and recite player stats by heart. He frowned at her when she booed the other team. He was the one who paled every time she mentioned getting her period, but always asked if she was okay when she cramped.

He was the guy she let pull her pigtails in middle school because he didn't know how to be affectionate.

She'd always blamed his abusive parents for that. She'd tried to hug him once after they'd won a local kids' ball game, but he'd stiffened. After that, she would punch him in the arm, he would tug her hair, and all was right in the world. How simple things were back then.

Liza slid her gaze to him and took in his rugged profile. Piercing

eyes razed the streets as he drove. His knuckles whitened on the steering wheel. His shoulders tensed. The suit's stretch of fabric over broad shoulders and biceps reminded her of how he looked beneath it... and how he looked fresh out of the shower. She smiled quietly to herself, turned her gaze to the busy city street, and then realized they were a location known for prostitution. She hadn't even felt a twinge in her gut, which meant sitting near Joe was canceling out her sin-sensing.

Her smile turned to a frown. She'd have to go out on her own if she wanted to make real progress. Catching Johns in the act was a great way to elicit information in exchange for a warning instead of an arrest.

"This is the third known vice spot we've been to," Liza mentioned. "Can't one of the others canvas the rest?"

Joe shook his head. "You know these girls. You went undercover with them. They'll speak with you."

"I went undercover over two years ago," she replied. "Turnover is high. Most of them are new, and the rest don't remember me."

"We have to keep trying. You know this part of the job isn't fun, but we have to be thorough."

Liza squirmed in her seat. She might not be feeling sick from the sense of lust, but sitting in a confined space with Joe had been another kind of agony. Now that she'd accepted he was her mate, and after their almost kiss, her body was in a constant state of arousal. Every time he moved, he filled the air with his alluring masculine scent, and he had no frickin' clue it drove her mad.

Until last night, he'd been in another relationship. She couldn't go telling him everything now. He needed time, and she needed to repair their friendship.

"We're not going to get far at this time of day," Liza pointed out. "There will be more girls in the evening."

Joe shot her a skeptical look. "If we had another lead to go on, then great. But canvassing known spots is all we have."

"We could always try the Port Authority. Keep an eye out for spotters. The trafficking rings could be linked."

"Geoff and Houlahan are there. I'd rather follow this direction. My gut says it's not trafficking related."

Liza slumped. When did Joe become so relentless? It was getting hard to reconcile the Joe she knew then with the one sitting next to her. The hardness in him had come from somewhere, and if his abusive childhood hadn't made him hard, then what had? Working with the FBI? Had it been so bad?

Or was it really as her guilt whispered... her fault?

She wanted to talk with him, to grab a beer, and watch a game like they used to. But she wasn't even sure if Joe liked watching baseball anymore. He'd thrown their ball back at her.

The car drove past the alley she'd vomited in.

"Stop," Liza blurted.

Tires screeched as Joe maneuvered the vehicle into the alley. They jolted to a halt.

"I may have a lead," she explained and stepped out of the car.

Joe followed her into the alley.

"I was here the other day." She pointed to the bloodstains on the ground. "A spotter tried to lure a teenage runaway. Mirabelle."

Maybe it was linked to trafficking, after all. But maybe the spotter wasn't a spotter. Maybe he was the killer.

"Whose blood is that?"

"I had to use excessive force on him."

"Did you arrest him?"

She shook her head. "But I took Mirabelle to a shelter. She might still be there. We can talk to her and see what she remembers."

"And what do *you* remember?"

That was the question. She'd blacked out for half of it. Maybe this wasn't a good idea. The girl might say something about Liza's loss of control.

"I need a coffee first," Liza said. "Heaven's not far. Let's also grab a bite to eat and talk about it over lunch. Some of my family are probably there. They'd want to see you."

He stutter-stepped and frowned at her. "Have lunch with your family?"

"Look, I know you don't like my family much, but—" She wanted to say that he'd have to get used to them. Whatever disagreements he'd had with her brothers back in school had to be forgotten. As her mate, he'd have no choice but to get along.

She blinked. She was making a lot of assumptions. Joe didn't *have* to do anything. Since he had come back to town, he'd been throwing mixed signals. Maybe it was as he'd said. He didn't want to be her friend anymore. But if that was the case, then why did he request her for the task force? Why did he almost kiss her? It couldn't all be her pheromones luring him in. It had to come from somewhere.

Hope was a tiny kernel of redemption growing inside her soul. A rush of warmth bloomed at the thought of Joe's forgiveness.

"Is that what you think?" He stopped at his car. "That I don't like them?"

She shrugged.

He made an incredulous sound as he opened the car door and slotted himself inside. When she joined him, he'd already shut down the conversation, choosing to focus on the driving.

She sighed softly. "If you drive to Heaven, there's a private parking garage beneath. It will be easier."

The only sign that he'd heard her was an almost imperceptible nod before he flattened his lips and turned silent and brooding. The temperature dropped to ice cold.

Thinking about it now, Liza was lost during those years Joe was gone. Somehow, she'd never connected the dots until he'd returned and she felt whole again. Finding out he was her mate was like the missing puzzle piece, the reason she could never quite get him out of her head. As it turned out, he must have felt somewhat the same, because when they parked in the garage beneath Lazarus House, he blurted, "Why did you stop taking my calls?"

"I don't know," she lied.

The truth was, after Wyatt's ex had faked her death, the family had drifted apart. Liza was ashamed of both herself and her family. She threw herself into work. Then when the siblings started pairing up with their mates, things started to pick up, and her family ties grew stronger. The thing was, in that time, Liza had embedded herself in the law, in doing things the right way. The expectation to be a vigilante scared her. She didn't want Joe to be part of that world. He was untainted and innocent. Loyal, righteous, good.

And she wasn't. He was right when he said she'd become jaded. Mean. She couldn't argue with that.

So instead of answering his question, she asked, "Do you like me, Joe?"

"Why are you wearing the gloves?" he deflected.

"They're good for robbing banks," she joked.

"In all my life, Liza, I've never known you to wear gloves."

"We hardly know each other anymore, Joe."

"Sometimes I wonder if I've ever known you."

As usual, they slipped into old patterns, sparring verbally like old beat up boxers, neither willing to concede. She thought he would continue, but he surprised her. One minute, he was inside the car, the next he wasn't. Liza blinked, trying to mentally catch up, but he already paced outside like a caged animal.

She got out and called over the roof, "Joe. We need to talk."

Frenzied eyes met hers, then skated away.

"Joe," she implored. "What happened? Why did you get out of the car? We were talking."

"Because I can't breathe," he growled, still pacing. "I can't *think*."

She crossed to his side. "What? Why?"

"This was a mistake. You and me working together. Bad idea."

Hurt sliced her chest. She wanted to rub the sore spot but reached for him. She should have known not to startle the wild animal. He reacted, clamping her wrist and twisting until her arm locked behind her back. He pressed his body against her, forcing her against the car. Like a criminal. A cheat. A liar.

And she let him, just like she'd let him pull her pigtails.

This was *Joe*.

Liza remembered when he'd been pinned like this by his father against their old Dodge pickup. It was the night before Liza had left for her seven years of training. At fifteen, she'd snuck out of home and ended up throwing pebbles at his second-level window pane. She'd wanted to give him the baseball for safekeeping. He was sixteen and growing out of his gangly stage, so when he'd climbed down the trellis from his room, he'd snapped the wooden planks and tumbled to the ground. The ivy came with him.

Looking back now, Liza realized Joe must have heard the screen door open because he'd pushed Liza into the back of the Dodge, and hid her under an old piece of canvas before his father came out to the yard, furious. Joe urged her to stay hidden. She couldn't move as Joe's arm was locked behind his back, and he was forced against the truck. She could still see the tears in his eyes as his arm was almost pulled from its socket, and fists boxed against his ears. Stupidly, Liza's dumb thoughts were of Joe's neat hair being messed up as his head snapped sideways like a rag doll.

And through it all, Joe's eyes had locked onto Liza's as though she was his lifeline. She saw not the cry for help, but the plea for her to stay hidden. So she had, knowing that Mary had lectured Liza to never show her strength in public.

Joe's father stayed outside for a cigarette after he'd sent Joe limping back into the house.

That first puff of smoke, the exhale that sounded like relief, it had triggered something within Liza. That night she had her first taste of what her soon-to-be Shaolin Warrior Masters called the Violent Calm. Mary's training rushed to the surface. Liza's instincts had stilled like she was underwater. She wasn't angry. She was at peace because she knew exactly what would happen next.

Retribution.

She had methodically, and systematically jabbed Joe's father in all the right pressure points to make him collapse in a paralyzed heap. Then she'd kneeled on his throat, put pressure on his carotid, and whispered as though the devil himself were inside her, *"If you ever touch him again, I will hunt you down. If you ever mention this to Joey, I will hunt you down. And if you are ever anything less than the perfect father... I. Will. Hunt. You. Down. Capeesh?"*

Wetness pooled on the broken ivy underfoot. He'd urinated in fear.

It took many years of exhaustive training and meditating to access that calm but violent space again, and Joe had never found out. His father never touched him again. But he failed at being perfect. He'd kicked Joe out of home when he finished high school. Liza had always wondered if she'd caused that, but being half a world away, she'd been powerless to stop it. Reuniting with Joe at the academy had been one of the best days in Liza's life.

"Liza." Joe's voice snapped her back to the present. He shoved her into the car and she winced. "Why are you wearing gloves? What aren't you telling me?"

Of all the things to focus on. "They're just gloves."

Movement at her wrist, at the glove. She panicked, whirled, and wrested out of his grip. Faster than she thought him capable, he recaptured both her wrists and pinned them to her side. He used his body to hold her against the car.

The man before her was furious. Neck tendons popped. Veins protruded. Pupils dilated. He was on the verge of a psychotic break, and exactly the kind of person she couldn't reveal her secret identity too. He was the spitting image of his father, but nothing like him. She hoped. This was Joe, the man she'd wanted to protect her whole life, but who didn't need it anymore.

Liza nudged her hips into him. There was something in her pocket he needed to see. She nudged again.

His mouth twitched at the corner. His eyes darted down. "What is that?"

She smirked. "It's certainly not my gun."

Amusement warred with anger until he wrested his expression back to stern.

"Why are you lying to me, Liza?" His voice deepened with threat. "Answer my question."

"Frisk me, and find out." She dared another push forward with her hips, a poke into his lap with the bulky item in her front pocket. A tease.

It was meant to be a joke, but once the words were out, she couldn't stop thinking about Joe's capable hands swiping up her legs, her thighs, her stomach, her—

Heat rushed between her legs. Her inner thighs clenched, and she stifled a moan as her body chose for her. Desire was a fizzy toxin, already winding itself through her system, replacing her blood with champagne. She'd never felt like this before. Not without the inevitable hangover that came with the drunken lust. The vomiting, the sickness. This was pure lust of her own making, and it was *intoxicating*.

She wanted more.

Joe turned Liza to face the car and slammed her palms against the windows.

"Keep your hands there," he ordered and kicked her feet apart.

But his voice was rougher than before, less sure. Satisfaction and anticipation climbed within Liza. Heat burned hotter as his hands lingered over hers. Ragged breath shifted hair at her ear. Tickled.

"Toe to top," she whispered hoarsely, upping the stakes, testing. "Just in case you've forgotten how to do it."

A hitched breath behind her. A pause. Nothing. No response. She pushed her rear back until it pressed against his hard front, but then the heat of his body disappeared.

Liza held her breath. Had she gone too far? Did he want to play this game, or was it all in her head?

The item he wanted was in her front pocket. He knew that. She knew that. There was no need to start at her toes. If he didn't want this as much as she did, he would go straight to her pocket, and she would have her answer.

She waited.

Fabric rustled as he moved behind her. Light pressure at her ankle moved up her leg, rasping tightly over her jeans.

"Slower," she burst out.

He paused.

Then resumed slowly. Two hands. He took her leg, inch by trembling inch. The higher he went, the more air released from her lungs until he got to her inner thigh and stopped.

They both knew this wasn't a game anymore. This wasn't appropriate. This was nothing friends did, and certainly nothing co-workers did.

He massaged her thigh, pushing his thumbs into the pillow of her bottom. His fingers hit her apex and her husky moan shot out. She bit her lip to stop the sound, but it was the trigger on her heart, her breath, her desire.

His touch slipped around her front, lingered at her stomach, and then fluttered down to where he found her bulging pocket.

No. *Too soon.*

She didn't want this to end, but he plucked the item out. She winced and dipped her forehead to the coolness of the car window. She shut her eyes and waited with bated breath.

His silence was deafening.

"Don't give up on us, Joey," she whispered, knowing he stared at their baseball, at the childish signatures scrawled over it, and at the two little words she'd added last night.

I'm sorry.

When no answer came, her throat closed up. She blinked rapidly.

"We're not the same people anymore, Liza." His sad voice rasped over her heart.

"Maybe that's a good thing. Maybe we're better like this. Just give us a chance."

Was it selfish of her to want him? Was it only because of the bond making her think and act like this? Or the fact that she knew she'd be able to have sex with him and actually enjoy herself. Would she have felt the same for him without her hormones telling her to need him so badly she wanted to burst, or her pheromones seducing *him* to want *her*?

"Maybe we're worse," he muttered.

Do you like me, Joe? she'd asked. He hadn't answered. But neither had she. And if she was going to take a step away from that mean, jaded person, she had to let him know how much he meant to her. She had to grow up.

Goddamn feelings are hard.

"I *like* you, Joe," she said, still facing the car. Her fingers flexed against the solid surface, wanting to ball into fists. "Do you understand?"

Ker-thunk. The baseball hit the pavement.

Defeat sat heavily on her shoulders.

But then a tickle at her neck sent electricity zipping down her spine. She straightened, shocked. Joe shifted her ponytail. Soft, velvety lips landed on the flesh beneath her ear. It was so gentle, so hesitant, so vulnerable. Her knees weakened. Her heart *burst*.

"I like you too," he whispered.

And then he was gone.

nine

JOE LUCIANO

JOE LUCIANO'S world had been turned upside down and he didn't know how to respond.

I like you, Joe.

I like you, too.

What were they, twelve?

He strode down the sidewalk toward the restaurant Heaven and didn't look back. Maybe he was a coward. Maybe he should have stayed and talked it out with Liza, but part of him didn't believe her words. Or his. The butterflies in his stomach roared. He could barely hear logic banging in his head.

Why now? Why after all these years?

Joe's doubts screamed at him.

She's lying. She's using you. She doesn't want you. Never has. You'll never be good enough for her.

Strange how that voice always sounded like her brothers. The same ones he was going to have lunch with. The same ones he would send to prison.

"Joe." Liza's footsteps thudded behind him. "Wait up."

His lips pinched at the sides. He stopped just outside the glass door entrance.

She handed him the baseball. "You forgot this."

He put it in his jacket pocket and opened the door. "After you."

There was one thing Joe knew to be true about Liza Lazarus; it was her inability to let go of a sore subject. She'd once raved about a poor umpiring decision for her favorite team for two days. She'd even gone so far as to replay the video and thrust it on anyone who'd listen and then draw diagrams on napkins to explain her reasoning. He'd only replied, "*The umpire is always right.*" Which, of course, infuriated her further. The look she sent him now was just like then. She wasn't done, but she would let him have some space.

Inside Heaven, the smell of butter and garlic made his mouth water. People were crowded into booths. A waiter dropped a tray, the female chef shouted something from the kitchen, and there was a line at the cash register.

"Maybe we should go somewhere else," he suggested.

"Bullshit," she replied. "This is fine. I'm starving, and there's a private room out the back."

The head waiter noticed Liza and came over from the kitchen.

"Liza," he said, then glanced at Joe. "I'm afraid there aren't any tables free, but if you and your guest don't mind dining with the rest of your family, there is space in the VIP room."

She nodded. "I thought they might be here."

This should be interesting. Perhaps he'd garner more information during this lunch meeting than he could at a poker night with the guys from the station.

Joe followed Liza through the busy restaurant to a space near the corridor that went to the bathrooms. The waiter knocked on a frosted glass door. Conversation within hushed. The waiter paused, glanced at Liza, and on her nod, opened the door.

Inside, six people sat at the long table. Although Joe hadn't officially met them all, he recognized most from his case files or from seeing them when he was younger. Sloan and her fiancé, Max, sat on one side. Max was Caucasian and looked like he spent his time at the beach rather than the inner city. Liza's mother and father, Mary and Flint, were on the other side of the long table. Flint's long arm rested over Mary's chair.

Next to him sat a brown-skinned woman wearing a black bomber jacket with a security emblem. It matched what Max wore, so Joe assumed this was Bailey Haze, Tony's fiancé, who also worked with Max at Nightingale Securities.

And then there was the last person, sitting at the head of the table. Joe had to stifle his visceral reaction of contempt for the man— Parker Lazarus. The tall, aristocratic, and egotistical asshole probably deserved to act the way he did. He had the looks, the hair, the body, and the brain. The man was the genius who'd invented many life-saving and environment-saving devices in demand around the world. He'd single-handedly made Lazarus Tech a Fortune 500 company.

He'd been none of those things when he'd said Joe would never be good enough for Liza and then warned Joe away with his very convincing fists. From where Joe sat, it was the Lazarus family who wasn't good enough for Liza.

He stared at the man whose piercing golden eyes watched him back. Parker picked up his napkin, wiped his mouth, and stood as Liza began the introductions.

"You remember my parents, Mary and Flint," she said.

He met their eyes and nodded. *I'll investigate you later.*

"And this is Bailey, Tony's fiancé. She works with Max there, and you know Sloan."

"S'up, bras." Sloan gave a crooked, amused smile.

Max reached around Sloan's shoulders and rested his arm in a possessive way. He gave Joe a cordial tip of the chin, but his eyes betrayed his wariness.

"And, of course, that big meathead over there is Parker."

The air tightened with stress as they waited for Parker to react. His eyes slid to Liza, his brow raised, and then he stood. With dramatic flair, he buttoned his designer blazer and then strode over.

Joe's trigger finger twitched.

Joe hated that he had to look up to meet Parker's gaze. Something wild and feral prowled behind Parker's tawny stare that disagreed with his careful deportment. But he hid it well. Parker never once conceded his gaze, but this time, Joe didn't back down. He'd never do so again.

"You two in love, or something?" Liza scoffed. "You want me to leave?"

Parker held out his hand. "Welcome back."

Joe squinted at it.

A man's metal was tested by the way he shook hands. Limp and sweaty, or hard and firm. Did he lock eyes, or look away? Did he dominate, or submit?

Joe grasped Parker's outstretched hand—*firm, calloused, warm*—surprising.

"It's good to be back," Joe replied.

Parker held Joe's grip, stared, and then bared a toothy grin that looked more like a warning snarl from an apex predator. Parker let go first and then turned to Liza.

"I'm needed back at the office. When I get home, we'll talk."

Joe watched Parker stride away. The man never once looked back. Predators rarely did.

But they should.

"Joe." Liza's voice drew his attention back to her. "What do you want to eat?"

She sat down in Parker's vacated seat, which left a spot next to Sloan, or Bailey. He chose Bailey.

She smiled warmly and handed him a menu. While he perused, menial conversation picked up at the table. After he'd ordered a fillet steak, and the waiter left, he turned to Bailey who'd been waiting to talk.

"You're a Fed, right?" she asked.

He nodded.

She pointed at herself. "Ex CIA."

"Right," he said as if he didn't know. "And how did you fall in with this lot?"

She rolled her eyes. "I made the mistake of falling in love with Tony."

"Mistake?"

She laughed. "Only because we can't seem to stay away from each other. He's not here. He's volunteering at a half-way house right now. What about you? How do you know Liza? Through work?"

"You don't know?" he asked.

"He used to pull Liza's pigtails," Sloan interjected.

"I didn't," he scoffed.

"Yeah, you did. Never pulled mine, though." She waggled her brows.

He shook his head, cheeks heating despite him willing them not to.

Sloan laughed. "Little Joey liked her. Just admit it."

A thump under the table. Cutlery jumped and tinkled. Sloan's eyes narrowed and shot to Liza.

"Ow," Sloan said through her teeth.

Liza glared back.

"What?" Sloan lifted her palms. "I don't need my—"

Another thump.

Mary cleared her throat. "Behave, children."

Liza sent Joe a tight-lipped smile and then stood. "Sloan. Can I see you outside for a minute?"

Flint used the opportunity to steer the conversation. "What brings you back to Cardinal City, Joe?"

"An investigation," he replied, and looked him directly in the eyes.

ten

LIZA LAZARUS

LIZA YANKED her blabbermouth sister outside the private dining room and dragged her partway down the hallway that led to the restrooms.

"Ow," Sloan whined. "What gives?"

She shrugged out of Liza's hold. Simultaneously, both winced as their sin-sensing came back now they'd reached the limit of their mate's nullification.

Liza rubbed her gut.

"Yeah," Sloan murmured. "It takes a little getting used to."

Liza took a few deep breaths. "Is it always like this?"

Sloan nodded. "The second I leave Max's radius, I feel it. Sloth, everywhere. Why do you think I'm stuck to him like glue?"

They stood together, bonded in shared pain. Liza had been about to chew Sloan's ear off for almost giving away their secret, but now it seemed rather pointless. Joe would find out eventually, but how long did she wait? She saw the way he looked at Parker. There was deep-seated animosity there, and with Wyatt around, it would only get worse.

Liza had no idea why Joe hated her two eldest brothers so much.

"He doesn't know," Liza conceded.

"About… us?" Sloan frowned, and then turned her head back toward the room, as if she could see through the frosted glass. Sloan was an empath. She could not only sense emotions, but make people feel things too. She'd once sent a busload of people to sleep by accident.

Liza had believed Sloan was the deadliest of them all. She looked down at her own glove-covered hands. Maybe not anymore.

"When did you know you could trust Max?" Liza asked.

Sloan shrugged. "He already knew. Parker told him."

"That's right."

"Joe's your mate, right?"

Liza nodded. "But he's throwing mixed signals, and he's resisting my advances. He's not the same person I used to know. I feel as though he's keeping something from me."

"I'll keep an eye on him." Sloan's gaze dipped to Liza's hands. "You going to tell me what the deal is with your new fashion choice?"

"What has Mama told you?"

"Something about poison."

"Sounds about right."

"And?"

"And, what?"

"Why do you have your hands covered?"

"Why do you think, dumbass?"

"It comes out of your hands? So that's why Parker wants to talk to you. The sooner you get that under control, the better. Trust me."

Liza was about to make a sassy retort, but a sharp, keening twinge in her gut meant only one thing. Her fingers wrapped around the grip of her gun in the holster.

Sloan stiffened. "What is it? Someone getting lucky?"

Liza crept back toward the restaurant. Alarm prickled her senses. "No. It's the other kind of lust. And it's getting closer."

It was the type of lust when someone wanted something deeply, perhaps even enough to kill for it. It hurt more like a sharp twinge in her gut than a slow ache. Liza took two steps past the private room and then came face to face with the reason for her caution.

Standing two feet away, dressed casually in jeans and a white hoodie, was their eldest sister. The one who'd been working for the enemy. Long silver-white hair draped down her shoulders and hid the faint burn scars on half her face. Vibrant violet eyes blinked at them from an ethereally beautiful face.

"Holy fuck," Sloan whispered. "Daisy."

Every time Liza saw Daisy, it was a shock to her system. She was as stunning as Liza remembered, but her eyes were empty. They used to be so full of life.

"Daisy," Liza said, and waited to be corrected.

Every time they'd met, Daisy had preferred to be called Despair. But naming each other by their sin was something the Syndicate did. It dehumanized them, and the Lazarus family had made the choice long ago to be better.

Daisy held her palms out in surrender. "I want to talk."

ANTICIPATION BUZZED down Liza's spine as she walked toward a recently vacated booth in the main part of the restaurant. The window to the street was to one side, and on the other, the main bulk of the restaurant.

Daisy was unarmed and alone. She claimed she only wanted to

talk. Liza couldn't risk Joe finding out about the sister they'd thought dead but had been left behind and now worked for the enemy. It would be too much for him to take. He held no loyalty to Liza's family, and she knew, without a doubt, that Joe would arrest Daisy, right there and then if he knew the crimes she'd committed.

Liza motioned for Daisy to get into the horseshoe-shaped booth before sliding in herself. Sloan took the other side of the booth, essentially blocking Daisy's exit. They were at the opposite end of Heaven from the private room. A myriad of people dined between them and Joe, but Liza couldn't help feeling nervous. Daisy had spurned their previous offers for her to come back to the family. What had changed?

"Make a wrong move," Sloan warned, "And you'll regret it."

"Sloan. Liza." Daisy tested the names as though learning them. A slight frown marred her pale forehead. "I want to talk. Just us girls."

"Then Mama should be here." Liza pulled out her cell, intending to send a quick text message.

"You mean the *Sinner*," Daisy replied. "She's not our mother."

"Maybe not in blood, but she is in every other way that matters." Sloan scowled at her.

"If it's all the same, she is the one who left me behind. I'd prefer not to have her here."

Sloan and Liza studied their sister. There was no way to decipher her true intentions, but Liza couldn't argue with her point. It was Mary who'd made the tough decision to leave Daisy after she'd run back into the burning building to save their biological mother, a futile feat. Gloria had died anyway.

"Speak," Sloan ordered.

"I... I want to..." Daisy shook her head. "You don't want me here. I'll leave."

Sloan pushed her back down. "You tortured my fiancé. Of course, I don't want you here."

"Sloan," Liza said. "We've all done bad things. Let's hear her out."

"Easy for you to say, she hasn't tortured your mate. But there's still time for that, isn't there Daisy?"

Daisy's eyes crossed to Liza's. "You've found your mate?"

Idiot, Sloan! Liza glared at her younger sister. Now Daisy knew that Liza's genetic makeup had been unlocked. The Syndicate had been after a sample of their blood as soon as their powers hit. They wanted to replicate the genetic experiments, this time growing powered clones in tanks, ones that could be controlled and manipulated.

The Deadly Seven were meant to be weapons of mass destruction. Julius wanted a new world, and he'd wanted the Lazarus siblings to help him. But when Mary and Flint helped them escape from the lab that created them, Julius's plans were temporarily foiled.

Liza could see the contemplation in Daisy's eyes, but she made no move, despite Liza tugging her gloves off beneath the table.

"Congratulations," Daisy said.

"That's it?"

"That's it," Daisy confirmed. "I do not wish to hurt you, or your partner. I'm done with Julius."

The news hit both Sloan and Liza like a slap to the face. They jerked. Blinked. And then squirmed uncomfortably. Wasn't this what they'd wanted all this time?

Then why wasn't Liza's doubt assuaged?

It was that lust she felt... the needy kind. It was laced with something gritty Liza couldn't put her finger on, only that it made her sick to the core.

Movement across the restaurant drew Sloan's attention, and Liza followed her gaze, surprised to see Mary leave the private room and come striding over. Liza sent questioning eyes to her sister. Had she alerted Mary?

"Daisy." Mary's eyes glistened with hope. Her hands trembled as she reached over the table for Daisy, then snatched her hand back to her side. Instead, she slid in next to Sloan.

"She wants to talk," Liza offered. "Said she's done with Julius."

"Then you need to come upstairs, *Mija*. We need complete privacy for this talk. It's been a long time coming."

Sloan shook her head. "No. We're not inviting her into our homes. No fucking way. Wyatt would have a conniption."

Sloan was a baby when they'd escaped the lab. She would have no memories of Daisy. But Liza did. She remembered a lot. She remembered how Daisy had trouble lying. How when she had to, she'd sweat. Liza also remembered how Daisy used to sing a song to calm their nerves before receiving a shot from the scientists. They owed it to let her speak.

She wasn't sweating now.

"Give her a chance, Sloan." Liza put her gloves on the table.

"Are you serious? It's a trap."

"I'll tell you anything you want to know," Daisy offered. "About... where I've been working."

Mary looked at Sloan. "What do you sense, Sloan?"

"Nothing. The woman has zero emotions."

Or she was very good at hiding them. But Daisy hadn't been able to conceal the lust she felt.

"Not all of them," Liza added. "She wants this meeting with us. Bad."

"Because she wants your DNA, Liza," Sloan growled through clenched teeth.

Daisy shook her head. "They don't need it anymore. They have enough."

Another stab of pain in Liza's gut had her doubled over. Sloan did the same. They met eyes with dread.

Deadly sin. Lots of it. Coming in fast.

Liza searched the restaurant and came up short, but then a ruckus exploded outside. Through Heaven's windows, a disturbance grew on the street. White robed and masked soldiers flooded the sidewalk. People screamed in terror.

Sloan's gaze landed on Daisy. "I hope you choke."

Daisy's eyes widened. "I didn't bring them. I swear."

Another curdling scream. Sloan hit the button on her wristwatch, triggering the alarm to every member of the Deadly Seven, then she launched out of the booth and bolted for the front door.

Liza gave Daisy a severe glance. "You say you didn't bring them. Then prove it. Fight with us."

Mary already had her cell phone out, but Liza didn't stay to see who she called. She jogged to the front of the restaurant, pivoted, and held her CCPD badge out.

"CCPD!" she shouted. "Everyone stay calm. Stay indoors. Stay down and away from the windows."

A shout outside cut mid-cry. A thud. A shudder against the window. Liza glanced over her shoulder to see blood spray on the glass door.

"*Shit.*" She couldn't leave Sloan out there on her own. The rest of her siblings weren't available. Only Wyatt was upstairs in the building, and there was no way Liza was letting him come down. Not with Daisy here. Misha would be left without protection.

Sloan could be right. This could be a trap.

Daisy jogged up to Liza's side. "You need help. Give me a weapon. I will join you."

"I'm not giving you my gun." Liza gaped.

"Then…" Daisy looked around, locked onto a steak knife at a nearby table, retrieved it, and then pushed her way outside.

Fuck!

"Liza?" Joe stood, not five feet away and coming closer.

"Stop!" She held her palm out, saw the yellow mist oozing from her pores, and snatched her hand back. "Stay here. Keep everyone inside."

His nostrils flared with defiance, but somehow, he knew this was important. He listened. He unclipped his firearm and retrieved his identification. With her mind awhirl, she turned her back on him and trusted that he would keep the crowd inside, calm, and safe.

Liza held her firearm steady as she shouldered through the exit. She only had one magazine. A limited number of bullets, and a set of cuffs in her back pocket. She had to make them count. When she emerged, her breath caught in her throat.

White robes swarmed everywhere. There had to be at least a few dozen Faithful. Down the street from Heaven were many cafes and restaurants, stores, and apartments. Pedestrian bodies lay on the sidewalk in a brutal display of violence. Cars had halted in the street. Traffic horns blared as Faithful jumped on top of vehicles, wreaking havoc. There was no escape.

Anyone caught in the area was trapped.

A woman screamed at Liza's right.

A Faithful crouched on the roof of a Prius. Somehow he'd clawed into the metal roof with one hand, while his other fed through the driver's side window. A middle-aged brunette slapped the hand away, but he'd caught her hair and tried to drag her out, heedless of the broken glass cutting into his arm. Liza aimed. Fired.

Pop!

The Faithful jerked but recovered.

She fired again. And again. Until she got the satisfaction she

needed when the figure fell to the ground, his white robe fluttering like the wings of a fallen angel.

Each enemy held different weapons. Some had none, but they weren't powerless. Through their blank, white Halloween face masks, Liza glimpsed bloodshot eyes.

The Syndicate had a serum that induced psychosis and gave the user a temporary boost in strength. Perhaps they were infected with it. Or it could be some new cocktail of chemicals. The Syndicate had created mutated plant monsters and demonic animals that sensed sin. Anything was possible.

Where was Sloan?

Liza's heart hammered in her chest as she searched but found another sister instead. Daisy's long silver hair flared like a fan as she twirled and stabbed Faithful with sewing machine repetition. Blood bloomed on white robes, but Daisy didn't wait to see how her opponents faired. She moved silently and swiftly onto the next and efficiently stabbed her knife into vital points. Jugular veins, carotids, femoral artery. Someone had taught Daisy the meaning of death. And she excelled.

In Liza's experience, there were only two ways to become that good. Innate talent, or fear.

A movement to Liza's left caught her attention.

Sloan.

She'd jumped onto a car for a better view. From there, she proceeded to stare down Faithful, sending her silent but deadly power into the minds of their enemies. Some screamed in fear, others simply fell into a dead sleep.

But Sloan wasn't in costume. She could blow her identity.

"Sloan!" Liza shouted. "You need to get inside."

The wind lifted Sloan's dark hair to curl around her fierce face. She shook her head.

Damn it.

Sirens wailed in the distance, but they were too far.

A heavyweight knocked into Liza. She careened to the side. Another knock. A Faithful's fist in her face. Her firearm disappeared from her hand. A swarm of sweaty, grunting white fabric covered men hit her. Her body moved on instinct, blocking, and retaliating, but it was the poison leaking from her hands and mouth that did the most damage. The instant she touched broken skin, or yellow fumes were inhaled by her opponents, they wilted in dead weight, foaming and convulsing.

Holy shit, this was dangerous. And frightening. Any bystander nearby could be hurt—from her—and she had no way of controlling it. Afraid to shout, to scream, or to do anything but hold her breath, a mad panic bubbled in her system.

What if she did this around a child? What if she was kissing Joe?

Pushing the weight of a Faithful from her body, Liza scanned the ground for her gun.

Pop! Pop! Pop!

An explosion of shots fired like a shooting range.

Liza ducked, scanned wildly, and found Joe at the door to Heaven, gun pointed and shooting any threat he could safely aim at. He wasn't the only one. Max and Bailey were on the street, guns aimed and discharging.

"Liza! Behind you," Joe shouted, eyes locked on her. He moved his aim to Liza's right and fired. The Faithful behind her went down, a bloom of red spreading on his robe.

She got to her feet and nodded her thanks.

Dead bodies piled up, both innocents and criminals. This was a shit-show. There would be an inquest. The captain would have her badge if he didn't believe they handled it properly. She had to trust that the evidence would back her up. She had to trust that no one saw or captured their abilities on camera.

Joe started for her, but she backed away. She couldn't be near him with her emotions heightened, with the poison still coming from her mouth and hands.

"Sloan!" Max bellowed.

Liza looked to where she'd last seen Sloan and found her no longer on the roof of the car. From the way Max manically fought his way there, he must have seen her go down. But he knew she was stronger than she looked. He *knew*. So why was he panicked?

Unless she'd been taken out.

Shit.

Pushing her thighs into action, Liza ran. No time to worry about appearances. She vaulted over bodies and sprinted to where Sloan had gone down. An undulating sea of blood-stained white blocked her way, snarling and ready to fight. Too many. She wouldn't make it through. Not in time.

Daisy appeared at Liza's side, plucking Faithful away, stabbing, jabbing, shrieking like a harpy in the biggest display of emotion Liza had seen come from her. Elation and hope momentarily lifted in Liza's soul. Daisy blinked at Liza, surprised. And then Max went down.

Liza screamed in frustration.

"Save Max," she ordered Daisy, and pointed to him. "Max!"

Covered in war-paint of streaked red and dirty sweat, Daisy nodded. She changed tactics.

This was it. Liza couldn't both save Sloan, and hide her powers. She had to make a choice and move. Liza did what had to be done. The valve on her power burst. Mist oozed from her mouth at an alarming rate as she fired the last of her bullets, aiming for heads.

Out of ammo.

She dropped the gun and shifted to manual combat. Strike. Jab. Snap. Her body flowed like water. Her fists like iron. Each time she moved, the poison not only seeped from her hand but shot out in an almost imperceptible tiny dart-like projectile that burned her palms on release. Each time she exhaled, her breath came out in a sharp, steady, and focused tiny toxic gust. She plowed through body after body, discharging toxin until the air misted into yellow, making it hard to see and her eyes sting. But it also provided her cover to act unhindered.

Eventually, Liza was on the floor, crawling through falling legs and tumbling trunks of white robes, and then she found Sloan, passed out. Liza launched, covered Sloan's body with her own, and...

Electricity crackled, metal creaked, blue fire flashed. Katanas and leather-clad warriors descended from the sky like battle-born dark angels. The cavalry had arrived. In what seemed the blink of an eye, an eery silence descended, and then sirens blared.

SWAT was here.

Too afraid to move and check, Liza covered her fallen sister. And then Sloan groaned. Liza almost wept with relief, but her poison hadn't received the memo to switch off.

Please stop. Please stop.

"Don't breathe in, Sloan. It's poison," Liza warned. She sat back on her haunches, staring agape at her stained hands. "Stop. *Stop!*"

Too much yellow mist. She had to get out of there.

"Crawl out of the mist, Sloan," she ordered. "Hold your breath. I don't know if you'll be—"

Liza cut herself off with a realization. She wasn't affected by the poison. Would Gloria give her this toxin and not make her siblings resistant to it? No, she wouldn't. They could heal fast. They were immune to sickness. Perhaps they'd all resist this too.

Liza waved her hand and tried to clear the toxic mist.

"Max," Sloan croaked. "I heard him."

"Daisy's protecting him."

They cleared the yellow mist and Sloan bolted to a sitting position, her eyes wide. Liza helped her to stand and then tucked her hands under her arms. The poison seemed to have stopped, or had run out, thank God.

The wind blew, and more mist dispersed, revealing a concrete war zone. Max bled from shallow face wounds and was down on his knee, cradling Daisy's head in his lap with his hand over her rapidly bleeding chest.

"She's hit," he said.

Daisy's expression tried to stifle emotion, but the pain was clear in the pinch of her eyes.

"What happened?" Sloan asked.

"She stepped in front of a bullet aimed at my heart," Max answered, face pale.

Liza checked around. Any evidence that her siblings had been present in battle gear was long gone. They knew that once the immediate threat was over, they had to flee and leave the mopping up to the authorities. That used to be her job. But now Daisy was hurt. There were more important things.

"Take her downstairs," Sloan said.

Liza put her hand on Sloan's leg. "Are you sure?"

"She saved Max's life."

"Go. I'll—" Liza finally summoned the courage to look for Joe. How much had he seen? How much had he deciphered? From the flex of his hard jaw, and the coldness in his eyes... a lot. "I'll sort things out here."

Liza took a step toward Joe, but he flinched and then turned away to check the fallen for survivors. Blood drained from Liza's face. When she looked at her reflection in the window to Heaven, she understood why he'd balked. Yellow ochre ran down her chin and neck in great, undeniable streaks.

Monster.

"Liza," Sloan urged, startling her. "Leave things here for the authorities. Help me."

With a look full of longing at her mate, Liza reluctantly nodded. Her family needed her.

JOE LUCIANO

A WHITE-ROBED OFFENDER was still alive when Joe yanked the Halloween mask from his face. He was alive, but having a seizure. Foam collected at the corners of his mouth as he gulped for air. Bloodshot eyes darted around.

"Why?" Joe asked.

The man's eyes rolled to Joe, and he garbled, "F-for a b-better life."

With the last of his breath, yellow bile emptied from his mouth.

Was it some kind of neurotoxin? A nerve agent? Cyanide? He sniffed, then coughed as a slight burn hit his olfactory. Alarmed, he turned his face to the side and gulped fresh air, waiting with dread to see if numbness exhibited in his body, but none came. Regardless, he lifted his shirt to cover his nose and mouth.

It hadn't smelled nutty like cyanide, but its effects were strong. He filed the information away for another time and made sure not to inhale more. For now, he needed to see to the victims, secure the scene, and talk to Liza.

She had some explaining to do.

Straightening, he surveyed the devastation in the street with grim defeat. Cars dented, crashed, and broken. Red blood mixing with a strange yellow liquid on the road. It had only taken a few minutes to turn from *Pleasantville* to a *Nightmare on Elm Street*. Victims' innards fell from their guts. Heads snapped clean off. The dead were a mix of innocents interspersed with the sea of white-robed extremists. The costumes said they were the same ones Joe had come across during his investigation of the Deadly Seven. The same terrorists the Feds kept sweeping under the rug.

And here they were again, causing more devastation.

Why was he investigating the Deadly Seven, and not them? If it wasn't for Liza and her family, the bloodshed could have spilled into the restaurant. Into the buildings. Down the streets… all over the city.

Exasperated, Joe wiped his sweaty brow with the back of his hand and searched for Liza. She was gone. As was the rest of her family. Vanished, as though they'd never been there.

The first lot of sirens turned up. Police, followed by an ambulance. Joe jogged over and showed his ID to the first responders, then had to wait as one of them puked onto the pavement behind his car.

The driver got out of the vehicle and met Joe. "What the hell?"

He was the senior cop, had graying hair at his temples, and a little too much weight around the middle. But he wasn't losing the contents of his stomach like the rookie who'd come with him.

"Prepare yourself," Joe said. "It's ugly. You're the first to arrive. We'll have to secure the area and alert the paramedics to any victims in need. The ones in white robes were the offenders. Anyone else takes priority. And be careful of the yellow substance. I think it's a chemical of some sort."

The cop nodded and went to work.

Joe's cell rang.

"Liza?" he said into the handset.

"Director Dixon."

"Sir. Sorry, I thought you were someone else."

"It's all over the news. What the hell is going on?"

News? Joe frowned and looked for a TV crew but found none. Then he saw the camera phones recording within the restaurant. *Idiots.*

Joe clicked his fingers at the cop who'd been puking. "You," he said. "Go into the restaurant and stop the filming. Remind them that this is an active crime scene, and we'll need their footage for the investigation."

The cop nodded and then jogged off.

"Sorry, sir, you were saying?" Joe said.

"Was it the Deadly Seven?"

Joe balked. The director had seen the devastation on the news, and yet the first thing he asked was that? "No, sir. It wasn't them who caused it. They're the ones responsible for stopping the situation escalating."

"Where are they now?"

"I have no idea. I'm knee-deep in bloody white-robed bodies."

A muffled sound came through the handset. It sounded like the director was frustrated and had put the phone down to rub his face. When he came back, he said with slow vehemence, *"You're in town to investigate the Deadly Seven, not these offenders. Let the locals pick that up. I want you chasing down leads. I want those vigilante assholes captured. The only reason you were picked for this assignment is because of your ties to the Lazarus family. Do you understand, Luciano?"*

Cold dread filled Joe. Yeah, he fucking understood. He understood that he was being used to get to the Lazarus family. He understood that if he refused, he'd probably lose his job. He understood that the Agency had its priorities wrong and Joe had to be clever about how he handled things.

The director sighed. *"I get it. It's a shit-show. But it's not your shit-show. Homeland will be there soon to mop up."*

"Homeland?" Since when were they involved?

"The assholes who did this, they're terrorists. That's all you need to know. Let them do their job, and you can do yours."

"Sir, but if it wasn't for the—"

"Luciano!" the director snapped. *"They're vigilantes. If every Tom, Dick, and Harry thinks they can get away with taking the law into their own hands, we'll have chaos. You know that."*

"Yes, sir."

"I want leads, Luciano. Evidence that ties the Lazarus family to the disaster we've just witnessed. If we can prosecute them for murder, they're all going away for a very long time."

"Yes, sir."

"Good. I expect a full report tomorrow. If I don't get it by the evening, I might need to find a new lead investigator for this case."

"You won't need that, sir. I'll have something for you tomorrow."

The call ended, and Joe put his cell away. When he slipped his hand into his jacket pocket, he felt the baseball.

"Shit," he muttered.

twelve

LIZA LAZARUS

"DON'T TOUCH ANYONE!" Parker shouted at Liza as he wheeled Daisy on a gurney into the medical room of the basement headquarters in Lazarus House. "You need to shower the chemical off. Go!"

Liza flattened herself against a wall as they rushed past.

Daisy's violet eyes were stark. She blinked at the ceiling. Max was on the gurney, kneeling over Daisy, pressing his palms to the wound. Blood welled from beneath his fingertips. They made it to the medical room where Griffin and Evan waited, both in battle gear, hoods down. Parker was a genius. He knew a lot, but he wasn't a surgeon. Would he be enough? Could they keep Daisy from bleeding out?

"She's going to make it, right?" Sloan asked, coming up to Liza. "I mean, she's got the same fast healing ability as us, right?"

Uncertainty stretched before them like a gaping abyss. There was so much they didn't know about their eldest sister. As Mary and Flint rushed into the hallway, faces gray with worry, Liza knew a turning point had been reached in their relationship with Daisy. Behind her parents, other members of the Deadly Seven and their partners crowded into the hallway, each with expressions of concern.

Daisy was one of them.

It didn't matter whether she had worked for the enemy, had committed atrocities, or loved them back. She was their blood, and they would take care of her.

Family first, Mary had always said. Because without this love between one other, there was nothing. There was doom, and the empty violent apocalypse Mary had foretold when she was younger.

Liza glanced at Sloan, also covered in an array of dust, blood, and yellow residue. Warm pride unfurled in her chest. Her sister had walked headfirst into danger and excelled. She'd almost died, too, but Liza had kept her baby sister safe. Sloan wasn't so helpless anymore. She was a strong, powerful, woman. And she was winning at life, far better than Liza ever was.

Sloan wrung her fingers, eyes glued to the windowpane leading to the medical room where Parker and Max triaged Daisy.

"Are you okay?" Liza asked, voice still trembling. "I mean, the toxin… it hasn't…"

Sloan shook her head. "I feel fine. A little numb around the lips, but fine." She met Liza's eyes. "What the hell was it, sis? You had yellow smoke curling from your mouth and shooting from your hands. If anyone else got that in their system—"

"Don't you think I know that?" Liza's eyes blurred as she recalled what had happened. The way the Faithful in her path had paralyzed, seized, and convulsed. "I need to wash this shit off. You too."

"I'm fine."

"If Max touches you with that stuff on, it could kill him. Mama. Papa. Anyone not genetically modified will be at risk."

"Damn it. I'm coming."

The two of them jogged to the locker room and then into the

bathroom with three shower stalls against the wall. On the other side were the mirrors and vanities. Liza turned on the first shower faucet and ushered Sloan in.

"Clothes and all," she said, and then turned on the faucet in the second stall before dunking under herself.

Water saturated her body. Yellow mixed with the blood of her enemies and dribbled down, leaving a swirling pattern of orange as it disappeared into the drain. Opening her mouth, she let the water clean inside, spat, and then drank deeply. *So thirsty*. She peeled off her outer layers and remained in her bra and panties, all the while receiving flashes of the bloody devastation from the street.

What were the Faithful thinking? They'd attacked for no reason. There was no logic to their actions. Anyone and everyone in their way had been the focus of their wrath. But it hadn't been the first time they'd done this. They'd attacked randomly multiple times over the past two years. They didn't need a reason, this was what they did—incite chaos.

Waterlogged inside and out, Liza turned off the faucet and shuddered. If she hadn't done what she did, more people could have died.

She'd done the right thing.

There was no other option.

"Sloan!" Max's deep voice roared from outside the room.

Liza glanced over the stall to see Sloan's head lift, as though she'd raised on her toes.

"In here!" Sloan shouted.

Liza blinked, reached for a towel, and stepped out of the stall just as Max came hurtling into the bathroom, frantic and in search of the fiancée he'd almost lost. His hands were still covered in Daisy's blood, but he only had eyes for Sloan. She'd barely opened her stall when he charged through, joined her in the shower, and checked her for injuries.

"You were down," he said. "I couldn't see you."

"I'm fine. Liza covered me."

Max's wild eyes searched and found Liza's. Silent recognition and gratitude echoed her way. She nodded in return.

"Daisy?" Sloan asked, drawing back Max's attention.

"She's fine. Bullet's out. Bleeding has stopped."

"Thank God," Liza said.

But no one heard her. Max pushed the stall door closed. Liza caught a glimpse of his lips mashed against Sloan's, kissing her as though she were the air he breathed.

Usually, Liza would say something snarky about the lust spiraling from them, but she only had energy for hugging the towel and leaving the room in case she vomited.

Daisy was okay. Sloan was okay. They'd stopped the Faithful from spreading and wreaking more havoc, but... Joe's piercing eyes flashed in her mind. When he'd seen the yellow streaks on her face, he looked afraid. She shook her head to get the image out, but it wouldn't leave.

"Liza." Parker's deep voice lifted her head. He stood in the locker room, Deadly Seven hood down and around his shoulders. The blood had been washed from his hands. Wisps of auburn hair pulled free from the tie he'd tamed it with. He looked wild, wolfish, and pissed.

"I'm not in a mood for judgment, Parks."

"Too bad," he replied. "You've been sitting on that skill of yours for a few days, and you haven't tested your limits. That's reckless and dangerous. What you produce is worse than cyanide."

Her eyes narrowed. "How would you know that?"

The arrogance dropped from his expression.

"You know something," Liza accused. She strode toward her big brother and jabbed him in the chest. "And you've been expecting this, haven't you?"

He tried to backpedal. "I never said that."

"Then how the hell do you know what my toxin is made of if you've only just discovered it?" Silence greeted her. God damn. "You've deciphered Gloria's laptop, haven't you?"

Parker had always claimed he wasn't able to crack it. None of them could, so they'd left it. Mary and Liza had sought him out the other night but failed to find him. Turned out their instincts were right.

Parker's nostrils flared at her accusation. And that's when she noticed something she never thought she'd see in her brother's tawny-eyed stare. Maybe denial. Or something darker. Fear.

"You found something on that laptop. About you," she said. "And you didn't like it."

"We're not talking about me. We're talking about you. The chemical you produce is one of the deadliest neurotoxins on the planet. Tetrodotoxin is a hundred times more deadly than cyanide, and there is no known antidote. We'll have to make modifications to your battle suit, and you'll have to wear it. I'm not fucking around here, Liza. You'll need to get it under control. One slip around a civilian—or your mate—and you *will* kill them." He started murmuring to himself, something about proteins and antibodies in her blood, and then strode out of the locker room, leaving Liza quaking.

She could kill Joe with a kiss... if he still wanted to kiss her.

"Today, Liza!" Parker's shout filtered through the basement.

"Arrogant fucker," Liza mumbled, and then found a spare pair of baggy sweatpants and a crop top in her locker. She towel-dried her hair and tied it in a low ponytail. When she met Parker in the work-shop attached to the operations room, he scowled at her.

The workshop was half mechanical parts and wiring, and part labo-ratory with scopes and scientific equipment. Parker, Flint, and Sloan were the main users of the room. The rest of the family usually preferred to use the gym, the weapons room, and on occasion, the multi-screened surveillance in the operations room. They all had their talents, and Liza's wasn't in any of these rooms. She preferred to do her saving in broad daylight. Sometimes the weak weren't preyed on in hard and fast confrontations, they were taken advantage of over time. For them, cruelty was a slow poison seeping into their skins, and Liza was the antidote. She'd been taking pimps and murderers off the streets for years.

"You know, I heard that," Parker noted gruffly.

"Heard what?" She blinked innocently. "The fact that you're an arrogant fucker, or the sound of your pride slowly choking you?"

His scowl deepened as he stuck electrodes to her skin, on her chest and temples. "You can't manage on your own, Liza. None of us can. I'm not too proud to see that."

"Aren't you?" She raised a brow which he ignored.

"Despite what you think, I'm not doing this to lord over you."

"Could have fooled me."

His jaw flexed. He turned his back and placed his palms on the workbench. Tension tightened his shoulders, and without looking at her, he spoke. "I'm doing this because I love you. You're family."

Her shoulders dropped, and she sighed. "I know. I'm sorry."

"Can you control your power?"

She flattened her lips. "It kind of happens when I'm stressed."

"Then we'll work on triggering that response and then see if you can rein it in."

Parker hit the Deadly Seven emblem on his chest and said, "AIMI, let me out of the suit."

The AI he'd created with Flint and Sloan, AIMI, spoke out of the speakers in the ceiling. *"Yes, Parker, oh King of Ass-hats. Form-fitting function deactivated."*

"Fucking Sloan," Parker shouted in the direction of the bathrooms. "Reprogram AIMI again, and I'll remove your access."

Liza covered her smile. Of course, his small confession of affection would be obliterated by a growling lion. She supposed she was lucky to catch a glimpse.

Air rushed out of the suit's neck, and the fabric lost its tension. Once tight and snug on Parker's large and muscular body, it became loose. He stepped out of it and placed the suit on the workshop bench.

Liza looked through to the adjoining operations room where white, faceless mannequins in glass cabinets surrounded the center table. When no one wore their battle gear, Deadly suits covered those mannequins. Each one had a different colored fukumen face scarf. Liza's was fuchsia, bright, and clean as the day it was made. Hers, Wyatt's, and Sloan's suits were the only two remaining on the mannequins.

Naked except for his boxer shorts, Parker found a swab kit and took samples of Liza's toxin from his suit.

"While you're doing a stress test," he said. "I'll test the toxin for due diligence."

"Where is everyone else?"

Serious eyes met hers. "Most are with Daisy."

"How come you're not?"

"Someone needs to make sure you can handle yourself before you're set loose on the world again."

Liza didn't think that was the only reason, but if Parker felt anything like Liza, he was nervous as hell to be around Daisy. And it wasn't purely because she'd been working for the enemy for most of their lives. Liza and Parker were the eldest. They *remembered* Daisy. As children, she'd held them when they'd cried. She sang them songs to make them feel better and told stories at bedtime.

Daisy was living proof of a nightmare future they'd escaped. She was who they would have been if Mary hadn't made the sacrifice to save them at Daisy's expense.

Liza crossed her arms. "I handled myself just fine, thank you."

A lone, indignant brow arched. "And have you checked to see if you caught any innocents in your wake? Do you know what your toxin has done to the insides of those it caught?"

He had a point. Joe was out there still.

"He's fine," Parker said, reading her expression. "The poisonous mist dispersed quickly, and tetrodotoxin is at its worst when inhaled or somehow imbued into the bloodstream. A little on his skin won't kill him."

"How do you know?"

"Griff is on the roof, keeping an eye on things. The effects of your poison works fast. If Joe was affected, he'd be down by now."

Liza received another flash of the dead bodies and the blood-covered Faithful.

"It was a mess, Parker," Liza breathed. "Why would they do that?"

Solemn eyes met hers. "I don't know. But there's more to it. And I don't believe Daisy's suddenly turned a new leaf. The two are connected. We need to take precautions."

"She got hurt protecting Max."

"She got hurt knowing she would heal fast."

LIZA SPENT the next twenty minutes running at full pelt on the treadmill in the gym. Electrodes on her chest and temples fed information back to AIMI who compiled data for Parker on his laptop. He'd tested the biohazard samples from his suit and, true to his hypothesis, it was tetrodotoxin, the same chemical pufferfish produced. Similar to what the bombardier beetle squirted.

Parker had inspected Liza's mouth and identified glands at the back of her throat, but they found nothing on her palms. They must be too tiny or under her skin.

She rubbed her hands together as she jogged on the treadmill in the gym, eyes forward and steady on the wall before her.

"Stop," Parker growled from his perch on a workout bench, his laptop balancing on his knee. Sometime between testing the samples and coming into the gym, he'd sourced a pair of sweats, but remained shirtless and shoeless, which meant only one thing—he planned on sparring. "This is getting nowhere. You're supposed to be triggering your stress response."

She hit the stop button on the treadmill and waited for the belt to slow. "Keep talking, brother. Maybe we'll have success after all."

An eyebrow quirk was his response. With a smooth glide, he got off the bench, put the laptop to the side, and pointed with his finger for her to get on the sparring mat.

"I'll be back," he said and left the room.

Puffing, Liza strode to the mat. She eyed the boxer's tape on the floor next to the weightlifting chalk but dismissed the idea. Knowing her brother, he'd have an exact notion of how this sparring match would go.

While she waited, her thoughts shifted to Joe, and she knew she'd have to see him in the next day or two, or the sin in her system could shift to unbalanced in the blink of an eye. Panic caused her pulse to beat a staccato rhythm in her chest, bouncing against her ribcage. Parker had been right. If she wasn't careful, and she blacked out as Sloan had once, then anyone in her vicinity would die. Just like that.

There is no known antidote.

Sloan had accidentally sent her family to sleep, but Liza could kill them with poisoned breath. Sloan said her lips had been numb, and that was only from having a light mist touch her skin. But what if next time she inhaled an actual direct hit of the poison?

There were too many variables to consider, and she couldn't afford to see Joe until she knew the answer to all of them. There were no maybes in this world.

Parker entered the room with a collection of weapons. Liza couldn't help wondering if she was using this as an excuse to avoid Joe, and he was using it to avoid Daisy. She'd been around Joe for two days without any ill effect, and around her family for the same. She was fine sitting in close quarters in a car, or touching Joe intimately in the garage. Deep down she knew her lack of control over her power wasn't why she avoided Joe.

The same look echoed in Parker's eyes. This was a distraction for him too.

He liked to think he was infallible, but he wasn't. If only he let someone in, he might not have to deal with his issues alone.

"What's your poison?" He held out the weapons and then smirked at his joke.

"You're so funny, Parks," Liza mocked. Then made a show of shopping for the best weapon. "You should start your own comedy act."

He had a katana, nunchaku, and a ninjato sword. But it was the curved karambit knife that took her attention. Sleek, dark, and sharp, the blade resembled a raptor's claw, had an ergonomic handle, and a safety ring she was well versed in using.

Being a cop, she'd had little use for these sorts of weapons. Her hand hovered over the karambit and Parker gave a knowing snort.

"How did I know you would take that? Mary would be proud."

"Hello, old friend," Liza crooned and fitted the knife to her right palm.

She stepped back, swirled the blade around her finger in a showy display, and then crouched into an attack position, muscles loose but ready.

Parker discarded the two swords and kept the nunchaku—two sticks joined by a chain—returning her display with a flourish of his own. The fact he chose a weapon that didn't draw blood was cocky, arrogant, and so very like him. It said he didn't need that extra violent step, he could decimate her without it. With his free hand, he beckoned her.

Oh, how Liza would enjoy watching him fall.

She prowled around him on the mat.

He casually echoed her steps and left the nunchaku resting over his shoulder, as though going out for an afternoon stroll. He wasn't even trying to prepare himself. Liza narrowed her eyes.

"Remind me, what's the point of this?" she asked.

"I get you afraid, and you release the poison."

She feinted, he lunged back.

"And what if you get sick?"

He shrugged. "I'll survive."

A snort escaped Liza. She jabbed at Parker's smug face, using the knife ring on her finger as a knuckleduster for improved impact. He let her hit him.

She stepped back and cocked a hip. "This isn't going to work if you—"

He flicked the nunchaku at her head and hit her sternum with the heel of his palm. The wind knocked out of her, and she stumbled back.

"Jerk," she gasped.

"You're rusty, Liza," he scolded, looking down at her. "I let you hit me once, and you drop your guard enough for me to take you out."

"I can hook your artery and rip it right out of your arm."

He bared teeth. "Try."

Liza swiped, jabbed and lunged, but missed or was blocked every time. He was right. She was rusty, and she only had herself to blame.

"So," he said casually. But nothing was ever casual with Parker. "Your mate is little Joey. Figures."

She glared, readied her knife, and circled. "What's that supposed to mean?"

Sizing her up, he smirked. "All the others ran away quaking in fear, but he was the only one stupid enough to stick around."

A growl ripped out of her throat. She stepped forward, hooked his face.

Block.

"He's not stupid," Liza said. "You are." *Yeah, real mature, Liza.*

Jab-jab.

Block.

Then something he'd said baffled her enough that she stopped. "Wait. What did you mean by, *the others ran away?*"

She wasn't *that* jaded and mean.

A look crossed his expression—the cat got the mouse—and when he grinned, sharp canines made him look more beastly than man. "Think, Liza. Why would a family of genetically modified warriors, who knew how you'd feel every time you sensed sin, want horny teenagers away from their sister?"

"You warned them off me?"

He gave an evasive half shrug, but it was all she needed to see red. Thick, viscous anger surged in her veins. *Assholes. Complete dickwads. Amoebas. Fleas on rats.* No wonder no one ever wanted to date her. There had always been a Lazarus brother around to scare them away.

Yes, she felt sick when sensing lust, but wasn't sending them away her choice to make?

She rotated the karambit around her hand, repositioned it for deadly striking, and said, "You made a mistake, brother. A grave one."

All the hurt, denial, pain, self-loathing—it all bubbled to the surface, along with the poison waiting beneath her skin. It grew hot. It burned like a pressure valve needing release. And there was only one way to let it out. In two deadly strikes, she lashed out. First, the knife to the jaw. He dodged, but failed to see the follow up poison. A torpedo-like projectile launched from her other hand, hitting Parker's face. He flinched, let go of his weapon, and covered his jaw as he went to the ground.

Sizzling.

Oh shit.

"Parker?" Liza's voice trembled with hesitancy.

"Did you have to go for the face?" His voice muffled through his hands.

"Are you okay?"

"It's sizzling. Burning. *Christ.*"

"Quick. Go wash it off."

"No. Get a sample kit."

"Are you freaking kidding me?"

"I'll be fine, Liza."

"You're not invincible, dickhead."

"Close enough." He dragged himself off the floor, squinted, and found the swab kit he'd already brought into the gym. "Help me get a swab out."

Heart pounding in her chest, she did as was told and swabbed his face, still sizzling like he'd been hit with acid, not tetrodotoxin. She put the sample in a test tube. Once she was done, she used a saline solution to cleanse his jaw. After the poison drained, he was left with red, blistering skin beneath the coarse hair of his short beard. Guilt pierced her.

"Parker, you know I love you too, and that's why I can say this. That pride of yours is going to kill you one day."

His gaze flicked to her with a sad sort of recognition that hit between her ribs. She knew how he felt. All of the Lazarus siblings knew death by their sin was a very real possibility. Except with Parker, perhaps he'd resigned himself to the inevitability of it. Perhaps it wasn't pride making him like this, but the fact he'd given in.

"Did you have to provoke me?" she said softly.

"You weren't getting worked up without it," he murmured with another wince.

"You could be scarred. On your face." She joked, but there was a serious note to it. No one wanted to be scarred, especially not as a result of a whim, or a tease.

"I won't."

She made an incredulous sound through her teeth. Her compassion evaporated. "You're so conceited you think poison is afraid to hurt you."

His jaw clenched, but he said nothing, only packed up the sample kit, and headed for the door.

"Was it true?" she called after him.

He paused, turned back, and then nodded grimly before leaving.

"Asshole." She threw the karambit at the doorframe.

"You made the mess," he shouted back. "You clean up."

thirteen

JOE LUCIANO

JOE SPENT hours organizing the mess outside Heaven. As the only law enforcement officer on the scene at the time of the crime, he had many boxes to check and many points of contact to brief. But after the emergency response team was fully briefed, he was tired, grumpy and a little bit furious. Liza had left. Never before had she fled the scene of a crime. She would stick around and pester, and pull apart the scene until she had something to work with.

No matter what was going on between them, she should know better. She was different from her family. They dressed up in costume, wreaked havoc at night, and then fled the scene like it was every other day. It was common for them, but not Liza.

He didn't like the feeling in his chest when he thought about her falling into the same patterns as them.

It was time for him to get answers.

The public level of Lazarus House was a restaurant and a night-club, but in between Heaven and Hell was a corridor that took him to the lobby leading up to the apartments. During the short period

117

working together at the CCPD before he'd joined the Feds, Joe had picked Liza up once or twice but had never gone in.

The most memorable time was the day she'd moved into the building. Both of them were rookie cops and the building had just been purchased by Liza's brother Parker. Renovations at ground level were well underway, but the apartments above were safe to move in. It was all Liza had spoken about for weeks, so Joe had offered to help shift her belongings from her old apartment to this one. When they'd arrived with his truck full of boxes, the Lazarus brothers had met them on the street. They made him double park, relieved his truck of Liza's items, and then in no uncertain words, told him to piss off.

This time he wasn't waiting for an invitation. He strode into the lobby to find the elderly doorman reading a book behind the front desk. His aviator hat tipped to the side as though he'd been scratching his head. His name badge said, *Gus*. The book was titled *The Investigator*.

Joe cleared his throat. "Good book?"

Gus looked up, blinked as if just realizing he'd completely missed Joe's entrance, and then dog-eared the book and put it down. "Sorry, sir. I was in another world. Yes, good book. This new Norcross series has me hooked."

Joe reached into his pocket and pulled out his ID. He flipped the leather case open. "I need to see Liza Lazarus."

"FBI?" Gus rubbed his chin. "Ain't you the fella who used to hang about with Miss L a while back?"

"You have a good memory."

"I'm sorry to say that whether you're an old friend or FBI, you'll need a warrant to enter this building without permission, and…" He pulled out a clipboard with a list of names, or lack thereof. "You ain't on the list."

Joe pressed the bridge between his nose. "Can you call her?"

Before Gus placed his hand on the desk phone, it rang. He picked it up with a confused frown. "Yes? Oh, hello AIMI. His name is Joe. Luciano, yes. Alrighty then. I'll let him know." He hung up the receiver. "Miss Lazarus is indisposed. She won't be able to see you."

"Who's Amy?" Joe asked.

"Security." Gus picked up his book and then nodded toward the bench seat on the other side of the lobby. "You can wait there. But it might be a long wait. I suggest you come back another time."

This was ridiculous.

Joe paced a few feet, then realized he'd parked his car in the Lazarus House garage. With a tip of his chin to Gus, Joe quickly made his way back out into the street, dodged a few more of the emergency cleanup crew, and took the side alley street to where he and Liza had emerged earlier that day. The garage door was down and locked. *Damn.*

While he scanned for another mode of entry, a camera above the door watched his every move. If they wanted him to stop, they would come out. It was either pry the garage door open, or shoot the lock on the reinforced steel door beside the garage, and there was no guarantee that the bullet wouldn't ricochet and hurt him.

He pounded on the door with his fist.

"Liza!" he shouted. "You have two minutes to open this door."

He continued pounding. Nothing. But someone was watching. The camera moved as he did. He could almost feel eyes on him. His frustration surged. He ran his hands through his hair, disheveling the style that managed to stay neat until now. When he lowered his hand, he felt the bulge in his pocket. The baseball.

This had to work.

He held it before the camera.

"Last chance, Liza," he warned. "Do this the right way or the hard way."

A beat.

Another.

The door clicked opened.

Liza came out freshly showered, in sweats, and a white crop top that showed off her God-given gifts. High and firm breasts. Abs made of steel. Defined arms that were powerful, yet didn't detract from her femininity. She must have washed her hair because she smelled like citrus and berry. Joe's mouth watered.

He tossed the ball to her.

She winced as she caught it.

"Let me in," he said.

"I can't."

Pain flashed in her eyes. No, it was more than that. Helplessness. Like she was being washed out to sea and could see him on the shore as she drifted away on a raft. Her eyes watered. She bit her lip.

The fight left him. His voice softened. "I'm right here, Liza. Right here. I'm on your team."

She reached for him, yet still held back. Her fist clenched at her side.

Why?

That old, sick voice in his head said the same old thing on repeat. *You're not good enough. You'll bruise the ones closest to you.*

He would never fit in with her family... but did he want to? Nothing good would come of his investigation. He knew that. Yet, he still ran barreling toward the finish line with no care for his heart. It was this insane drive to be better than his father competing against his need for her. She was the flame, and he was the moth beating its wings in the opposite direction against the urges of his heart. Every cell in his body wanted to gather her into his arms, but he fought against instinct, just as he had all these years.

The more he studied her, he realized something. Her reaction wasn't about him. It had never been about him. She was... he searched her face as he struggled to come up with the right conclusion. There was so much pain and uncertainty there. Perhaps he'd been too caught up in his perceptions, and his position imposed on him by his director, that he'd not seen Liza's struggle.

She gulped air and then said, "I can't. I'm afraid. I'm..."

He touched her cheek, but she flinched.

"You shouldn't touch me. You shouldn't be near me."

"Liza, that's not true. Talk to me."

Her stare bored right through his chest. She shook her head, denying it all. Always with the tough act. But he knew her better than most. The tremble on her bottom lip, the dimple in her chin, the scream for help in her eyes. He'd seen the same things when she would tumble into his yard as a child. When she'd throw the ball into his second-story window, and climb the trellis. Back then, she only ever whined about menial things like chores, or her brothers, despite him sensing there were things she failed to tell him. They would share their silence, eat raspberry licorice, and it had been enough.

But he couldn't be patient now. Something had to give. Maybe it should be him.

"I know, Liza."

"Know what?"

"More than you think. You're fast, strong, and you come from a family of gifted people. Each of you disappeared for years, only to come back hard, and even more frightening than before. Out there on the street, I saw the stains on your mouth and the mist from your hands. That night on the balcony across from my apartment? I saw the dead rats. Now it makes sense why you'd left so fast. The evidence is irrefutable. You're one of the Deadly Seven, Liza. Please don't pretend you're not."

His words shifted something in her. The hard, invulnerable,

warrior queen emerged. She clenched her fists, as though she needed to defend herself.

"What did I just say, Liza?" he chided.

She pursed her lips and glanced down at the baseball in her hand. "You're on my side."

He nodded. "You always know who wants to date who at the office. You're the best closer in sex-related crimes. You're always harping on about sensing my lust, or lack thereof. You *are* Lust. Tell me I'm right."

Her head drooped. "I…"

"You're not like them—the rest of your family. You don't hide behind a mask and run from responsibility, from what's right. Why are you now?"

Her gaze snapped up. Wildfire flared in her eyes. "But you see? I've been pretending I'm normal for so long, I forgot what was coming for me. What's been inside me the whole time. There is no escape. I'm the furthest thing from normal."

"You're not making sense."

"*Lust.* Just think about it for a moment."

He narrowed his eyes.

Her voice trembled. "I feel sick in my stomach every time I sense lust. Whether it's sexual, or not. Every time I get close to someone, I feel sick. The last time I tried to have sex, I vomited on the guy." She held up her hands, her voice getting tight. "Poison. I make it. With my body. With my *mouth!* Like some sort of fish in the ocean or bug in the sand, I'm a freak. You saw those Faithful out there. They died the moment they inhaled my mist. I'm a monster, and I can't risk you, Joe. You're the only one I don't feel sick around. You're my—" She cut herself off.

She got physically sick from sensing sin? This explained so much. Her recent avoidance to date, her reluctance in having a long term

relationship, her snarky comments about his love life. The mean and jaded front she put up. She was messed up inside, but all she'd ever wanted was love, just as much as anyone else.

"Does your family know? About the sickness?"

She sniffed. "Why do you think they warn away every guy I meet."

"They know about the vomiting?" he pressed.

She dipped her chin and hugged herself. It broke Joe's heart to see his strong woman so downcast.

"You're the first person I've told," she admitted. "It's a recent development."

He studied her smooth skin. There were no traces of the yellow residue he'd seen before. The only time he'd seen the yellow mist was when she fought, or was perhaps stressed, like on the fire escape outside his apartment. He didn't think he was in danger. They'd spent plenty of time together, and he'd never felt ill or incapacitated around her.

And he was the only person she'd never felt lust from. She'd never felt sick from him.

His heart lifted.

He was special to her. He couldn't explain it, or quantify it, but he knew it in his heart.

"You're not a monster, Liza."

"What would you know?"

"I know that every time you walk into a room, it's like one of those lame 80s movie montages with the music and the drooling men."

She snorted. But he caught her smiling. So he continued. "It's true. You know the ones. The girl walks in, a breeze comes from somewhere and lifts her hair. Men everywhere fall apart. They drop cigarettes from their mouths, spill drinks, walk into poles. And all she does is walk in the room, trailing her sweet perfume."

"Deadly things come in pretty packages." A sardonic eyebrow raised. "I know how people feel about me. It makes me sick. Literally. Maybe I'm built this way to lure in prey and then kill them."

"I think that feeling is twisting your reality. You're the furthest thing from a monster I know."

She sighed. "That's the problem, Joe. You don't really know me. Not the real me, and it doesn't change the fact that I'm a health risk to anyone around me."

He squeezed her shoulders. "I'm willing to take that risk. Invite me up. Invite me in. We'll talk." He held his breath and waited. He dipped to meet her roving eyes. "Come on. There's a game on soon. Let's sit back like old times, have a few dogs and a beer or two, then just chill and talk. Invite me up."

A tentative smile tilted her lips, and it stole his breath.

"Okay, but not this way. There's an elevator in the garage."

"Don't trust me?" He eyed the door she'd come out of.

She flinched. "It's not just up to me, and... I don't know if I'm ready to show you all of me yet. There's more I need to tell you first."

"Okay. Lead the way."

She started walking, but his cell phone buzzed in his pocket. He pulled it out to find a message from the director: *I expect results tomorrow.*

Joe glanced up at Liza, waiting for him.

"Everything okay?" she asked.

"Just need to answer this for work."

He thumbed a reply: *On it.*

DESPAIR

DESPAIR MUST HAVE PASSED OUT. She remembered being carried and then wheeled into the secret headquarters of the Deadly Seven, but not having the energy to feel triumphant. The pain in her shoulder hurt more than she'd anticipated when stepping in front of the gun aimed at Max.

But she had to do it. It was the only way to gain their trust. And it worked. For now.

From within a cozy bed, she looked around the room. Small, blue, with brown furnishings and golden decor. A nice rug. Nothing fancy.

Voices filtered through a cracked door.

She moved her blanket and winced at the pain in her shoulder. A glance down revealed she'd been stitched and patched. A small stain of blood gathered on the bandage, but it was old. Another day and she'd have good mobility back. How long had she been out?

Flashes of her injury came to her. They'd all gathered to help. Mary and Flint had watched with concerned eyes. They tried to get her something to drink. They were... caring for her. She couldn't remember the last time someone did.

When she'd grown up with Julius, every knee scrape, or head wound, had been treated as a means to toughen her up, to thicken her skin.

This was different.

The bed was soft. Part of her didn't want to get out. But she must. Her everlasting soul depended on it. Julius may not care the same way as Mary or Flint, but he'd cared enough to include a strand of her hair in his locket with his beloved first family. That was special. When the replicate expiration issue got solved, Despair would be reincarnated as a clone after she died. And they would do so in a new world where sin didn't rule.

The voices raised in timbre, as though in argument.

She forced herself out of bed and tiptoed to the door.

Four distinct voices. Mary, Flint, Wrath, and the youngest, Envy.

"She's a hazard. A danger. She has to go," Wrath declared.

"*Mijo*, you know she came here asking for our help. This is what we've been waiting for."

"I don't care. I'll walk right in there and drag her out."

"Wyatt," Flint admonished. "You were once in her shoes. Don't forget. You left the family, then came back asking for help. We gave it."

A growl. "It's not the same."

"No, it's not. None of us wanted to leave her behind, but if we didn't, none of you would be here. She sacrificed everything for you all. She deserves our forgiveness. But we can only pray for hers in return."

"Has she given you any information we can act on?" Envy asked. The shuffle of papers sounded like maybe he had notes in his hands. "What about these?"

"We haven't had much time to chat," Mary admitted. "But I'll ask about the sketches as soon as she's awake."

"There's something else," Envy added. "I had another dream. This time, there's another face... well, see for yourself."

Mary gasped. "It's Daisy's face. Are you saying she's at risk, just as much as Misha, or Liza?"

Despair's heart palpitated. A hidden fear she'd long since repressed tried to break through. Growing up, she never knew her family had survived the fire. Julius failed to tell her. She'd feared that if she wasn't perfect, then he wouldn't want her anymore, and then use her for spare parts.

Silence.

A sound something like a chair scraping along the floor as it moved. Footsteps.

Despair hurried back into the bed, climbed beneath the covers, and rolled to the side away from the door. She shut her eyes and feigned sleep. Perhaps she dozed off because when she next opened her eyes, the house was silent. All except light footfalls in the bedroom.

When she looked over, Mary carried a small plant in her hands. She placed it on the side table.

"You're awake," Mary said. "How are you feeling?"

"Like I've been shot."

"We're grateful for your sacrifice."

It was Despair's turn for silence.

The small plant was an old and gnarled bonsai. Mary touched its leaves.

"Do you remember this?" she asked.

Despair focused on the plant but shook her head.

"You were carrying it when we escaped the laboratory. You left it behind when you ran back for Gloria."

Vague memories washed back. There *had* been a plant Despair cared for in their locked observation room. It was the only plant they had in the entire suite. The only plant they'd ever seen. Despair sat up and reached over to lift a leaf. She found a flowering bud. Somehow it had managed to grow beneath the shade of the top leaves.

"It's a daisy bonsai," Mary said. "We kept it alive, but it belongs to you. You should have it."

Despair didn't know what to say. They had left her. They'd thought she was dead, just like she had thought they were dead. But they'd kept her plant alive. Her throat dried.

"When you're ready," Mary said. "There's food in the kitchen. It's just Flint and me now, so take your time. We want you to feel comfortable."

Despair watched Mary leave and rubbed the ache in her chest.

She took the flower bud gently and leaned close to inhale deeply. A nostalgia she couldn't describe entered her body, and she quickly sat back.

"What do I call you?" came a strange, disembodied female voice.

Despair surveyed the room. The door was closed again. Mary had left. So who spoke?

"Who are you?"

Her head tilted up and found a white speaker in the ceiling.

"Who are *you?*" Despair snapped back.

"I'm AIMI. The Lazarus's Artificial Intelligence Management Interface. I manage this household. Usually Sloan or Parker update my system, or I scan relevant databases using facial recognition software to find an identity match for house guests, but you are listed with multiple identities. Are you Daisy, The Falcon, or are you Despair?"

The truth was, she wasn't sure. Before the computer had the chance to ask again, Despair left the room.

fifteen

LIZA LAZARUS

BUTTERFLIES FLUTTERED around knots in Liza's stomach as Joe followed her into the elevator that would take them up to her apartment level. This was the first time she'd invited anyone up, let alone a potential—

Her mind shut down. She couldn't let herself entertain the thought of intimacy. Not yet. Not when she wanted it so badly. Not when she still felt the residual effects of battle riding her system. It was more than adrenaline and more than her recent training session. It was the flashes of horror behind her eyelids, more terrifying because she hadn't just served and protected, she'd *ended* lives. Dead. Gone. No judge. No jury.

This was her future.

She could kill with her breath. And she could do it without even knowing it, blacked out in a berserker rage.

She punched the button to her floor and leaned against the cool wall as the elevator doors closed. Her gaze shifted to Joe and immediately softened at his familiar face. Once again she was struck by how it had changed. There had always been a hard edge to him, but now it was razor-sharp, honed by the same sort of trauma that she dealt with. Gone was the hope, the glint she'd seen in all rookies, the dream of making a difference. She knew the kind of work he'd done at the bureau was soul-crushing work. He faced the worst humanity had to offer, and he still showed up to work the next day.

When he'd come to the basement door and demanded entry, there had been a wildness to him. This was not the boy she'd grown up with, not the youth she became friends with, and not the man she came up in the Force with. There were things about him she was still discovering, just as he was learning about her. How much did one really know the other? The notion sparked another round of anxiety. Memories of the battle.

Foaming mouths.

Face masks sliding off.

The fear in eyes as death came. Then seeing her reflection in their eyes.

Heat swarmed her palms. She looked down. Yellow. It was pooling in her pores.

"No," she gasped. "Not now."

"Liza?" Joe reached for her.

She shut her fists, avoiding him. "Don't, Joe. You can't touch me."

"Why?"

She held her palms out. "I'm oozing toxin! I'm panicking. I can't… just stay back. You should go."

Shit. She couldn't even touch a button without leaving a poisonous residue.

"Liza," he said, voice eerily calm. "Your hands look normal. There are no yellow stains."

She blinked. "What?"

"Take a deep breath and look again." He touched her shoulder.

Inhale. Exhale. Look down. Gone. He was right.

"I could have sworn…" Her heart thumped in her chest. "It was there. I felt it."

His eyes turned stark. "I know that look. Seen it in the mirror too many times to forget. You're replaying the crime scene, seeing the bodies. Try not to see them. Think of something else."

Liza hugged herself. She should be better at this, but Parker was right. She was rusty. The years she spent training to master her emotions was a distant memory.

"How do you do it?" she asked.

"How do I think of something else?"

"Violent Crimes, right? I mean, you worked in that department for a while. You must have seen some shit. I've never been like this before. I've seen a frickin' murderous plant, but this… How do you block it out?"

His eyes skated to the instrument panel and pointed. "Luxury building like this has a pool on the roof, right?"

She nodded.

"Good." He punched the button for the roof, and then he met her eyes. "I swim."

Her first reaction was to shake her head. She'd already worked out and wasn't in the mood. But he was right. A swim might be good.

The Shaolin Monks had taught her to run her body ragged so that when they fought, there would be no emotion or anger causing mistakes. Sometimes they'd wake at dawn, do chores at the abbey, and then practice martial arts until dinner time. And then there would be more chores, and then meditation before bed. The quiet in Liza's mind during that year had been incredible.

The doors opened on Liza's level. She hit the "close" button and stayed in the lift.

"A swim would also dilute my toxin in the water until I have it under control." Meeting his eyes, she added, "Thank you. For understanding."

He shrugged. "I just want to talk. Makes no difference if it's on a couch or the poolside. And for the record, I think you're doing just fine."

The honey warming her chest was a shock to her system. A compliment from Joe. She felt like a damned schoolgirl, and completely out of her comfort zone. Any time a guy complimented her, she was usually ready to beat him back with snark to avoid the punch of lust to her gut. She fidgeted with the baseball in her pocket.

It would be so different with Joe.

The elevator opened to the roof and Liza stepped out. The sun was getting low, and the sky darkened with impending rain, but the Olympic sized lap pool was heated. A wide oak deck surrounded the pool, and a glass fence provided a barrier to the Cardinal City skyline. The boys used a broken pane as a launching spot for base jumping in their wingsuits at night. She'd never worn her suit, so hadn't tried the wing function. They kept telling her it was the easiest way to move around the city.

Vines crawled up pergola columns that surrounded the pool and provided privacy from the neighboring city buildings. Wooden tables with chairs tipped over showed a lack of use. Next to the pool area, a vacant helipad stretched over the rest of the roof. No one was up here. They wouldn't be brave enough in this weather. The air had a bite to it, and when the rain eventually came, it would cut like blades.

But Liza needed this. She kicked off her sweat pants and was folding them when she caught Joe's attention and froze under the weight of his gaze. She'd never censured herself around him before. In her mind, he'd never been someone she had to worry about. He'd never leered. He'd never propositioned her. And she'd never worried about propriety but, now, seeing the smokey heat in that gaze, it hit her. All those times she'd stripped down to her underwear in the locker room, or when they used to go to the lake as teenagers, or... God, she'd even teased him for being a prude when he'd excused himself to dress in private.

Her entire view of their relationship shifted.

Had he hidden from her because he'd been aroused?

It was too much to contemplate. Tearing her gaze from his, she dove into the water. Warmth embraced her like a hug. Sound dissolved. The world ebbed away. It was so calming. So peaceful. The turquoise mosaic tiles glinted and sparkled with the waning daylight. Soon the clouds would take it away, and it would be a dark, gaping abyss. Would it be as peaceful then?

Just like her brothers, Liza had trained with military units around the world. Part of their education required them to remain underwater for extended periods, both with a breathing apparatus and without. A SEAL could hold their breath for two to three minutes. Liza and her genetically modified family could hold for up to five.

It was the advantage she took now. She needed a moment to collect herself, for when she surfaced, Joe would want to talk, and she wasn't sure she was ready for that. His very presence threw her mind and body into a tailspin. The right way up was now upside down.

Her uncertainty caused a bloom of frustration to take hold of her nerves, and that made her even more annoyed. *This wasn't her.* The Liza Lazarus the public knew dominated, but when it came to matters of the heart, she was weak, a fucking rookie.

A splash jolted her out of her thoughts. Before her mind registered the blurry image fizzing before her, sturdy hands scooped under her arms and propelled her to the surface. She broke with a spluttering gasp.

"Joe?"

Wet, dripping, and still in his shirt and tie, Joe scowled at her.

"Are you okay?" he asked, voice deep. "Do you need to get out?"

She wiped hair from her face. "What?"

"I thought…" He frowned at her, fury flashing in his eyes. "You were down there for so long, I thought you were drowning!"

Oh. She stopped treading water and sank until her feet touched the bottom and the surface hit her chin. "I was hiding," she confessed.

"Hiding. Why?"

Panic tripped her heart into overdrive, and the very thing she'd been thinking about from the safe underworld cocoon blared in her face. *Here's Joe. Your mate.* The one man you can screw and not feel sick. And he's soaking wet, looking at you. Waiting.

Short dark hair stuck to his forehead. His lashes spiked with moisture. But it was the concern in his eyes that caused the biggest reaction within Liza. Her stomach flipped with anticipation. Her blood sang for her to join him. She *wanted*, and she'd never felt that way before.

Like a coward, she turned and started swimming. One hand over the other, stroke after stroke, until she hit the end of the pool, somersaulted, and propelled herself back in the direction she'd come. She didn't want to talk. She got halfway across the pool when Joe took hold of her hand and dragged her to the surface. The fury hadn't left him. It tightened his jaw, stretched his shoulders, and left him a hardened rock.

"I thought I could wait," he snarled. "But I can't. I jumped into the pool because I had no idea what you're capable of, or what you're built for. You need to start talking before I lose it."

"The poison…"

"Is fine. The water will take care of the rest. Talk."

This was it. She had to change, to open up, or she'd lose him.

"I'm a genetically modified weapon," she blurted. "My family was

born in a lab. Mary and Flint rescued us, but the people who created us are still trying to create weapons of mass destruction. They want to destroy the world and create something free from sin. It's impossible. Innocent people are going to die because of their antics."

Joe jerked as though hit. "What organization?"

"The Syndicate."

"Were they the masked terrorists you fought?"

"You mean the ones in the white robes? The Faithful?"

He nodded solemnly. "I've seen pictures of them, but nothing else."

"Figures." She snorted and started paddling circles around him.

"What does *that* mean?"

"They're Syndicate fanatics, and since the Syndicate has their hand up the ass-puppet of law enforcement, it's no wonder you've heard nothing about them."

A coldness entered Joe's gaze, darker than the encroaching clouds. "Are you accusing me of something?"

"No!" she splashed him. He dodged. "I'm not talking about you. I know you'd never willingly work for them."

Joe was a saint. Loyal and moral to the core. But after her words had come out, there was no taking them back. A chain reaction of doubt started to swirl in her head, and suddenly, she wasn't swimming in a heated rooftop pool, she was in shark-infested waters.

Why was Joe back in town? Because it certainly wasn't to bone her. The Special Agent was high profile enough to be put on the plant-monster case, something that seemed incredible but wasn't. Liza didn't remember anything in the news about a plant that came to life and ate people. So did that mean Joe was in on a cover-up? Or had they come to a different conclusion? Maybe they'd reasoned that attack away as something more plausible.

But now he was in town chasing a serial killer, something so sadly human and depraved that it wasn't on the same level as a Syndicate crime. He wouldn't skip from one sort of case with higher clearance and then be demoted to something with less.

She didn't buy it.

God, she was dumb. How could she miss this? She'd been so hopeful, so desperate for attention that she'd ignored all the warning signs. Her breath solidified. She swallowed and paddled to the side of the pool where she kept her back to him while she sorted through her mind. If he read the suspicion on her face...

Hairs on the back of her neck lifted.

Was she in danger? Had she let the wolf into their home? They'd all been worried about Daisy, but maybe it was Joe. Someone she couldn't read. Someone her family had treated poorly. Someone who, up until a few days ago, had wanted nothing to do with her.

She tried to let that settle in, but her mind raced.

A while ago, they'd established that even though those mated in the Seven couldn't sense sin around their partners, it didn't mean their partners weren't *feeling* sin. Misha still felt wrath. Bailey still felt gluttony. Their bond triggered when they had none. Since Liza had never sensed Joe's lust, their bond had half-triggered in their youth, only now releasing her powers upon a time in their adulthood. But between that first time and this last time, Joe had grown. He'd become someone else, perhaps someone who would reject their bond.

Water splashed gently behind her.

He's coming.

She tensed. Did she have it in her to take him down? Tears stung her eyes.

No, she didn't.

If he was the trojan horse sent to take the Lazarus family down from the inside, then Liza was the one who opened the gates with welcoming arms. She wanted him too much. She needed him. To hold. To hug. To be there.

The line of his body pressed hotly against her back. He braced one hand on the pool's edge. The other landed on her shoulder and squeezed. For a bated breath, she feared the worst, but then he traced his touch up to her ear and tucked her hair affectionately. Shivers danced down her spine.

"I'm sorry." Joe's voice came out a hoarse whisper. "I shouldn't have snapped."

She tensed, but he didn't move. He pressed his body harder against her back. She ached at the closeness, craving the bodily connection she'd missed her entire adult life. Above the chlorine of the pool, she could smell his masculinity. Salty, sweaty, and a hint of aftershave still clinging to his skin. Her eyes fluttered closed and, God help her, but she pushed back into him. Her rear found a hardness that sent her hormones rocketing.

The hitch of his breath.

The burst of an exhale.

The softness of reverent lips on her shoulder.

"Liza," he groaned, teeth scraping, turning his touch wicked. "The five years we spent apart were torture."

She faced him and found anguish in his expression. "So why did you leave?"

"Because I had to prove I have what it takes. That I'm as good at saving lives as your family. I wanted to be *better*. Do you understand?"

"Why on earth would you want that?"

He gaped. "*You*, Liza. Because I want to be good enough for *you*. It's all I've wanted. You kept me in the friend zone. I always thought maybe it was because of my father, who I might become. Or maybe your family was right, and I'd never be good enough. So I left. I had to see if I could be more. To be better than my roots. Then maybe... maybe you'd see it too."

Time seemed to stop. The rumble of thunder rolled through the skies like a soft warning that continued in her heart. *Thud-thud.* But she refused to listen. It was the residual alarm system her body used when lust sickened her, when it wanted to protect itself from inevitable pain when she found herself in this kind of situation—wet, with a perfect specimen of a man, and horny as hell. Only, there was no sickening in her stomach, just desire.

"Fuck my brothers. Fuck your father," she growled and took his lapels in a firm grip. "I know it's their fault you have these doubts, and maybe that's my fault, so fuck me too. I'm sorry I said nasty things to you. It was only ever to mask my insecurities. I never wanted a hero, Joe. I just want someone to hold. Someone to kiss without the pain."

His gaze dipped to her mouth. "Someone on your team."

"Yes, you dum—"

He swallowed her words with a crushing kiss.

sixteen

JOE LUCIANO

THE HONOR CODE was something every FBI agent recited upon joining the bureau. Joe could hear himself pledging as clear as it was the first day he joined the FBI academy.

I devote myself to the pursuit of truth and knowledge.

I subscribe to the highest standards of honesty, integrity, fidelity, and honorable behavior.

I will not condone the actions of those who would use dishonest means.

It screamed at him from the back of his mind. He shouldn't be in love with this woman. She represented everything he fought. He was a lawman because it was the furthest thing from his father's brutality. He swore he would do better. Be better. If he gave in to this, it could be the first crack in his hard facade, the first step down the path to becoming the beast he descended from. But all he could focus on, all his body wanted, was the implacable woman turning pliant in his arms, for him. Desire was a heady drug working its way through his system. Finally. After decades. She was his.

He pushed his code aside and then pushed Liza firmly against the wall of the pool. She let him. She let him push his tongue into her mouth and drive deep. She let him put his hand to her breast, squeeze, plump, and roll the nipple. Her resounding moan into his mouth made him harden even more.

She let him take the lead.

The notion blanked his mind. He pulled back.

"Liza… how many times have you been with a man?"

"What the fuck?" She grabbed his hair. "We're kissing, and you bring up shit like that. Do you hear me asking about your scorecard? I've had plenty of men, just none I never, you know—"

A stupid grin stretched his lips as he pressed them against hers. He slid his hands around her firm waist and tugged her close. A delirious swell of pride hit him. He would be the first to show her true pleasure. To bring her to blissful oblivion. He liked that idea. A low, possessive growl rumbled in his throat. All this time he'd been torturing himself with images of her with other men, but it made no difference. He would be her first in pleasure.

He shouldn't be this happy about it.

In his fantasies, she'd been the one who'd taken charge. She'd walk into his room dressed in lacey lingerie and then cuff him. She'd climb on top and use his body, and all he could do was submit because she was the one who came to *him*. She wanted him, not just the other way around.

But he liked this more.

With mouths entwined, and fingers roaming each other's hot, slick skin, Joe shifted Liza back toward the steps of the pool. He lifted her to sit on the ledge, spread her legs, and fit between them.

The water had turned her crop top transparent. Two dark nipples touched the surface of the white fabric. He lowered his mouth, took one in, and sucked. She arched into him with a muttered curse that left her squirming.

Satisfying.

Another smile stretched his lips. He moved his attention to the other side, suckling and paying homage to her perfection. She was so responsive, so ready, and so long overdue. Her legs tightened around his waist. Cold air brushed their skin, but he ignored it. Nothing would get him out of this pool, or off this roof. Not unless it was with Liza in his arms.

She speared his hair with her fingers and held him steadfast to her chest, but he resisted. He moved down her stomach, licking, tasting, getting bolder with every moan and whimper she made. He swirled his tongue around her belly button, then kissed lower—to the top of her soaked white panties where he kissed her mound, reveling in the high-pitched mewls she made, the writhing, the tightening of her thighs around his head. And when she pulled his hair sharply on a reflex of rapture, he tugged aside her panties and worked her slick center with his tongue. He gave her pleasure until she crumbled. Until he felt her release against his lips. Until she shouted his name to the star-filled sky.

Breathing hard, she collapsed back against the cold tiles. "Holy Jesus Jehosefu-*uck* Christ. I can't believe I *ever* thought you felt no lust."

He should probably have said something witty, something she would remember until her dying days, but all he could do was push himself out of the water, and climb on top of her.

"I'm not done," he said, and fitted himself between her legs.

Awe shined back at him, and it was too much. Unreal. A dream. An echo of some unnamed emotion beat in his chest. A voice. An oath. A code.

"...eventually you'll bruise the people closest to you."

He shook his head with a jerk.

No. He'd been waiting his whole damned life for this. *Don't think about your father. Don't think about your job.* Not now. Sweet, fucking hell, not now.

Two fingers smoothed the groove in his brow, and for a beat, she contemplated his anguish, seeing right through him. Then he buried his face in her neck. Inhaled her. Groaned. She reached down and lifted his shirt. The moment she touched his skin, there was no more doubt. There was only her.

"Undo my belt," he rasped.

She fumbled with the fastening. He tugged her panties down. All the way off.

She was a goddess. Built from divinity. What had she said? Genetically modified perfection. And he was going to appreciate every inch.

The belt unbuckled with a metallic tinkle. She wrapped her fingers around his erection, tightened her grip, and stroked. "You like this?"

Christ. He squeezed his eyes shut and nodded. Sensation coursed through him. He couldn't move. Couldn't think.

"I can't believe we're doing this," he murmured, still not believing. "After all these years."

"I can't believe you're my mate."

He kissed her neck and drove into her hand. "What?"

"Nothing." She stroked. "I'll tell you later."

He drew back to stare at her flushed face. Glazed eyes focused on him. She tried to distract him with her touch, but his oath screamed at him.

Honesty, integrity, fidelity.

Why couldn't she tell him now?

"Liza, what did you mean by mate?"

All the way back, he tugged his pants up and sat on his haunches. A dark look ghosted her face, and her wall of defense slammed up like a tangible thing.

"It's not a bad thing," she groused. "It's a good thing."

"So explain it."

"Each of us is linked to one person who embodies our sin's opposing virtue. This person balances the sin in our system." She displayed her yin-yang inner wrist tattoo. "The more I'm around lust, the more I get out of balance. This tattoo shifts to show how much sin is in my system. If I'm out of balance, I can black out and go all berserker rage against anyone I sense lust from. But now that our bond has triggered, now that I know it's you, of all people, I don't have to worry again."

"Me? Of all people?" Talk about a bucket of cold water. *Goddamn.* He got up and squelched to where he'd thrown his jacket and holster. Her words replayed in his head. He may have spent his life pining after her, but she'd clearly never felt the same. The only reason she was with him was because he embodied her sin's opposing virtue. "So I'm what, some kind of lottery winner. I'm the one you get?"

Their hearts had nothing to do with it?

"Joe." She scrambled to her feet and jogged after him.

"I refuse to be your consolation prize, Liza."

"But you're not! You're the opposite."

He rounded on her. "You just said 'you of all people' meaning you had others lined up, meaning, I was the last person you expected to fit this role. Admit it, I was never your first choice. I'm just the one you get."

"Okay, I admit it was a surprise." She reached for him.

He shook her off. Fuck this shit.

Turned out her family was right all along. She didn't pick him on her own. He was stupid to think he ever stood a chance of being seen. She might never love him, only the relief he brought. And maybe *that* wasn't good enough for *him.*

JOE WENT STRAIGHT DOWN the elevator to the garage. His shredded heart and battered mind couldn't take it anymore. The reality of Liza Lazarus was nothing like the fantasy that had fueled his soul for most of his life, and he couldn't quite work out if that was a good thing, or not.

The Lazarus House garage was a study in performance luxury. From slick custom-made cars, to muscle motorbikes and dark-tinted vehicles. His boring sedan stood out with two dings on the side, a scratch on the fender, and peeling paint on the roof from too many days sitting in the sun with no protection. Parker leaned casually against the hood, tracking Joe's movements across the floor.

Joe kept his squelching strides long and sure. He gripped his dry jacket in one hand, and his holster in the other. He stopped before Parker, again hating that he had to look up. Joe was a tall man, but the Lazarus family was taller. Now he knew why. They were created in a lab.

He laughed at the irony. He'd spent his life trying to be better than beings created in a goddamned lab. His father, he understood. But these guys?

Parker's eyes narrowed at Joe's burst of humor.

"What?" Joe demanded.

When Parker didn't answer, Joe shook his head and unlocked the car. He didn't give a shit what that cocksucker thought anymore. Hell, he wondered if he ever had. Joe opened the car door, but a big hand slammed it shut.

Oh no, he fucking didn't.

Blood boiled in Joe's veins, coursing around, kicking up a storm. He tensed. And then turned to meet Parker's golden, smug stare.

The man wore a tight black muscle shirt and slouch jeans that probably cost more than Joe's car. With long hair hastily pulled back at his nape, day-old scruff that, for once, didn't seem manicured from an in-house barber. A red blistering welt covered one side of his face.

Shit. Parker was disheveled.

Joe's lips quirked. He gestured at Parker's wound. It looked like how Liza had left some Faithful. "Disagreed with your sister?"

Another squint of Parker's eyes. Joe could practically hear his thoughts calculating: *How much does he know?*

Enough. Joe knew enough.

Parker leaned forward with menace. He opened his mouth, but Joe spoke first.

"Save me a repeat of the speech you gave me twenty years ago, Parker. I don't give a shit what you think. We're not kids anymore. What's between your sister and me is just that—between us."

A low animalistic snarl ripped out of Parker.

Instead of returning Parker's anger, Joe was only tired. This man had no reason to be shitty. Joe had done nothing to him except ignore his warning to stay away from his sister.

And there it was. Like a lightning bolt of clarity.

"You're Pride, and you can't stand the fact that you're not right about something." Joe laughed harshly. "I mean, you fucked up, right? You didn't want me near your sister and, as it turns out, I'm the only one she can be near. Liza hasn't been lonely all these years because of the sin she senses, it's been because of you and your arrogance. If you hadn't warned me off, I would have made a move a long time ago. So from where I'm standing, it should have been me warning you away from her." It was as though the words stoked a long-dormant fire in Joe. Vehemence rocked to the surface. His fists clenched as he glared at Parker. "*You* ruined everything."

Parker's violence dissipated, and what replaced his demeanor was more alarming: calm. It turned the man into something so deathly quiet that Joe felt like Aesop's mouse who'd scurried over the sleeping lion's outstretched paw... only to be caught. His life now hung in the balance, dangling over sharp teeth and a gaping chasm, at the mercy of the lion's whim.

Amused eyes leveled on him as Parker dusted imaginary flecks from Joe's wet shoulders and said, "You think because you're with the Feds that you're untouchable?"

"Fuck off."

Parker stepped back. He didn't say anything else. He didn't need to. He prowled away with the cocky sureness of the lion walking away from a mouse.

Joe got in his car and drove out. He didn't stop until he got to the precinct. It was either go there, or go home to his empty apartment, and he wasn't ready to face those ghosts.

He used a locker room shower to clean himself. He changed into a spare suit he kept in his locker, and then sat at his desk and wrote everything he knew about the Lazarus family and the Deadly Seven.

There was one part of that fable most people forgot. The lion ended up owing his life to the mouse. Parker should take care who he pisses off.

seventeen

LIZA LAZARUS

LIZA CHECKED her cell for the tenth time since waking. No message from Joe. After he'd left her at the rooftop pool, she'd called and called, but hit voice mail every single time.

This morning, she'd completed her workout, another stress test with Parker, jogged five miles, and then came back to her room and tried him again. Nothing.

Lying on her unmade bed, she daydreamed. For her, yesterday had been a wondrous revelation. She could still feel the touch of his lips down her spine, on her stomach, lower... a pleasant shiver ran through her and she pressed her thighs together with a lazy smile. He was incredible. *My Joe.*

The very thought of his name sent butterflies zipping in her lower belly. Since he'd left, a nagging in her soul had ruptured. She longed to be with him again, but the betrayal in his eyes last night had been so deep. He truly believed she would never have picked him if given the opportunity.

But maybe she had.

Maybe the way she felt for him factored into it.

She glanced at the tattered baseball on her nightstand, an ever-present reminder of their shared life. Picking it up, she realized her need for their bond had been very different from his. Running her thumb over the signatures, she realized her pleas for help had been nothing but childish defiance and flexing her newborn independence. The unfairness of having to pick up Wyatt's share of the chores when he'd left for seven years of training, the trapped feeling when Mary wouldn't allow her to go to a party, or an argument she'd had with Flint about the way she dressed. She'd run to Joe's house and used *Codename: Baseball* to justify her anguish. Seemed so childish now.

But Joe...

She rubbed her thumb over his signatures.

He'd used the ball for very different reasons. He'd never once tried to get out of responsibilities. Instead, he'd cashed in *Codename: Baseball* for comfort after having his eye swollen shut by a fist from his father, or needing someone to sit with him at Emergency for X-rays, or simply just to sit with him when he received no affection from his family on his birthday. Liza had filled a hole in his life. He'd needed her like he'd not needed anyone else.

She longed to go back to that simple time. To have nothing between them but clear, undiluted love. Because that's what it was back then, she realized. Love. Only, she'd been too young to comprehend.

She sat up.

He wasn't some second choice; he was the first. Always had been.

Putting the baseball down, Liza took up her cell and tried calling Joe.

No answer.

But a text came through. Family meeting in her parents' apartment for breakfast. That could only mean one thing. Daisy was up and talking.

"Fuck it," she growled and got out of bed.

There were more pressing things to worry about than Joe's rejection. The sister who'd spent her life working for the enemy was downstairs.

Liza showered, dressed, and gathered spare clothing for Daisy. She ventured down to her parents' floor. Mary sat with Daisy on a sectional in the living area. They weren't alone. Tony, Griffin, and Parker also sat pouring over some of Evan's sketches from his psychic dreams. The artist himself was conspicuously absent.

She put her keys on the bench in the kitchen, smiled at her father cooking bacon and eggs, and then joined the rest of her family. Tony, Griffin, and Parker were on one side of the couch. Mary and Daisy on the other. She handed Daisy the small pile of clothes.

"I thought you'd want something to wear other than sweats."

Daisy's violet gaze sparked with an emotion that gave Liza a glimpse into her old self. Then it was gone. Daisy took the pile of clothes with a smile that didn't quite reach her eyes, but she hugged the clothes in her lap as though they were a blanket that would protect her from the ghosts of her past, sitting and staring at her from across the couch.

"Did Evan have another dream?" Liza asked, eyeing the rough charcoal sketches on the table. She'd seen the one with Daisy in it earlier, but they not shown Daisy.

Tony shook his head grimly, but his gaze skated to his brothers. Liza knew that look. No amount of acting classes could get rid of that look on Tony's face. He had made that face as a toddler who stole Liza's last Oreo from the dessert plate. And usually, it was when another brother had told him to do it. Guilty and colluding.

Liza scanned the rest of her brothers. Griffin sat stiffer than usual in his corporate attire. Parker looked especially pompous with his casual arm rested across the length of the couch and eyes zeroed in on Daisy like she was about to rob the bank.

Liza had to shut that down quick-smart. She wasn't ready to attack Daisy just yet.

"Hey Parks," she called and ditched a pillow at his lustrous hair. "The nineties called. They want their shampoo commercial back."

He sneered at her in a way only a brother could. But she achieved her purpose. He may be kingpin in the field, but he wasn't at home. They were all equal.

Daisy had offered to tell them anything they wanted to know about the Syndicate. And here she was, sitting in borrowed sweats and shoeless. Mary was by her side, stoic and ominous in her dark yoga attire. The woman had a spine straighter than an arrow, and yet, today, she managed to look smaller and more fragile than any of them. It was the first time Liza had ever imagined her adoptive mother as anything other than invincible. But Mary was getting older, as they all were. Mary's latter years had been full of gut-wrenching nerves. The children she'd raised to be loving yet implacable warriors for good had come undone, stitched themselves back together, and come undone again.

And here was her greatest regret, Daisy. The obvious hope in Mary's eyes kept flicking to her lost daughter, who tucked her long skinny legs beneath her bottom and kept to herself.

"Bit early to discuss the end of the world, isn't it?" Liza asked.

Parker slid unamused eyes to her but said nothing.

Griffin, already dressed and slick in his corporate attire, indicated the sketches. "Daisy's been telling us what she knows about the Syndicate."

"Oh?" Liza took a seat next to Daisy and tried not to look too invested, but this was the moment they'd all been waiting for. "Shouldn't we wait for Wyatt and the others?"

Tony snorted. "As if Wyatt'll leave the seventh floor before Misha gives birth."

"That's not true," Griffin said. "He's cooking family dinner at the end of the week."

"I think Daisy was about to explain the sketches Evan's made," Parker interrupted, in no uncertain terms, effectively silencing everyone. "Please continue, Daisy, and tell us what you know."

Daisy's violet eyes shimmered beneath a frown. "The truth is, not as much as you'd like to hear. I've been having blackouts."

Mary took Daisy's hand and met Liza's stare. "Julius has no further use for her, and since she's not triggered her powers, a blackout isn't going to get her far in terms of world devastation. Not when you are all powered. Apparently, they haven't completely dismissed the possibility of turning you all rogue. Daisy believes her life is in danger."

Liza wasn't the only one unconvinced at this excuse, but Mary swallowed it. They had to tread carefully or they'd break her heart. Uncovering Daisy's true reason for being here was like surgery. They needed the right tools and the right surgeon.

When Evan and Sloan sauntered in with a mobile tattoo kit, Liza understood. They were going to use the bio-indicator ink on Daisy. Having the yin-yang tattoo was just one level of secrecy they could peel away from her. The ink would show everyone just how close she was to blacking out, if she was a risk, or if it was all a lie.

"This is going to take some time," Parker said, and then looked at Liza. "You should go to work." He stood and guided Liza to the door, not even giving her a chance to say goodbye, but Liza knew better than to publicly dispute him. He almost always had a valid reason.

She didn't have to like it to know it came from good, or smart, intentions.

At the elevator, she murmured, "What is it?"

His brow furrowed in a surprising show of concern. "Be careful."

"Me?"

He nodded.

"Don't worry, I feel more in control this morning. I'll keep my hands to myself, and I have a backup plan if shit goes down. I'll be fine once I see Joe."

"Will you?"

"What's that supposed to mean?"

"It's not exactly comforting to see a Fed walk out of a known criminal organization's headquarters in a dark mood."

Liza flinched. She hated it when he called their family criminal, but it was true. "He'll be fine. He just needs to process."

An indignant eyebrow shot up. "It's Joe."

"Exactly."

"You know, on second thought, you should be heading straight to the basement and working on your control. One slip at the precinct and you give us all away, even if your mate decides to keep our secrets to himself. You need to seriously consider if it's time to give up the day job."

"What?"

"You heard me. Tony's done it, and he was balancing both lives well enough. You've *never* been capable of balancing your alter egos. So you'll have to pick one. Time for you to get into your suit. I'm almost finished with upgrades to handle your poison. We're going to get the information we need from Daisy and then shit is going to happen. Are you in?"

Pain shot in her teeth from the tightness of her clenched jaw. How could he say that? How could he make demands?

"You know I'm right," he said. "We've let you entertain thoughts of a real career, but I think it's clear you're a Lazarus. You can't run from it."

"Fuck you, Parker."

"I'll meet you downstairs in ten."

JOE LUCIANO

A FLYER WAS SLAMMED onto Joe's desk.

He looked up and found Letisha from admin. She waggled her eyebrows and glanced at the flyer.

"What do you say, Loochie? You joining the team?"

"Stop asking me." He shifted the flyer away. "I'm not part of this precinct anymore. I'm just visiting. Find someone else to join your— what is this?" He squinted at the flyer. "Softball?"

She nodded emphatically. "You haven't played in years."

"That's because I left the city," he replied drolly.

"Don't take that tone with me, Mr. Snarky Pants." She snatched the flyer back. "It's the least you can do since you cost us our best player."

"What are you talking about?"

"Liza pulled out."

"Why is that my fault?"

She pursed her lips. "Boy, I've been around since the day you two walked in with your academy shirts and matching green faces. You think I don't know the reason our girl's taking her first sick day, so soon after you arrive in town, isn't because of you?" She made an incredulous sound through her teeth. "Puh-lease. It's always the man."

She went to leave, but Joe stood suddenly. "Wait. Liza's sick?"

A raised brow and a gesture at the flyer. "You going to join?"

"I'll think about it. What do you mean about Liza?"

Liza told Joe last night that she needed to be in contact with her mate, or her internal balance was volatile, or something like that. Whatever she'd done to maintain her equilibrium before might not be enough now. If she'd called in sick, maybe it was his fault. Maybe she was actually sick, and he'd walked away from her.

Letisha shrugged. "All I know is that her brother said she was unwell and won't be in for a few days. He also said to remove her from all extracurricular activities, hence the need for a replacement player on our softball team."

"Her brother said that?"

She tipped her chin affirmatively.

He sat in his chair and fumed. When Letisha left, he pulled out two Manila files from his locked drawer. He'd spent most of the night compiling his report on the Deadly Seven, but the moment he'd finished, he immediately started another report. Both of them were so sensitive, that he hadn't been ready to enter the data into the computer. The second report had been about the white-robed terrorists Liza called the Faithful, and their Syndicate boss. By the time he'd crossed the last t and dotted the last i, he knew he needed more information before making a final decision about which report to hand in. One file was thick. The other was thin. He needed more evidence.

The previous night had left him exhausted, both spiritually and bodily. Old bitterness rose to the surface at how Parker had treated him on the way out. Parker thought he was so much better than everyone, and maybe he was. Maybe that was the reason Joe wanted to see his downfall. If Parker didn't think he was so perfect, then Joe didn't have as high to climb.

A knock came at the door. A glance up and his heart stopped.

"Liza." Joe surged to his feet, almost knocking the case files wide open. Scrambling to order them, he quickly locked them back in his drawer before meeting Liza's eyes.

"I thought you were..."

"Sick?" she finished for him, and then slouched into the guest chair at his desk, making herself comfortable by kicking up her boots and stretching back in a way that affected him in dark and deep places.

The passage of night and the murky thoughts of apprehending her family had not dulled the ache in his body for want of her touch. She looked picture perfect. Brown glossy hair. Tanned face, sharp and stubborn jaw, wide lips. Curious eyes laced with awareness too clever to miss anything. She knew he studied her longer than appropriate, and she welcomed it by stretching her arms behind the chair to expose the swell of her breasts beneath her white blouse. Her bra was black today. A rosette pattern of lace. Had she made a mistake or was she deliberately trying to heat his blood?

The answer would come when she either buttoned her jacket to hide the lace or left it open before leaving the room. He supposed he could always just ask her.

He cleared his throat. "Letisha said your brother had called in sick for you."

Two brows squished together. "I know. Can you believe that asswipe? He thinks I need more training, but I said I have you now, so not to worry."

Her blind faith in him pinged a spark between his ribs. Hearing her blow off Parker's orders sent another spark kindling. He liked that she came to him for support, but... she was wrong.

He planted palms on the desk and splayed his fingers before leaning toward her, returning her glib contemplation for something more unwavering. "What makes you think you don't have to worry around me?"

She paused. Her brow flinched as if she was trying to assess his veracity, but then shrugged it off. "Because you've always had my back, and I've had yours. I may have lost my way a little. As you said, I got a little jaded, but now we're partners again. I'll be fine. We'll be fine."

Her gaze lingered a beat longer than normal, and then she pulled out her cell. "I think we should head to the shelter today. I'm not sure if that runaway will be there long. Most of them bail after the first night."

"No," he said.

"What?"

He went to his door, shut it, and then turned to her. "We're not going anywhere until we talk. We're not going to sweep last night under the rug."

She gaped, scoffed as though she would rebuff but then softened and said, "Yeah, well, maybe I was afraid that if I talked, you'd run away again, just like you always do."

"I don't run away."

"Yes, you do." She held up leather-clad fingers and pointed them out. "Exhibit A, last night. Exhibit B, in my garage when I told you to get the ball from my pocket. You said you liked me and then bolted. Exhibit C, in seventh grade, you were supposed to meet me behind the blue trash can in the cafeteria on Valentine's Day and we were going to swap puddings. You failed to turn up. I rest my case."

He arched a brow. "Seventh grade? Really?"

"Yes, you dick. Seventh grade. Pudding. Valentine's Day." She widened her eyes with an attempt at intimidation. "I remember everything, Luciano."

He scratched his head. The pudding incident had been the year after they'd started hanging out. The summer they'd met was well and truly over, and Parker had just left for his first year "studying abroad" but his warning to stay away from his sister had been fresh in Joe's mind, and Wyatt's ever-looming presence had seemed to grow darker without his level-headed, older brother to keep him in check.

"I don't remember it being Valentine's Day," he muttered.

"The point is, you tend to avoid tough conversations. Even the ones about your..." Her voice trailed off, but then she rallied and looked him in the eyes. "About your parents. We never talked. We just sat there and shared the silence."

"I was a kid back then, Liza. I'm not now."

Her gaze sharpened as she took him in with feminine appreciation. "I know."

"I'm just trying to figure out how I fit into this."

Liza stood and pulled something out of her back pocket before putting it on the table. It was a folded picture of the two of them grinning at each other on their first day in the police academy, dorky T-shirts, dull haircuts, and bright cheeks. He remembered it vividly. They'd both been so surprised to have enlisted in the same class but were giddy with excitement at having someone to share the experience with. Well, Joe had been giddy with plenty of other feelings too. Liza had grown from a fifteen-year-old budding beauty to a hard-as-nails hidden rose. Anyone else who tried to talk to her got a brow-beating, but not him. All the male rookies had been jealous of him. He'd been so smug.

She pointed at the picture.

"You think you had no choice in this, but neither did I." Her eyes glistened. She swallowed with barely restrained emotion, and when

she spoke, her voice had turned tight. "But from what I'm seeing there, we couldn't have been happier to know our partner was someone already proven to be trustworthy. I know when I left to train, we drifted apart. But somehow, we found each other again. And now, for the third time, the stars have aligned and we're here." She tapped his chest, and then hers. "That's not a consolation prize, Joe. That's destiny."

"Liza Lazarus talking about destiny?" he asked sardonically, then winced at his attempt of disrupting the intensity of their conversation.

"I have to believe it," she insisted. "Because without it, then all I have to go on is that life is shitty. I was born in a lab. I put my life on the line when there is corruption and sin around every corner. And loving someone only brings me pain. I don't want that life for myself. I don't." She choked up and turned away, stiff.

He didn't know what to say, so picked up the picture. They did look happy. Innocent. Hopeful. Naive. He complained about not having a choice, but neither did she. No one did in life. You're born into your circumstances, but you can build your way out of them. Hard work was his version of destiny. And if he wanted to make his own, then he had to lay the first brick himself.

A knock came at the door a moment before a hurried shout. "We got a body!"

Liza wiped her eyes as his phone pinged with an incoming text.

"There's been a homicide," Liza murmured, eyes grave.

He nodded and pulled out his cell. When the message hit his brain, a sinking feeling leveled his gut.

"Same MO as our guy," he said.

Shit.

THE DEAD BODY belonged to a fifteen-year-old girl. At least, that's what the medical examiner was currently telling Joe. She was unrecognizable from all the blood, viscera, and gore. Naked from the waist down, her body had been dumped on the muddy banks under the Vermillion Bridge near the South-Side industrial area.

A bearded homeless man pushing an overflowing cart cursed when he was stopped from getting to his shanty tent, right next to the crime scene. Another homeless man threw an empty bottle of beer with a shout to not touch his things as an officer finished cordoning off the area.

Liza's subdued murmur floated in and out of the occasional angry shout as she took witness statements. He'd never known Liza to avoid a body like this, but the minute they'd arrived, her face had paled, and she turned away without another word.

Joe used his pen to lift wet hair from the girl's face. A plastic pink clip fell from her hair. It was the kind you bought at a dime store or won in those little coin machines you found at the mall. She was so young. Innocent. Probably a first-time runaway.

At the thought, a cold stone dropped in his stomach. Hadn't Liza said she'd come across a runaway? He glanced at her, and then back to the girl. If this was who they were meant to see at the shelter yesterday, it would explain her reluctance.

Joe straightened. The examiner's bald head shone with sweat. His long fingers plucked a hanky from his pocket and blew his nose.

Scenes like this could get to even the most seasoned.

"What else have you found?" Joe asked.

"Just like the other ones," the examiner said. "She's been brutalized, cut open with surgical precision, and has organs missing. I'll know more at the morgue, but at first glance, it seems like a liver, a kidney, and her uterus. Lack of blood on the ground suggests this happened elsewhere."

"*Christ.*"

"She got in a few good scratches, though. We've retrieved samples from beneath her fingernails."

"Good. Let me know what you find out."

"Will do."

Joe put his notebook away and strode toward where Liza interviewed a woman wearing a blanket and a beanie. He was sure he'd already seen her speak to that person.

He cleared his throat to let her know he was there, but then stayed at a respectful distance until she finished.

With bleak eyes, Liza said, "It's not safe out here." She wrote something on a card and handed it to the woman. "Ask for this person at the shelter. She'll look after you."

The woman nodded but didn't look like she'd do it. In Cardinal City, a dead body down here was something they saw every other day.

"What have you got?" Joe asked Liza.

She flipped through her spiral notebook. "We're estimating the body was dumped sometime between two and five this morning. No one heard a scream."

"Examiner thinks she was killed somewhere else. Lack of blood. She was either brought here after or killed quietly."

Liza looked away. Her bottom lip quivered.

"You good?" he asked.

She nodded. Then shook her head. "It was the teenage runaway. Mirabelle."

He let out a sigh. "I thought it might be. It's not your fault. Don't get attached."

Thunder clouds clapped at her dark look. "Not my fault? I could have stopped it. Wyatt should have let me finish him."

He'd seen the dried blood on the alley floor.

"Are you talking about that man you used excessive force on? Liza, listen to yourself."

With a grinding of her teeth, she wrenched her gaze from his and scowled as Mirabelle's body was bagged and zipped. Her fingers flexed, creaking her leather gloves.

"Come on," he said, voice soft. "I'll get you a coffee with a straw, and we'll start going over the old case files Geoff and Briggs have been rounding up."

But she wouldn't leave. Her eyes had turned distant, as though she was still in that brutal world where Wyatt had interrupted her.

"Liza?"

Wide eyes locked on him and Joe felt her panic to his core. Something wasn't right. A curl of yellow at her mouth revealed why.

Joe searched their surroundings, looking for cover. His thoughts tumbled through different scenarios, thinking of ways of keeping her secret hidden. They couldn't use the car, the two of them locked inside would be deadly, unless he locked her inside on her own.

He curled his fingers around her neck, intending to guide her to the car, but she put her hand over his and stopped. He sent her a questioning look.

Are you okay?

Relief poured through her gaze. She gripped his hand tighter and nodded. "You relax me. Don't let go."

He nodded. "Can I do anything else?"

Her eyes fluttered closed. "Just this." She squeezed his fingers. "No... say something. Distract me."

"Like what?"

"I don't know."

He blurted the first thing he could think of. "Barry Bonds: 2986 games; 762 home runs."

He paused, waiting for her reaction.

"More," she said.

"Hank Aaron: 3298 games; 755 home runs. Babe Ruth: 2573 games; 814 home runs—"

Liza snorted. "As if."

"Just checking to see if you're listening."

"You can't make up stats, even for the Babe."

"Especially for the Babe," he chuckled. A wisp of her hair floated from the push of his breath. He wanted to catch it and smooth it down, but refused to lift his hands from her.

After a few more minutes of him reciting baseball statistics, she nodded again and let go of his hand. "I'm okay."

"Wait there."

He retrieved an unopened bottle of water from the car and gave it to Liza. She gratefully accepted, cleaned her hands, and then washed out her mouth before spitting.

It wasn't an odd scene. Many officers puked at a homicide like this. If anyone noticed, they'd probably put it down to a queasy stomach.

"You sure you good?" he asked.

"See? You have my back."

He returned her tight smile and ignored the twinge of guilt in his gut, but knew he couldn't avoid it forever. He expected a call from his superior by the end of the day.

nineteen

LIZA LAZARUS

AFTER RETURNING from the crime scene, Liza spent the afternoon filling out copious paperwork regarding the Faithful attack. Joe went straight into his office and shut the door. The ride home with him had been interesting. She'd thought, perhaps, her poison-slip had ruffled his careful Italian feathers, but his hair remained tidy, his shirt tucked in, and his tie in a perfect Windsor knot. His eyes were schooled and stark. He wasn't ruffled.

But he cracked his knuckles continuously.

It reminded her of the time he'd applied for Quantico and was waiting on the results.

Joe sat reclined, long legs sprawled under his desk next to Liza's. He cracked his knuckles and stared at the phone, foot tapping on the linoleum floor.

Liza put down her phone receiver and glared at him. "Jeez. Enough already."

She reached across the expanse between their two desks, pressed her finger to a dark freckle on the back of his hand, and then made a buzzing sound.

He looked at her. "What?"

"That was me pressing the off button," she replied, then raised her brows. "You're cracking your knuckles again. Relax. They'll call."

He was probably still flexing his hands behind his closed door. She glanced at the solid wood barrier, a spear of concern momentarily hitting her, but then scowled back at her paperwork. With it done, she switched her mind to the recent homicide and felt sick all over again. It was hard not to let it get to her. Mirabelle had been so innocent. She didn't deserve the fate death had dealt her. Liza pulled out her notebook from her jacket pocket and flipped through what she'd found.

Bubkis. Nada. Zilch.

The homeless people saw nothing. No witnesses. No motive. But the nature of the crime matched the MO of the serial killer Joe's team was hunting.

With a heavy sigh, Liza leaned back in her chair. For the first time in her life, she felt inadequate as a detective. Joe had specifically requested Liza on his team for her expertise, yet a new crime had occurred on her watch. A lot was going on with Joe at the moment. The serial killer, the bombshell about her secret identity, their feelings for each other. He had her back at the crime scene. She used to always have his back, despite him never talking about his problems.

She should do something nice for him.

Roses? Chocolate? She grinned. Not really her style. But catching a killer would be the perfect gift.

The man who'd accosted Mirabelle in the alley came to mind. Liza had beaten him pretty badly. Her knuckles still smarted with an echo of righteous pain. Would he have retaliated, tracked the teenager down and then lured her to her death because Liza had put him in his place? But the idea that this same man was also the serial killer Joe had been hunting was almost too coincidental.

Liza continued her internal dialogue. She found a conversation always helped her make sense of things. Like this fate business. Take Evan's psychic drawings, for example. Or Mary's old visions that had pulled her away from the Hildegard Sisterhood. Mysticism was never something Liza put her faith in. Especially not after the way she and her siblings were created. Besides, Mary always used to say, magic is just science we don't know yet… or some shit.

Liza suspected the saying had originated with Gloria, their biological mother. It didn't sound like a Mary thing to say. Mary was a *bruja* trained as an assassin pretending to be a nun, and a Catholic convert. And that religion came with an awful lot of mysticism and arcane devil and angel voodoo woo-woo. Who was to say what was a coincidence, or like Liza had said to Joe earlier, destiny?

She wrote the word "destiny" and circled it.

If it was real, then there was a reason Liza had been in that alley a few days ago, and it wasn't to puke all over a potential one-night-stand. The reason had to be bigger than giving a runaway an extra day of life. She just needed to figure out what it was.

Banging, shuffling, and the sounds of desks being packed away alerted her to the late hour. The working day was done, and she hadn't discussed a plan of action with Joe yet. She collected her notepad and headed to his door. She lifted a fist to knock—the door opened.

Joe walked out with his suit jacket on, his car keys jangling in one hand, and a stack of Manila case files in the other.

"You're leaving?" she asked.

"Day's over."

A pause.

"You need something?" he asked.

A flinch inside Liza's chest. "Um. I just thought that we should head down to the shelter and interview anyone who might have spoken to Mirabelle."

"Already sent Geoff."

"What?" She blinked, affronted. "But I was the one who suggested the lead."

"I know. But we don't have time. I have a thing, and you shouldn't be out without me." He glanced down at her wrist tattoo. "If I can't join you, then you should go home, right?"

"I'm not some woman who needs to be kept," she growled. "I'm quite capable of handling my shit."

His brows lifted. "That's not the impression I got today."

"That's a jerk thing to say while I'm in this teething period. Once I'm used to... you-know-what, I'll be fine."

"I thought you said if you're not seeing me at regular intervals, you can black out."

"It's... it's easier if I see you. Much easier. But not impossible. A couple of days apart is fine. I just need to be wary of it or revert to my old process. Anyway, shouldn't we be working on the case?"

"There's not much we can do until forensics are back." Dark eyes contemplated. "Why don't you go sit with a sketch artist and get a likeness of the alley attacker?" He reopened his office door. "Better yet, I'll get you the old case files on the Ripper killer and you can get acquainted."

He shuffled through some files in his cabinet and cursed softly. "They're at my place. I'll bring them in tomorrow."

"I'll get a start on the soft copies tonight."

"Hard copies are better." He frowned. "But, fine. You do what you need to do. I'll see you tomorrow."

Then he strode out, leaving her staring at his retreating broad-shouldered back.

"He just gave me the brushoff," she murmured.

THE FOLLOWING NIGHT, Liza stood outside Joe's apartment with a box of freshly printed case files, some of Evan's sketches, and Chinese takeout. This was it, the moment she laid it all on the line. She'd even brought a peace offering—a tiny wrapped gift.

He had been suspiciously absent from work today. No call. Just a vague *"I've got Bureau stuff to do"* as an explanation. She'd considered giving him space, maybe going to the church for a sin-equilibrium reset, but she didn't want to. He'd either react the way she'd hoped or... well, she didn't want to think about what she'd be forced to do if he responded badly.

With her hands occupied, she kicked the door instead of knocked, and hoped with all her heart that Joe would open wearing only his towel again.

Sounds came from inside. Unlike last time, she was in full nervous mode and felt her underarms prickle with sweat. What if she was pushing too hard? Sure, there was work to do and, sure, she'd had a breakthrough when Evan had offered to draw a picture of her assailant, but maybe Joe needed more time before making a big leap of loyalty to her family.

She could have tested the waters by calling him first, but there was also no reason for her to stay home. They already had a twenty-four-seven guard watching Daisy in case she made a wrong move. Liza couldn't stand another minute in Parker's orbit. During their training earlier, his judgment was too critical, despite her control of her poison getting better. The dude seriously needed to get laid.

So did she.

The door opened.

"Liza?" Joe's brow furrowed as he took her in. Still dressed in his suit, he must have recently arrived home. She probably should have checked that. He *did* say he had a thing yesterday. Maybe it ran longer.

His eyes glided down from her face to the box. "I thought we said we'd do this tomorrow."

"It is tomorrow, and I have ideas," she said. "And I brought food. Your favorite."

He looked confused for a moment, but then an inquisitive dark brow arched toward her package. "Beef and Black Bean?"

She grinned, already feeling a win coming.

"Come on," she pressed. "I didn't see you all day. You're probably starving. Plus, Evan drew a likeness of the guy from the alley. There are coincidences we need to discuss."

Liza wasn't aware of the breath she'd held captive until it escaped upon his release of the door. He collected the box from her hands.

"I got it." She tugged it back.

His jaw clenched. Nostrils flared. For a moment, Liza thought he would instigate a tug-of-war, but he let go and stepped into his apartment.

"I'll get the wine," he said.

Another small win. When Joe shifted from beer to merlot, he relaxed. Unable to contain the grin on her face, she entered and kicked the door closed. An evil laugh cackled in her mind, and she gloated at his back. She was going to break through to him. He stood no chance against the Liza Lazarus maelstrom. No chance.

"Did you say something?" he asked as he retrieved two glasses from the overhead cupboard in the kitchen.

"Huh?"

Had she said that out loud?

"I'll just put these over here." She went to the couch by the window, but it reminded her too much of that... other woman who shall not be named. The small two-seater table between the couch and the kitchen was better.

Liza set the box down and realized there was no room for food, so shifted the box to the floor and put the takeout on the table. The chopsticks had just been snapped when Joe handed her a glass of red wine. He sipped from his glass and sat down with a long, drawn-out sigh.

"Long day, huh?" she joked, then winced because anyone making light of the past few days was stupid.

Another sigh was her answer.

Jitters rode her system. She feared she'd never be done with them, so took a big swig of merlot, and then dug into the food. Joe watched her with a small smile kicking up one side of his mouth.

"What?" she snapped. "I'm hungry."

He made a noncommittal grunt, and then picked at his food. She used her chopsticks to trap his against the plate.

"What was that look for?" she asked again, refusing to release his captive chopsticks.

"You eat when you're nervous," he explained.

She let go and slit her eyes. "You crack your knuckles."

"I'm not now." He flexed the fingers of one hand.

"But you were all yesterday afternoon."

His gaze leveled on her.

Not so much fun when the spotlight's on you, huh?

She stole a piece of his beef and popped it into her mouth. "What's got your panties in a twist, anyway?"

"Nothing you can help with," he murmured with a dark look at his food.

Oh. This was serious.

It suddenly occurred to her that maybe he'd never talked much about his problems, because she'd never offered to listen, and she

never told him her problems. Not the real ones, anyway. If she wanted him to open up, she had to do the same. By the end of the night, she resolved to let him know more about her family.

"Hey," she said. "You'd be surprised at what I can help you with. You won't know unless you tell me."

He shook his head, seemingly throwing off his tension, and then removed his suit jacket and hung it over the back of his chair. He sprawled long legs and loosened his tie. That's all he did. But the paring of his decorous mask revealed rampant masculinity. A sliver of heat unfurled in Liza's lower belly, and she allowed herself a moment to appreciate him in a way she'd neither the propensity nor courage to do in the past. Her gaze lingered on his long legs, moved up his trim torso, snug in a button-down shirt, and then shifted to his sleeves rolled to the forearms. His Adam's apple bobbed as he ate. Rough scruff grew dark and thick along his square jaw, accentuating the angle. He would need a shave soon. She'd like to be the one who shaved it. And then she'd lick that neck. Maybe she'd lick it now.

A blush hit her cheeks.

Another spear of desire pooled low and insistent between her legs.

She squirmed a little and kept eating. After a few more moments of companionable silence, she said, "This is nice."

When his obsidian gaze met hers, she couldn't decipher his thoughts. His finger rimmed the wine glass while he watched her with unblinking contemplation that made her want to squirm.

What was he thinking? Feeling?

She knew she'd never sensed his lust, but it had always been there. Other moments like these popped into her mind—when he'd simply stared at her while toying with the rim of a soda can, glass, or something else.

"What are you thinking?" she blurted.

"I'm thinking you need a straw." The gravel in his voice shuddered down her spine. "You usually use a straw."

Her breath hitched.

A breathy sound came out of him. It reminded her of something an animal made when it warned another from its food. A short, sharp grumble of warning. His eyes weren't on the food. They were on her lips.

He cleared his throat and pointed at the box of case files. "What did you bring?"

Whatever tension had been hanging in the air was gone. She frowned, shoved the last mouthful of food in, and then shifted over to the box on the floor. The surface area down there was the biggest, so she laid down the forensic crime scene shots and placed the sketches beside them.

Over the past few months, Evan had been amassing quite the collection of dream sketches, or she should say nightmare sketches. Included among the subject matter were faceless women lined up, sleeping, often with strange faces looming over them. There were also pregnant women crying through shallow holes for eyes. And through it all, Evan's hurried frenzied charcoal strokes and smudges cast an all together haunting aesthetic. One could almost believe they were simply art pieces in a horror show and not windows into the future.

When Evan had drawn the likeness of Liza's assailant, he'd been struck with familiarity. He'd recognized the same man from previous sketches and had retrieved a few for Liza.

"Evan dreams the future," she murmured, laying the last of the pictures out. "He's seen the Syndicate taking women, and Daisy has confirmed it."

"Daisy?"

Here goes... sharing. *She could do this.*

"My sister."

"You mean, Sloan?"

"No. I have another one."

"How many siblings do you have?"

"She's the last, but... we thought she was dead. She wasn't." Liza picked up the sketch Evan had drawn of Daisy in peril. "You might have seen her when the Faithful attacked in the street. She helped put them down. That was the first day we've worked together, on the same side."

"Why?"

"Daisy was unfortunately left behind when we escaped from the lab, and the Syndicate took her. But she's come back to us now."

"That's her?" Joe pointed to the paper in Liza's hands of Daisy's face sketched in angry, painful lines.

"Yes, this is her." Liza's gaze darted between Evan's sketches and the Ripper crime scene shots. "It's all starting to make sense now. They're kidnapping runaways. The Syndicate needs stem cells to finish replicate experiments—clones."

Joe blinked. "Did you just say clones?"

"Trust me, I know how it sounds, but we've seen them."

"Do you have any proof? Anything I can bring back to the director?"

"Unfortunately, Evan destroyed the last lab we know of. There was a black site where the plant came from, but it was heavily guarded and sanctioned by some sort of military connection. We infiltrated once, but apart from some experiments, incriminating files weren't on site. It seemed more of a Plan B sort of place. We need to find the clones."

"I want the address of that place," Joe said. "Anything I can get to build a case."

Liza nodded and wrote it down. "I'm not even sure if they're still there. After we made them, they abandoned the site. But, who knows, you might get lucky and find something."

Joe rubbed his day-old scruff. "What about those sketches? Why does it look like Daisy is in pain?"

She winced, not wanting to tell him despite every instinct saying she must.

His eyes tracked across the line-up Liza had created and paused at more sketches. His finger touched the sketch, then lingered on the one of her. "These look familiar. Also in pain."

"Misha, and... me."

Intelligent eyes crossed to hers. "You're in danger?"

"It's fine." She pointed at the Ripper crime scene shots. "The killer has been removing organs, including the uterus. Have they been screened by forensics to see if the victims were pregnant?"

"Liza."

"The report says there were traces of chloroform around the mouths of victims, meaning the killer knocked them unconscious before—"

"Liza!" Joe took her shoulder and lifted her from the floor to face him as he studied her. "Are you in danger?"

"I'm more in danger of becoming unbalanced. But with this sort of stuff, I can take care of myself. You know that."

He didn't really. As far as he could see, the pictures told him nothing about the sort of danger she was in, except she'd end up in pain. It was Liza who hoped he'd assume the pain was physical, and nothing to do with her internal battle.

But her words did little to assuage the concern turning to cold, hard resolution in his eyes. He scrubbed his hands through his hair and paced away.

"You're always going to be a target until this Syndicate organization is taken down, aren't you?"

From the way he waited for her reply, she knew she had to keep opening up. She had to trust him with everything. Lying to him would come back to haunt her.

"Yes. They invested billions of dollars in creating us. There are representatives around the world who want us in their custody. And if they can't have us, then—" She pointed at the sketches of her and Daisy. "Then they'll use us for our biological matter, study us, and create replicates that will actually do their bidding. We can't allow that to happen. Can you imagine an army of us, only with no conscience, and no mate to balance them out?"

"How can this not be on our radar?" he murmured to himself.

She ignored his comment and went back to the murderer. "The Ripper killer could be harvesting cells, whether the victim was pregnant or not. There is more than one type of stem cell, and perhaps the Syndicate needs them all. They're also in our spine, our brain, our—"

"Enough," he snapped. "I don't want to hear any more."

He strode away and disappeared into his bedroom. Liza cocked her head when she heard strange scrapings and strained her hearing. It sounded like tape, or paper being ripped.

Hesitantly, she followed him to his room. "Joe?"

The bedroom was simple. A double bed. A bedside table. A wall covered in evidence from an investigation. Pictures, notes, reports, red string leading from one pinned piece of evidence to another. It was like a murder board from the station, but instead of dead bodies and suspects, the pictures showed Liza's family tree. Joe had been tracking them for years. Since Evan's power was triggered. She stepped closer for a better look, but Joe continued to rip down everything like a man possessed.

"Stop," she said, and tried to take his hand, but a manic demon had taken hold of his body. He ripped through everything like it was going to kill him, and he wanted to get to it first. She latched onto his forearm, halting him. "Have you been investigating my family?"

Two pained eyes met hers. His jaw clenched.

She stepped back. Puzzle pieces started to connect. "This is why you came back to town. This is why Parker told me to be careful with you. Is this why you..." The memory of the two of them on at the rooftop pool hit, and betrayal flared in her gut. She squeezed her eyes shut to stop the burn. "This is why they chose you. It's all so you could get closer to my family. It's why you've been with me."

"No." His voice came out a harsh bark.

Papers and pictures fluttered to the ground. He took her face between his palms. "Look at me, Liza."

She shook her head.

This was what she was talking about. This was why she never put her heart on the line. It was inevitable, this hurt. It was always going to come for her. Destiny. She was so stupid to think she'd caught a break. That the fate she'd been resigned to her entire life wasn't real. That maybe there was another road for her.

But Liza was born for one thing only. To kill lust.

Joe's thumbs scraped her cheeks. "Please, look at me."

JOE LUCIANO

WHEN JOE WATCHED Liza's eyes open, there was no affection, no love, only the cold bleak stare of an enemy. It settled on him like the suffocating weight of his worst nightmare.

It choked him, blocked words in his throat. He'd already told his director that his report was delayed, but after hearing Liza's words, knowing the Syndicate killed indiscriminately to get the supplies they needed, that they were creating clones of the Lazarus siblings and wanted to unleash evil… it was inconceivable, but the very possible end to the world.

And Liza and her family were the only ones standing in their way.

He wanted to tell her that she was everything to him. That he'd been stupid to ever believe she, or her family, could be evil. But the words wouldn't come. Nothing was good enough. She looked at him as though he were the villain, and it broke him.

"Liza." He shook his head, struggling to explain.

I'm not going to investigate you.

I'll investigate them.

I lov—

A punch to his face sent a shockwave through his system. Pain exploded in his jaw. Vision blurred. Black dots swam before his eyes. He reeled to the side, coughed out the pain, and then worked his jaw to test its function. Rallying his senses, he straightened and leveled his gaze on her.

Her bleakness had been replaced with electric anger. Fists flexed at her side and, for a split second, Joe thought she might actually kill him. He was a loose end, a threat to the survival of her family.

She struck. He blocked.

Goddamn, she was *strong*. The fact he fought back incensed her. Joe could see it in her eyes. All she wanted was to pulverize him, and he would let her. If it made her feel better, if it made her understand the depths of his feelings, he would let her grind him to a pulp.

"You've hated my family since the beginning." She shoved him.

His back hit the wall. "That's not true."

"Don't *fucking* lie to me, Joey."

There was no reasoning with her, she came at him again. A fist hammered into his gut. A knee cleaved toward his groin. He caught the strike on his thigh with a wince. With a quick twist, he shifted out of the kill zone against the wall but didn't get far. She came at him again. He didn't want to hurt her but had to protect himself. He gave a tactical one-two jab. She dodged effortlessly.

"I never hated all of you." He escaped a fist to his face. "Never you."

Somehow that was the wrong thing to say. An animalistic growl ripped out of her, and she launched, catching him around the middle and propelling them onto his bed. Then it was all hits and blocks. A backhand to his face. He elbowed her jaw. Long brown hair whipped like corporal punishment. A harpy's scream, and then they grappled. They rolled. He had the surreal sense he should be in worse pain, that she pulled her punches. She *allowed* him to touch her. She knew every weakness he projected, but still ached for love so hard, she welcomed his attention, even if it was pain.

It was the hope in her eyes dying a slow death. It gave him scores of insight. She'd never had physical affection from a lover. She'd always avoided touch from the opposite sex in case it led to arousal and inevitable pain. This tough wall she erected was her line of defense.

But when the light of her hope died its final death, she pinned him on his stomach, kneed him between the shoulder blades, forcing his face into the mattress. She wrenched his arm back in a stronghold.

A metallic cricking rent the air as something cold locked around his wrist. She yanked his other hand behind his back and cuffed his wrists together before rolling him to face her. She straddled his thighs. The wild woman looking down at him was a thing of primordial beauty. Her hair came loose from a braid. Electric brown eyes. Flushed cheeks.

But the fear and hate were not Liza. This was not the woman he'd dreamed about being in this very bed. This was not his fantasy. She was an avenging Valkyrie, ready to smite with no mercy. He couldn't even lift his arms to protect himself. Her time for pulling punches was over.

She curled her fist, drew it back—

"Stop!" he shouted. "For the love of God, just stop and let me talk."

"There's nothing you can say."

"I love you."

She physically jerked. Blinked.

Silence.

His heart hammered in his chest, rattling his ribs, but he pressed on. "I've always loved you, Liza. Always. Never stopped. Never will."

Her face crumpled. "You're using me."

Suddenly shock lit up her face. She glared at her palms. Little pebbles of yellow started gathering along the crease lines. The defiant burn of her gaze turned wild and panicked.

In a heartbeat, Joe knew what to do. He spoke calmly, voice low and soothing. "Barry Bonds: 2986 games; 762 home runs. Come on, repeat it."

Every iota of Liza's body language said she would rather choke on her own vomit than acquiesce.

"You know this works," he insisted.

She held his gaze and then spoke through a raspy throat. "Barry Bonds: 2986 games; 762 home runs."

He nodded. "Hank Aaron: 3298 games; 755 home runs."

She repeated, and then he moved to the next statistic. They went down the ladder of all-time baseball statistics until no more yellow appeared at her palms. She kept mumbling the stats to herself, eyes wary on her palms, then disappeared into his ensuite. He heard the faucet turn on a moment later and dropped his head back on the bed with a heavy exhale.

Her footsteps shuffled next to the bed, but he kept his gaze on the white ceiling.

"I was using you," he admitted. "I thought I could steer you away from your family. I thought you were too good for them and they didn't appreciate you, but I didn't know the whole story. I do now. Listen to me. I was tearing it all down to get rid of it. Liza. I'm on your side, now." He paused. He forced the next words out with a trembling voice. "I can't sleep without dreaming about you. I smell you, and I go weak at the knees. I see you, and I can't function. I had to leave the city to become better and failed. I even tried to attempt a normal relationship to get you out of my head, but it never worked, and that's because it's always been you, wrapped around my heart." He slid his gaze back to hers. "I *love* you, Liza Lazarus."

As though snipped by scissors, the thread holding her composure unraveled. Her eyes watered. Her lips flattened. Fear. That's what he saw in her eyes. She was on that raft, floating away, afraid to drown in her sea of overwhelming emotions. Disbelief, pain, incomprehension —it all warred on her face, drawing her brows together so tight they became two straight slits across her forehead. When she spoke, it was a heart-rending confession.

"I thought I'd never hear that," she rasped, sobbed. "Ever."

"Hear what... that I love you?"

She tried to hold it in, but a sob burst out. Her chin dropped. "I thought I'd never get it. From anyone."

Aw, hell. *Shit*. "Liza. You've always had it. From me."

"I didn't know!" Her voice tightened, almost accused. She dropped a knee on the bed and then hit him on the chest, but there was no power, only tears. Tears she'd likely never shown anyone. But him.

"Come here," he urged. "Kiss me, and you'll know."

She climbed onto him and pressed her lips to his. He pushed back until their teeth knocked, and then they kissed as though starved. A sharp pinch. A taste of copper. The snare of his wrists and strain of his shoulders as he arched to meet her. He barely noticed any of it through the ecstasy of feeling her mouth on his. He would kiss through the end of the world if it was her fused to him like this. Her sweet, heady taste hit his system. Euphoria. Bliss. *Desire*. He groaned, or maybe she did. He tried to deepen the kiss, but she held him captive beneath her, at her mercy. And, fuck, that made it hotter. She *wanted* him.

"Liza," he rasped, begged, chasing her lips as she pulled away.

But she was gone, lost in another world that started somewhere around his neck and jaw. She twirled her intrepid tongue over his skin, inducing a thready sigh from his lips.

"Uncuff me." He shuddered as she found his ear.

But did he want to be freed?

Not with her mouth on him, taking what she desired. Perhaps she read his mind because she denied him, instead opting to slide her bewitching slick tongue down his neck, to his throat, to his collar. With a low, throaty growl, she ripped his shirt open, popping the fastenings. *Jesus.* Buttons landed on the bed, rolled, and tinkled to the hardwood flooring. Seeing her lust-filled, feminine appreciation caused the swell of deep satisfaction in his chest.

"When did you get so fucking hot?" The low pitch of her voice connected with his cock, hardening it to steel.

She scraped nails down the coarse hair on his chest, circled his nipple, and scratched the ridges down his abs. A shuddering hiss burst from his lips. She kneaded his flesh as though taking her due, touching and tantalizing him everywhere. Then her lips were back, savoring him. Wet, hot, and cool sensations followed her mouth until she found his belt and unbuckled. He thrust into her touch, threw his head back, and rolled his eyes to the ceiling. *Yes. There. Put your lips there.*

"I'm so fucking hard for you, Liza," he groaned.

"I need to see. I have to know." She frowned as she worked his fly, lowering the zipper. "I can't sense you. I—sweet *Jes*—"

Her words abruptly cut off. Her fingers wrapped around his raging cockstand. His mind blanked. His heart kicked in his chest, thumping like a bucking bull.

"Put your lips on me," he pleaded softly.

A breath. A pause. She took him into her mouth. There was nothing else. Just her and a thousand sparks of paradise shooting through his body. After two slides of her tongue, he knew he wouldn't last.

"Uncuff me," he insisted and struggled against the restraints. "Now."

She dug into her jeans pocket, retrieved the key, and then fumbled behind him to unlock a single wrist. Metal tinkled as he brought his arms to his front, intending to take the lead, but she captured his cuffed wrist.

His brows shot up. What...?

She smirked and then cuffed his hand to hers—his right to her left. She threw the key. It clinked down the bed's headboard and sifted between the wall space to land somewhere beneath.

"In case you feel the urge to run away again," she explained.

A low growl of intent rumbled through him. "Honey, I'm not going anywhere for a very long time."

Liza's eyes turned lazy and full of carnal promise. She threaded her cuffed hand into Joe's and held it firm at the side of his head, pressed against the quilt covered mattress. They stared at each other, almost in disbelief—*they were finally here, doing this*—and then he lost all sense of reason. He rolled them so he was on top and kissed her hungrily. He pulled at her blouse with his free hand, and she helped wrench it off with hers. The cuffs prevented it coming all the way off, so they left their tops dangling between them. They were a team, thinking as one. Next were her pants, and then his, until he was naked and she was in her provocative black lace bra and panties.

She lay beneath him, looking like his dream. He tugged the tie on her hair and helped it unravel.

"Perfect," he muttered as brown cascading softness fanned out on his bed. She was everything he'd imagined and more. She watched as he slid his cuffed hand down her smooth as satin front. She echoed his movement with her trapped hand, so they touched her together as one. Her low moan of desire hardened him to the point of pain.

He had to have her now. His fingers rasped over the lace between her legs and felt the wetness there. He stroked the fabric. She thrust upward, needing more sensation. His eyes rolled when her hips hit his erection.

"I'm leaving these on," he said hoarsely, looking at her lace. "It's the least you can do after teasing me with them at the station."

A wicked, self-satisfied grin curved her lips, and it was that smile he wished he could capture to remember forever. It sent his heart hammering against the black doubt that had kept it caged all these years. He guided her cuff-free hand to her panties.

"Hold it aside," he ordered.

She used the fingers to hook onto the lace at her crotch, tugged, and gave him an unhindered view.

He slid his blunt tip over her slick center until she squirmed and begged him to fill her with whimpered pleas. She was his. He claimed her. He showed her by tunneling into her tight heat with a hard thrust to the hilt.

All senses shut down. Both of them stilled. He felt nothing but the simple sensation of her surrounding him. When the irresistible stillness became too much, he dropped a hand to either side of her head. One holding hers, joined irrevocably, gripping tightly. He pumped into her. She encouraged him with her legs kicked high, pressing into his rear.

Their first time was supposed to be a marathon, to last like he'd promised. He loved her more than anything, and he wanted to show it. But it was hopeless. Her sweet smell, her smooth skin, and glowing cheeks. She barked demands for him to go faster, to hit her deeper. He was powerless to her whim. He always would be. With hard pants, cries, and sweaty movements, they reached their bliss together.

He collapsed onto her, still grinding absently, wringing the last of their throws, kissing her neck, muttering sweet nothings until their breathing returned to normal and they entered a different kind of quiet. A shared stillness.

For long moments they stayed silent, simply holding each other, and then she spoke.

"I didn't puke."

He chuckled and kissed her gently. "Never again."

"Again starts tonight, right?"

7

twenty-one

LIZA LAZARUS

LIZA WOKE in Joe's bed. The sun was yet to shine, but she could feel it in her blood. Sunrise had always been like that for her, a tangible sensation, an anticipation. Perhaps it had something to do with the training she'd received. Much of it had been outdoors. She'd learned to trust her body clock on more than one occasion. And right now, her body clock was ticking along deliciously with tugs of recently pleasured aches. *Joe.* She grinned. *Joey.* He didn't like her calling him Joey, which was precisely why she was going to do it.

Stretching languidly in the sheets, she put her arm out and searched for him, but found the bed empty. Her heart clenched, panic bloomed, but then she heard movement in' the living room... no, kitchen. The sizzling of bacon. Eggs... Holy shitballs, her man was making her breakfast.

Scrambling to find her clothes, she settled on his shirt and threaded her arms through the sleeves. She plugged the only two surviving buttons closed. She padded into the kitchen, only to pause at the threshold.

The sight of her mate caused a visceral reaction in her body.

Everything froze, lured by his messy morning appeal. Joe stood with his back to her, stirring the sizzling pan. A black apron was tied to his front, but his rear was naked as the day he was born. The globes of his taut ass dimpled as he tensed and relaxed with movement. Olive skinned. Broad-shouldered. Almost too good to be true. He looked good. He cooked. He made love like a machine. All night, they'd lasted. In every position. *Mine*, she thought, and licked her lips.

With barely contained mischief, she tiptoed over and jumped onto his back like a monkey. He let go of the spatula and steadied her with a small grunt of amusement.

"Morning, Joey." She kissed him on the prickly cheek, loving the raspiness of his stubble.

"It was going to be a surprise," he said, voice deep and throaty. "You should go back to bed."

She slid down his back, pinched his rear, and then fit herself under his arm.

"Sleeping in isn't my thing," she said, eyeing the delicious omelet and bacon.

"What is?" he asked. But before she replied, he answered. "Morning workout. I forgot."

She smiled up at him. "I can take my jog tomorrow. Or a swim. Maybe you can come with me."

Affectionate eyes met hers. "I'd like that."

They'd finished eating and were halfway through washing the dishes when Liza finally dared to ask something that had been playing on her mind forever.

"What did my family do to make you hate them?"

Joe wiped his hands on his apron and faced her with an evasive shift of his eyes. "It doesn't matter now. The reason is moot."

"Now *that* makes me want to know the truth. Tell me."

He gripped the back of his neck and looked at his feet for a long time before lifting his gaze. "I don't want to start anything. It doesn't matter. We're together. That's all that matters."

"What the fuck did Parker do?" she growled. Because it had to be him. He was the ringleader in all things. "Tell me, or I'll force it out of him."

A long exhale left Joe. "Do you remember at the end of that first summer, we'd arranged to meet up and I had a question to ask you?"

Liza folded her arms. "Of course I remember. That's the day you gave me the baseball." She pointed at her face. "You were all bruised up from your dad..." She studied his face, and it wasn't the kind of expression that proved she was right. He was downcast and cleaning that pan as though it held the answer to his problems. If he was so reticent to let her know, then it could only mean one thing. "Oh, shit. It wasn't your father who beat you. It was them. My brothers!"

He winced.

"What did they do, Joey?"

"They told me to stay away from you. They said I'd never be good enough, and that I'd only hurt you."

"Bastards." How dare they decide what was right for her? Ire built like a rising tide, filling her veins and muscles with tension. She was going to *kill* them. Murder them in their sleep. Better yet, she'd shave Parker's hair off. That would teach the asshole.

"Liza," Joe said, reaching for her. "It doesn't matter. They were wrong."

"Which ones?" she asked, jaw clenched. "Parker? Wyatt?" her mind traveled back. Tony, maybe, but he was too concerned with having fun back then. It was more likely the eldest two.

"Forget it."

"You realize we both suffered because of him sticking his nose where it doesn't belong. We could have been together years ago if you'd only asked me out."

He gave her a sad smile. "Maybe the bond wouldn't have finished triggering back then, anyway." He sighed and pinched his nose. "Parker couldn't have known that I was afraid I'd end up like my father, that his comments would cut so deep. He had no clue what was going on in my life. Or maybe he did. It pains me to say this, but he was only trying to protect you."

She slumped. "I'm sorry. It should never have happened, but while we're on the subject of confessions..." She forced herself to meet his gaze. "I have something to confess."

He folded his arms with a smirk. "Oh, yeah?"

"Yeah." She bit her lip. *Here goes.* "The night before I left for my, um, extended training, do you remember I gave you the ball, but you fell down the trellis to meet me in your yard?"

He nodded with a frown.

"Well," she continued. "After you fell, and your father hit you, I kinda... sorta... threatened to kill him."

"What?"

She shrugged. "I was so angry. I put him in a choke-hold, and he peed his pants, and I said if he ever touched you like that again I would come after him and kill him."

Joe stilled. His nostrils flared as he grappled with his thoughts until he finally concluded, gripped her shoulders, and stared intensely into her eyes, so hard that she felt it through her body.

"You risked your secret, for me," he said. "When you were fifteen."

She gave a hesitant laugh. "I guess, I loved you even then. I just didn't know what it was, or how to show it. I'm sorry, I should have—"

Joe's lips slammed down on Liza's. He dragged her to the ground, right there in the kitchen, ran his hands up her thighs, and slid his fingers between her legs.

"Oh," she gasped, surprised, as he kissed his way down her front, ripping the last of the buttons on his shirt off. "If I'd known this was my reward, I would have told you a while ago."

"You said you loved me," he murmured against her skin, then kissed the hollow of her belly button.

She smiled. "I guess I did."

WALKING into the precinct with Joe was surreal. Maybe it was that their relationship had shifted, solidified, and they walked in, united, but the place *looked* different. Felt different. It seemed as if everyone watched them, but Joe didn't stall. He strode strongly and proudly. Liza did too.

"We'll touch base with Briggs and Geoff," Joe said as they pushed through the front door. "We also have your portrait artist sketch, so can perhaps canvas with that."

"What about your… other investigation?" she asked.

"You leave that to me." They got to Joe's office, but found Captain Morais standing there with two uniformed officers.

Morais checked his watch and gave Liza a grim look.

Her stomach dropped. Her pulse quickened. She turned tentatively to Joe—could he have betrayed her? No. Not after last night. Their relationship was solid. She knew that deep in her soul. He looked as flummoxed as she was.

"Liza Lazarus," Morais said. "We've received a formal complaint of unwarranted use of excessive force. While the matter is under investigation, you'll need to hand in your firearm and your badge."

"You're suspending me?" she gaped.

Morais held his palm out, waiting for her things.

Liza met Joe's stare. "It's him. The Ripper suspect."

Joe grabbed Morais' arm. "Is he still here?"

The two police officers stepped forward, ready to intervene, but Joe let go of the captain.

"You know we can't reveal the personal information of a victim of police brutality," Morais said.

Even though she saw red, Liza unclipped her firearm from her holster, and removed her badge from her belt.

"Liza," Joe said. "You don't have to do this."

"Yes, I do," she replied. "There will be an investigation. We can use it to find him. Investigate him back."

Joe looked like he was going to complain but thought better of it. "I'll drive you home."

twenty-two

DESPAIR

IN THE BASEMENT level of Lazarus House, Despair submitted herself to tests of all sorts. She'd had her blood drawn, brainwaves monitored, mobility checks, a lie detector test, and more. Pride completed a thorough study of her, and just when she thought he was done, he came up with another test. Right now she submitted to the dreary task of a heart rate monitor taking incremental readings. She wasn't sure what purpose it served, but it kept him complacent while he studied biological samples down a microscope on the workshop table.

Nuts, bolts, and oil spilled across the beat-up wooden table surface. Flint and Sloth tinkered with something with wires and occasionally crossed to a room the supercomputer server was in. They pretended not to watch Pride's progress with Despair, but now and then, Sloth would cast her eyes Despair's way, assess, and then flit back.

She held a grudge for what Despair had done to her fiancé, even though she'd then saved his life. Perhaps they'd sent her down to monitor Despair's emotions, but Sloth's empathy powers would sense no red flags. Despair felt nothing. Was nothing. Only one light existed at the end of her tunnel, and it existed inside a tiny locket hanging around Julius Allcott's neck. If all was going according to plan, Julius and his top scientist had completed most of their trials on regular human stem cells. Once Despair delivered the life giving cells from Wrath's child's umbilical cord, they would know exactly what to do. Nothing would go to waste. It was their only immediate hope of getting the data they required to extend the shelf-life of replicates beyond a few months.

Despair looked across the table at Pride looming over his microscope, contemplating samples of her blood. From what she knew of her younger brother, he was one of those "can-do" geniuses who learned anything he was curious about. If the information was there, he found it. And then he broke new barriers, turning that information inside out. But he wasn't self-aware. She'd been watching him. He thought he had a handle on his sin, but it handled him in ways he was yet to comprehend.

His DNA was still locked, which meant he had no powers, nor could he procreate until he met his mate. Despair was the only other sibling left in the same boat. The two of them had no future, but which one would go first?

In the lab that raised them, Parker would compete with Despair. Sit taller, walk faster, be better. But she'd only ever sing in his face. It had been fun ruffling his fur.

She shifted her gaze back to a blank spot on the floor before her.

Keeping them impotent had been Gloria's best idea. It was the only thing that saved Despair from being used and impregnated as a test subject by the Syndicate. She had other stem cells in her body they could use, but they wanted to exhaust embryonic cells first, or the next best thing, umbilical cord cells. If they decided Despair's worth had expired, then... No. Her father loved her. He'd placed a strand of her hair, along with the strands from his first family, in his precious locket. He wanted Despair with him in the new world, as much as them.

"I'm not sure what you're looking for, Pride," she murmured.

He lifted his golden gaze to meet hers. "You don't need to know. And it's Parker."

Back to the blank spot on the floor. Despair let herself become one with it. Finding something mundane to focus on, explore, and turn marvelous, had been her only source of entertainment on many lonely nights during her youth after the fire at the lab. At first, Julius hadn't been kind to her. He also hadn't been mean. He'd just been the one who rescued her from the flames and healed her. They all thought he was a cruel man, but she'd sensed his despair, and how it lessened when he visited her. Sometimes a person's true colors showed from the dark cages of their body.

Eventually, she'd been moved to a facility where she was the only person in a room, watched and studied much like she had been in the lab with her siblings. Only this time, there were no carers. There were no friends. Only her, four walls, and a bed and toilet.

The walls became her friends.

The bed, her solace.

The toilet, a place to drown.

"He's just making sure you're healthy," Flint said, his deep voice piercing her reverie.

She slid her gaze to him. A vague memory of him existed somewhere in her psyche. She knew because she felt something tug deep inside her chest when she looked at him. But apart from that, he was no one to her. He helped stage the rescue that sent Gloria into a kamikaze state. He was a father to Despair's siblings. And it was either

he, or Mary, who kept a constant, yet compassionate, eye on her while she lived in this building.

Despair often watched him to ascertain what Mary saw in him. A quiet, yet sturdy presence. He was attractive for an older man, but he wasn't a leader like Mary. He existed only to support his makeshift family, spending his time in the workshop, making weapons, playing with computers, and fixing tech gear. Despair couldn't understand. Each of the mated Lazarus siblings was drawn to their partners through the biological urge programmed into their DNA, the one that pushed them toward a person embodying their sin's opposing virtue.

She might not understand why they loved each other, but she did know love was a weakness. Mary would do anything to save Flint's life, and he would die for her. Despair counted on it.

"How's the tatt going?"

Despair lifted her head and found Envy looking down at her. The youngest of the Seven had been the most blasé about her reemergence. Even now he stood in casual torn jeans. Nothing about his appearance said he took this business seriously. Tattoos crawled up his arms, twining in patterns that accentuated his physique. An odd beanie covered his unruly medium length hair.

When Despair didn't respond, he took her hand, and gently checked the freshly scored skin on her inner wrist. He tilted it to catch the light and squinted at the Yin-Yang symbol.

"Looks almost healed," he noted, then met her eyes and held. "And almost in the black. You need to find yourself some hope, sister, or you'll blackout."

She shrugged.

His brows puckered, but he let go of her hand and then strolled over to Pride where they spoke in hushed tones. Despair went back to studying the floor. She knew they spoke about her. She knew no one trusted her. But she didn't need trust. She only needed for them to keep her in this building until her plan came to fruition. She would find trust in her next life... or rather, her replicate would. That's all she wanted—an end to this misery and a rebirth of her old self. She wanted it so badly, it consumed her.

A strange grunting and choking sound came from the basement hallway entrance. When Despair left the solace of her dot, she found Lust clutching her middle as though it hurt and eyeing Despair with suspicion. Her mate rubbed his palm on her back.

"You okay?" he asked.

Lust nodded grimly, straightened, and took a deep breath.

She senses my lust.

Despair tried to empty her thoughts, hopes, and dreams. If she was found out at this late stage in the plan, it would all have been for nothing. Thankfully, the rest of the family noticed Lust's entrance and started talking.

"I thought you were at work," Pride said, with a clear note of derision.

Despair had caught the underlying tension between the two earlier, but now it felt palpable in the air. Lust's gaze darkened upon landing on her brother. She took a step forward with clenched fists, but her partner stopped her. He whispered something in her ear, and she calmed.

Treasonous longing slashed through Despair. To have someone so trusted in her corner, like the way Lust's mate was for her, it begged the question of love without boundaries. Did they have them? Did they put caveats on their love, the way Julius had kept Despair striving harder and higher for his? From the way they looked into each other's eyes, the way they softened from a simple touch, yes, she believed they loved freely. She knew this because she'd never experienced the same.

"You have some nerve," Lust said to Pride.

He sat back on his stool, leaned an elbow on the table, and arched a righteous brow as if to say, *This should be interesting.*

Lust seemed to bite back words, and instead said, "I got suspended."

"Good." Pride strode to one of the white mannequins in glass cases surrounding the operations room walls. Each held one of the Deadly Seven augmented suits. One looked pristine and untouched. The one with the fuchsia face mask. He opened the cabinet. "You can finally try on your suit. Flint and Sloan have worked around the clock to make the upgrades."

A sort of grumble broke from Lust's throat, but she dragged her feet over to Pride. While she did, Envy approached Joe and shook his hand.

"I suppose welcome to the family is appropriate if you two are walking in together like this."

Joe gave a curt nod of acknowledgment, and then Sloth gave a "Wassup" from her spot. Flint also greeted Joe with a smile. Pride's inaction toward Joe was as good as recognition. Their acceptance of the new stranger was troubling. They put so much faith in this soul-mate business, that they simply accepted a federal agent into their secret headquarters. They'd also accepted her. A killer. A thief. A liar. Such was the stringent loyalty this family showed for one another. Such was the power of their love and devotion. Their hope.

Despair looked down at her tattoo. The black seemed a little less.

Her heart kicked in her chest. Sweat broke out on her brow. The vague warbles of conversation flittered into her perception, but it compounded with her heartbeat rushing in her ears until everything became a cacophony of voices, those long silenced from within, and those without. She ripped the electrodes from her chest.

"Enough."

All eyes swiveled her way. Perhaps she'd overreacted. Her mind scrambled to come up with a solution, and then she remembered the tail end of Pride's conversation with the agent.

"... we need more hard evidence before we can entertain some kind of conviction against the Syndicate."

Perfect.

She turned to their expectant faces and straightened her spine, but the dizziness in her mind still threatened to topple her. Her words intended to come out firm, but instead breathed like the wind. "I think I know how you can get some."

A stillness came over the room. Pride left Lust at the cabinet and strode to Despair. "You said you knew nothing."

"I can't give you locations where the replicates are held because I don't know. That's the truth. You confirmed with the polygraph."

"Anyone in this room can beat one of those tests."

"So why give it to me?"

His face deadpanned. More secrets he was unwilling to share.

"Give her a break," Sloth mumbled. "Let's see if her intel pans out and go from there."

Lust nodded. "I agree. Daisy made the first step, it's our turn to trust her."

"What do you call bringing her into our homes?" Pride replied, didn't wait for a response, and turned to Despair. "What's your intel?"

"I know where a Faithful hideout is. There's a single replicate tank on display." She turned to Joe. "Will that be sufficient evidence?"

His expression turned thoughtful. "It will depend if we can link it to the actual Syndicate organization somehow. If not, at least it's proof of unlawful activity by *someone*." He leveled his gaze on Pride. "Genetic modification and cloning of humans are illegal. It might give us probable cause to open an official investigation."

"Great," Envy said, looking more excited than he should. "Let's suit up."

Pride slapped him on the chest. "Tonight. For now, we prepare."

Today, tonight, it didn't matter. Despair was ready with the next phase of her plan. She just needed as many of them as she could out of the building.

twenty-three

JOE LUCIANO

JOE HAD WANTED to join the Deadly Seven and their raid of the Faithful hideout, but first had some loose ends to tie up at the precinct. He had a serial killer to catch, and he had to figure out a way to get his director to drop the investigation against Liza and her family. The best way he could think of was to steer him in another direction, toward the Syndicate.

Before he'd left Liza this morning, he'd spoken briefly with Sloan. As their resident computer guru, she had records of interactions and evidence they'd gleaned from Syndicate sites. The ringleader, Julius Allcott, worked out of a tall building in the city's Quadrant, but it was filled with unassuming business corporations, and was seemingly innocent. They could be fake companies, but Sloan couldn't find evidence of fraud. For all intents and purposes, the offices were real. So it wasn't the Syndicate base of operations. Not the scientific base, anyway.

Joe's laptop had pinged continuously during the day with more information from Sloan. He knew they kept their cards close to their chest, but the documents she sent were incredible, and nothing he'd

be able to obtain without many months of hard work. Some files contained data from the black site the Seven had infiltrated. It showed experiments of all sorts going on, but none of them were the replicate program. He filed them away for a time he could get tech forensics onto it.

Joe looked up when a knock came at his office door.

"Come in." The door opened and gestured for Geoff to enter. "What did you find?"

Geoff ambled in and dropped a file on Joe's desk, then opened it to show a rap sheet with a mug shot of the man who'd pressed charges against Liza.

"You didn't get this from me," Geoff said.

Joe studied the sheet.

Gareth Smith. He looked like a junkie. Hollow eyes, bad skin, long face with scarring on one side.

Geoff took a seat and started talking. "Two DUIs, a bunch of misdemeanors, one aggravated assault, which was later withdrawn, and a slew of unpaid parking tickets."

"Who withdrew the assault charge?"

"His father. Seems like Smith comes from a long line of Meat Royalty."

"As in cattle and a slaughterhouse?"

"Yep. Except, he was disowned after that last assault. From what I gather, Gareth's shenanigans cost his father a meatpacking plant. Had to shut the whole thing down and declare bankruptcy to cover his son's debts."

Joe whistled through his teeth. "This is the guy who pressed charges against Liza?"

It wouldn't stick.

"He came in with pictures taken at a hospital and claims a witness can verify his assault." Geoff leaned forward and flipped the case files to the next page, pausing at the picture of a heavily beaten face. You could hardly reconcile it with the man in the mug shot.

"Shit," he murmured.

"You think Liza did it?" Geoff asked. "I mean, I don't know her from a bar of soap, but you do."

Joe studied the picture. He knew what Liza had been thinking—not much at all. She'd said she blacked out. This was brutal, in his face, evidence of Liza's deadly potential. The same went for her entire family. And this assault had nothing to do with their superpowers. If the Syndicate had their way, or if one of the Deadly Seven lost their marbles, then this violence was only a taste of what was to come.

A moment of doubt hit him. Should he be supporting this vigilante family, or making sure they were carefully quarantined and safely secured away until a failsafe could be put in place? The latter had been his original instinct, but after the night he'd spent with Liza, he knew it wouldn't be possible. They were too strong, too clever, and if he supported the capture and charging of the Lazarus family, they would be spirited away to some undisclosed location, put under a microscope, tested, poked, and prodded. He couldn't do that to Liza, especially since she was born in that environment. It would break her.

And he'd never see her again.

Once the notion sank in, a profound protective instinct surged. He would do anything to keep Liza safe, even if that meant becoming the thing he hunted. He would break the law.

"We'll let the investigation decide that," he said to Geoff. "In the meantime, this man is a person of interest in the Ripper killings."

The moment Joe found Gareth Smith, his life was over.

"Why?" Geoff asked.

"A day before the Ripper victim disappeared, Liza intercepted this man from taking the victim."

"That's a definite link," Geoff said, eyebrows raised. "And motive to pull a stunt like claiming police brutality. Why didn't she say anything?"

Joe couldn't exactly tell him the truth, that Liza was more interested in following Gareth Smith to the source—the Syndicate. If they arrested him now, they'd never find out who he sold the body parts too.

"What did you find at the shelter?" Joe asked.

Geoff leaned back and blew a raspberry out slow. "Not much. We asked around. The girl said nothing while she was there. No one noticed anything strange about her. But if you ask me, we're fishing in a basket of empty water."

"What do you mean?"

"The only person at the shelter who wanted to talk to us was a woman who claimed to have escaped aliens who tried to impregnate her. She was high as a kite."

Joe rubbed his forehead. "All right. Let's keep digging into Gareth Smith. See if anything else comes up. Let's get eyes on him too. Geoff?"

"Yeah."

"Keep this between us."

"You got it."

Geoff went to take the case file, but Joe stopped him. "Leave it."

When Geoff left, Joe flipped back to the pictures taken at the hospital. A name on the report caught his attention. Gareth's witness was listed as Wyatt Lazarus.

LATE AFTERNOON, Joe arrived at the Lazarus House basement garage. It felt strange to drive in, have a computer recognize his vehicle, and allow entry. Only days ago, he was pinning pictures of vigilantes to his bedroom wall and trying to ascertain how to gain proof of their criminal activities. That Joe was naïve. He hadn't understood how deep the conspiracy went—beings with powers had been created by a criminal organization. Right now, they were contained, but in the future, they could become the norm. And unhinged. And the Syndicate had military backing, possibly up to the Pentagon.

There was no turning back.

There had to be a way to get the government on the right side, and he was yet to figure out how to do it. The first step was obtaining irrefutable evidence. It was why he was going on the raid with the Seven, to mop up, and then call it in as though he'd been tipped off anonymously.

After being let inside through a side door, he found the Lazarus family in full battle gear, gathered around a central table in the operations room. It was a sight to behold. A wall of television screens depicted news network and CCTV footage. Glass display cabinets around the room were empty, except one. Who hadn't put the suit on?

He searched the cluster of uniform-clad bodies gathered around the table... there she was. Liza as he'd never seen her before. As no one had.

Even with her back to him, he knew it was her, dressed in a skin-tight dusky gray suit made of some sort of fibrous material that hugged her like a second skin. She cocked her hip to the side and put weight on one leg. There was no fault to her shape.

For a few beats of his heart, he stood on the outskirts of the room, admiring Liza as she watched her family discuss the best points of entry to the Faithful hideout. She stood back with her arms folded, an opinionated eye on Parker as he gave a speech. Daisy stood quietly to the side. She wore a white hoodie and jeans. Somehow, Joe didn't get the sense she was humbled or submissive as her posture projected. Intelligent eyes took in everything.

The men in the group were ominous shadows, standing silent but with piercing gazes. But Joe's eyes kept tracking back to Liza—he would marry her one day. The notion was a certainty.

Sloan looked up with a secret smirk that said she knew what Joe was feeling. He cleared his throat and approached the table. Parker frowned.

"What are you doing here?"

Joe scoffed. "I'm going."

"Like hell you are," Parker replied.

But Joe was prepared for that. While he and Liza had discussed it that morning, he'd asked that she not share the news with her family. He would do it himself.

Liza smiled at him but said nothing. Her confidence bolstered him.

He met Parker's fierce gaze and said, "You'll let me go because you want an end to this hiding and fighting in the shadows. You want the law on your side. The only way to get that is to let me gather evidence in an official capacity."

"If you're caught working with us, it will be the end of your career," Parker warned.

"I won't get caught. I want to come with you. You do your thing, and then I'll call it in. I'll say I received an anonymous tip." He shifted his focus to Griffin who, without his spectacles, looked oddly different. "I think between Lilo and myself, we can expose the Syndicate. She can handle the press, and I'll handle government intelligence. If we go for this double-pronged way of getting the information out, then having it discredited, or swept under the carpet will be difficult."

"No," Parker said. "You can stay here with Daisy."

Daisy shifted uncomfortably.

"Screw you, Parker," Liza snapped. "You don't get to decide for all of us. This is a democracy, not a dictatorship. Let's vote. Hands up for Joe's plan."

Everyone raised their hand, except for Parker. He fumed.

"It's your funeral."

twenty-four

LIZA LAZARUS

LIZA WAS the last of her family to leave. One after another, they roared out of the garage on black, unlicensed motorcycles. It was late afternoon; the sun was still up. Usually they avoided daytime missions, but they wanted to catch the Faithful in the act. Daisy had said they congregated at the hideout to socialize. If they left it too late, no one would be home.

It was one thing to raid and find a replicate tank, but another to find suspects that tied the tank to the white-robed terrorists Joe needed to build a case.

While Liza preferred to go by road, some of the Seven had jumped from the roof, preferring to use the wingsuit capacity of their uniform to weave between Cardinal City buildings. Combined with grappling guns, the wingsuits almost gave them the capacity to fly and, even though they were probably seen by a few bystanders, they were too fast to be caught.

The same went for the motorcycles. They could weave in and out of traffic, cover their heads with helmets, and abandon the bikes if need be. Being caught by the cops was a risk they had to take.

Joe stood by the open door of his car, about to get in. But the gentleman waited until she was ready to leave.

She gave a trembling exhale, stomach squirming with nerves, and climbed onto a motorcycle. But as she took hold of the throttle, she couldn't rev. Her gloved hands froze on the handlebars.

Joe shut the door and walked over.

"You look like you're about to be sick," he said, eyes full of concern. "Are you okay?"

She flattened her lips. "Yep. Just give me a second."

"Is it nerves?"

She had thought so, but the unsettled feeling in her stomach had started the moment she'd put her suit on. It should be gone by now.

"I'll be fine," she said. "You go. You need to be ready for when it's safe to enter."

A divot appeared on his brow. He went to leave, hesitated, and came back to take her jaw in his hand. His thumb grazed over her cheek. A responding ache of longing echoed in her chest. She wanted to stay with him. She wasn't afraid to go, far from it, but some far away intuition urged her to stay. She feared after this night, everything would change, and she couldn't quite put her finger on why.

The raid was simple enough. Daisy had given them an address. She was also left under the watchful eye of Flint and Mary. Wyatt and Misha were locked safely in their apartment. The team would be gone for only an hour or two, tops. So why weren't the nerves quelling?

"Be careful," he murmured.

She forced a smile on her face, for his sake. "I'll see you there."

A curt nod, and then Joe got in his car and drove out. She watched him leave and had the sense it could be the last time she saw him.

What a stupid thing to think. It was only because of her self-sabotaging tendencies. She'd found happiness, and a part of her didn't believe it.

She shook out her arms to dispel the tension. Hardening herself, she covered her nose and mouth with her fuchsia mask, and then lifted her hood to hide the rest of her identity. She'd decided against the helmet. People would see her weapons, anyway. At least this way, she'd be unimpeded if she had to launch quickly into action. Two revs on the throttle, the engine roared in the hollow chamber, and then she surged out of the garage. She drove down the side alley and then stalled at the main street intersection. A look to the left showed patrons entering Heaven for their evening meal. She looked right and saw a patrol car coming down the street.

Shit.

She used her boots to back peddle and hugged the shadows next to a dumpster. If the officers looked down the alley, they'd see her. She had no helmet. Her bright face mask would be a red flag. Heart thumping in her chest, she kept her head down and waited. This was why she hated daytime missions. It was much easier to act as a cop. *Goddamn suspension.*

One.

Two.

Three.

The patrol car glided by on the main street. She waited for another few beats and then drove back to the intersection. This time, when she looked left, she almost had a heart attack. The patrol car had stopped at the front of Lazarus House. She glimpsed two uniformed officers disappear into the lobby.

Fuck. Shit. Fuck.

Why would they be there?

"AIMI, it's Lust," she said into the hood microphone. "Why are police entering the building?"

Static.

She waited a few seconds in case AIMI was busy with another request, but then realized AIMI was a supercomputer. She could handle more than one person using her at a time. She could handle millions.

"AIMI," she tried again, a note of urgency in her voice.

After another minute, dread unfurled in her gut. Something wasn't right. AIMI was offline. *Impossible.*

In no world would Parker leave their artificial intelligent management interface offline for this mission. AIMI was their eyes and ears in the streets. She alerted them to danger, both from local law enforcement, and the enemy.

Revving the engine, Liza planted a boot on one side, spun the back wheel, and turned around. In two seconds she was back at the garage, approaching the closed roller door. But it didn't go up. She slammed on the brakes, bringing the motorcycle to rest just inches before the metal door.

She looked up to the camera. It was supposed to recognize her and let her in. She waved. Nothing.

Don't panic. Everything is fine. Just because systems are down, and a patrol car is at the front door, doesn't mean a thing. But the sick feeling wouldn't go. In fact, it increased in intensity until it pierced her abdomen. *Deadly lust.*

And there was only one person in this building who'd been throwing that sin earlier—Daisy.

Liza's heart twisted with the realization of what it meant. Daisy was betraying them. They'd hoped so hard it wouldn't be true.

No time for regrets.

She had to get inside. It was either head out the front, potentially reveal herself to the police at the front entrance to her building, or climb up the seven-story facade to the roof and enter through the stairwell there. She could always try smashing a window, but that would get messy. She looked up the long line of the building to the cool winter sky.

The building had no fire-escapes. Only a single drainpipe. Then that's how she'd go. She tugged on the two karambit she'd synced to her battle uniform, but they wouldn't detach. *Fuck*, she realized with a jolt. The knives were stuck to the suit via computerized synchronization. The suit was made of some kind of kevlar polymer blend. It was virtually indestructible.

AIMI was definitely out. Daisy must have put a virus into her mainframe, effectively shutting down everything she managed. Elevators. Suit functions. Communications. Building security.

They were sitting ducks. Anyone could infiltrate the building.

The loud thwacking of a helicopter's rotor blades drew her attention to the sky.

"Motherfucker," she cursed.

Multiple scenarios ran through Liza's mind.

Could she use her poison to somehow weaken the synchronization?

No. It wasn't acidic based. The sizzling that happened on Parker's face was due to temperature, unlike she'd originally thought.

So, then what?

Pull the knives until her arms broke, or the connection did. She could get down with that. With a renewed sense of purpose, Liza pushed energy into her arms—almost screamed at the tension she emitted—and... nothing.

She tried again, and again, until eventually, her stubbornness won. The magnetic lock between the indestructible fabric and knives gave way, and she sagged with relief. Whether it was a flaw in the suit's system, a safety backup, or her strength, she didn't care. It worked. Making haste, she used the blades to claw the brackets on the drainpipe and climbed.

She climbed until her muscles burned and kept going. No doubt Daisy was going for Misha. Liza's apartment was adjacent to Wyatt's, two levels from the top. Wyatt's faced this alley. Perfect.

Before Daisy got to Misha, she'd have to get through Mary, Flint, *and* Wyatt. There was no way in hell she'd get past Wyatt. She'd have to kill him, and the man was invulnerable—bulletproof.

But Daisy had found a way to shut AIMI down. She'd infiltrated their home, counted on their weaknesses, and exploited them. She'd lured every other deadly Lazarus out of the building by dangling a Faithful sized carrot, and they'd fallen for it.

She had underestimated Liza's sin sensing. Everyone did. They all assumed the lust Liza felt was sexual. Even Liza had assumed Daisy's lust wasn't as serious as it turned out.

She'd never make that mistake again.

Approaching Wyatt's apartment, Liza ignored her protesting muscles and pushed past the point of pain. The drainpipe took her within arm's reach of a window. She tried to angle herself closer to the window so she could peek inside, but a scream from the roof had her sharply looking up. *Misha.*

Liza edged her way higher. *Only two stories to go.* As her face crested the top, she took stock of the scene.

A helicopter hovered above the roof, causing the water in the pool to vibrate and splash. Dangling from the chopper's open cabin were two black-clad mercenaries, machine guns at the ready. Neither had spotted Liza. Their eyes were on Daisy as she dragged Misha from the stairwell—they'd not taken the elevator. Made sense if the system was down. Daisy had blood on her face and arms, as though she'd fought... but they looked like knife wounds. *Mary.* Wyatt would have pulverized. Mary sliced. *Where was he? Were they both okay?*

Misha held her round belly with a pained expression as Daisy forced her to move down the decking toward the helicopter dropping a rope ladder. Blond curly hair caught in the wind, whipping into her eyes. They were coming from the right, the helicopter was to the left, and Liza was in the middle.

Misha cried in pain and doubled over. Good God, was she having contractions? Was she in labor?

Adrenaline surged through Liza. If she didn't get to them before they reached the ladder, there would be no hope. Knowing the suit would protect her from bullet spray, Liza vaulted over the ledge and ran to the decking, blocking their escape.

Daisy saw Liza the moment she vaulted. Violet eyes widened in shock, and she lifted her palm to the soldiers in the chopper. *Stop.*

Liza was too close. The bullets might catch Daisy, or worse, Misha and her precious cargo. Long silver hair floated from the helicopter's wind. Daisy looked right, left, and knew her only escape was back down the stairwell, or straight through Liza.

Liza's grip on her karambits tightened. *Try.*

An almighty crash sounded from the rooftop lobby. Liza refused to take her eyes from Daisy but caught movement in her periphery, and when the bellow of an avenging mate cut through the din of the rotor blades, Liza knew Wyatt had arrived. A glance and she caught him stalking like the devil himself from a punched and dented out elevator door. Black clothes, black hair, black eyes. He was darkness coming to reclaim his light.

He must have been locked inside when AIMI went down.

Clever Daisy. She'd lured Wyatt to the ground floor with the police, then shut the systems while he was in the elevator. And if she'd known there were police coming, then it was entirely possible she'd caused it.

"Let her go!" Liza shouted to be heard over the helicopter uproar. "You're out of options."

But Daisy did something Liza never expected. She dragged Misha by the hair and crossed to the edge of the roof. She kicked the glass pane, shattering the fence. Wind coursed up from the ground, buffeting their hair.

She's going to jump. She's going to kill them both.

"Stop!" Liza shouted at the same time Wyatt roared, "No!"

Liza tugged her mask and hood down. The clatter of metal barely registered as she dropped her knives.

A furious demon glared out from Wyatt's face. Veins pumped in his neck and forehead. His fists were ready to decimate. "I'll kill you, Daisy. You fucking lay a hand on her, and I swear to God I will hunt you down to the ends of the earth."

That threat might have worked for someone who cared. Liza inched closer to Daisy.

"Take me!" Liza shouted, holding her palms out in surrender, approaching cautiously as one would to a wounded animal. "Daisy, listen to me. You don't want to do this."

Daisy's face hardened. She gripped Misha around the neck and stepped closer to the edge. "You have no idea what I want," she shouted. "You've never known. Never cared."

Tears burned Liza's eyes. "That's not true. Give us a chance."

The cold hard resignation in Daisy's posture was a stake to the heart. The lust Liza sensed fizzled, signaling Daisy's resolve dying. She was giving up, and not in the way they wanted.

"I'll catch you!" Liza shouted, taking another step. "If you fall, I'll jump after you and catch you."

Another step.

Closer.

Daisy blinked. Liza wasn't sure if she'd heard, but then Daisy cocked her head curiously. That's right. Remember.

"Lu-ust," Despair's sweet, melodious voice sang. "Come here and give me my morning cuddle!"

"You have to catch me first, 'Spair." Liza's four-year-old legs jumped onto a table, slipped, and toppled to the side. She screamed.

Strong childish arms caught her. "Don't worry, Lust. I'll always catch you when you fall."

"Don't do it, Daisy," Wyatt added. He, too, had inched closer.

Daisy's face screwed up. She forced the emotion away and leveled her violet-eyed stare on Liza.

"You don't understand," she said. "I have to return with her and the baby. This is my last chance. We just need the stem cells from the umbilical cord. That's all."

"You don't really believe that, do you?" Liza replied.

"He'll take me!" Daisy shouted. "If I don't bring him something, he'll—" Pain ripped through Daisy's expression. "He'll suck the life out of me, every damned cell. He'll throw away my hair follicle from his locket, and then that will be it. I want this over. I want this never-ending nightmare over!"

"Then you give them me," Liza urged, not understanding half of what her sister said, but it didn't matter. Daisy's fear was real. "I've met my mate. I've unlocked my DNA. If they want embryonic stem-cells, they can use me. It only takes a few weeks to make them, right?"

She shuddered at the thought, but she'd cross that bridge if she came to it.

Thoughts collided behind Daisy's eyes. She was thinking about it. Liza's gaze darted to Wyatt. He stared back, bleak, and resigned. He knew this was the right thing to do. Misha had to live. The baby had to live.

Liza could take whatever they dished out. She clenched her jaw, steeled herself, and looked back to Daisy.

"What assurances do I have that you'll come without fuss?" Daisy called.

Liza lifted her palms. "You'll just have to trust me, the same way we trusted you."

"I betrayed you."

Misha cried out again, clutching her stomach. Tears streamed down her face, her blue eyes locked onto Wyatt in desperation.

"It's okay, baby. You're going to be fine."

"Wyatt."

Liza shouted, "You might jump, Daisy, but I'll catch you. These suits have wings."

"You'll catch *her,*" Daisy accused, looking at Misha.

Liza swallowed her heart and said something she could never take back. "She's too heavy. She'll fall too fast. You're my sister, Daisy. I'll save you."

It was a lie. Liza wouldn't be able to save either of them, and if given the choice, it would be Misha, but Daisy didn't know that. Hopefully. And from the way she contemplated, she also didn't know that their suits' functions were broken because of AIMI. Thank God for small mercies.

Daisy's eyes locked on Wyatt, trying to get closer. "Knock her out," Daisy said, and jerked her chin toward Liza. "You want your mate back, then you knock your sister out. Hard."

Anguish swamped Wyatt's gaze as it landed on Liza. She didn't need him to respond to know he'd do it, even though he'd hate himself after.

"It's okay," she said to him. "Knock me out."

Every line of his body said he was forcing himself to move. Every step he took was one his heart didn't choose. But he didn't hesitate. He boxed Liza's temple.

Agony spliced through her head. The ground shifted. Blackness closed in and she toppled to the floor. *Goddamn.*

The last thing Liza saw before darkness swallowed her whole was the shove Daisy gave Misha, her subsequent fall to the ground. A scream of agony, hands clutching her belly.

Boots pounded the pavement, closer.

Another punch to the head, and then darkness.

Please let the baby be okay.

twenty-five

JOE LUCIANO

LATELY, it seemed like all Joe did was mop up after crimes. Whether it was a murder scene or the aftermath of a vigilante family raiding a criminal's hideout, he was the one coming in *after* the deed was done. He'd rather be preventing it from happening in the first place, but he supposed he had to start somewhere. And this was it.

Ambulances, local police cars, and firetrucks gathered at the downtown laundromat where the raid had gone down. A burst water-main sprayed into the early evening sky, but the flames from inside the basement hideout had been extinguished. The Faithful that resided there had tried to burn the place down after the Deadly Seven arrived.

Joe had sat from the safety of his car while the Lazarus family did the hard work. At first, he was annoyed to not be included, but the moment it was safe, they called him in and then left just as suddenly. They'd said their communications system went down. Since then, Joe's stomach had been filled with a bucket full of nerves. It hadn't escaped his attention that he'd failed to see Liza's fuchsia mask among the gray-clad warriors.

The beep of a packing truck reversing smashed through his thoughts, reminding him to pay attention. As he gestured for the truck to keep reversing, a news crew arrived. He pretended not to see. If all things went according to plan, it should be Lilo Lazarus, Griffin's wife. If the news crew caught the replicate tank on camera, then it would be hard for anyone to sweep it under the rug. The actual clone was still suspended inside. Coupled with the Faithful being carted into the back of patrol cars, there was no doubt this incident would be taken seriously. It was the second Faithful attack in as many days. The captain would receive recognition as the one who helped blow the conspiracy... well, part of it. They still had to tie the Faithful to the man running the show in Cardinal City—Julius Allcott.

"Special Agent Luciano!" Lilo shouted above the noise.

Holding the boundary, Geoff tried to keep her back. "This is a crime scene, ma'am, please stay back."

She plucked her press ID from her lanyard and held it out, as though it gave her immunity to do whatever she wanted. "Is it true these white-robed terrorists are more than just some disgruntled workers getting revenge like we were led to believe? I heard the inside of that place looks like it's been bankrolled by someone with expensive tastes. Can you comment on—*holy shit*. You got that on camera, Mo?"

The cameraman, a tall gangly guy in his late forties, aimed his lens somewhere behind Joe. Four firemen staggered up the laundromat's basement steps carrying the long replicate tank, sloshing with a viscous liquid and a naked man.

Geoff tried to block the camera, but Joe waved him off. "It's all right, Geoff. I got this."

And then he proceeded to tell Lilo and the camera about everything they'd found. He'd probably get an earful from the director, and perhaps the captain, but screw it. It was about time some of this leaked. He would use the opportunity to study the reactions of the higher-ups. He wanted to flush out the traitors, those under the Syndicate's thumb.

His job was to uphold the truth, not hide it.

When he finished talking to Lilo, she told the cameraman to shut it down and pack the things away, then she gave Joe her cell phone. The green look on her face made Joe think she was going to be sick.

"What is it?" he asked.

"They've been trying to call you, but no one knows your number, and AIMI is down so they can't, you know, *look for it.*" She waggled her brows at the last words, making Joe think she implied something else.

"The computer is down?"

She nodded. "Take it."

He lifted the receiver to his ear. "Luciano."

"It's Parker. There's something you need to know. Liza's been taken..."

The rest of his words were a blur. The ringing in Joe's ears grew louder until it brought his senses to a standstill. His arm holding the cell dropped to his side and he leaned onto his knees, taking deep breaths.

"It's going to be okay, Joe," Lilo said grimly. "I know it is."

With a purposeful exhale, he brought the cell back to his ear. "Explain that again?"

"It was Daisy. She lured us out, somehow knew when the police would come for a witness statement from Wyatt, and—" Parker made a disgruntled sound. *"She put a virus in AIMI, effectively shutting us down from the inside."*

"And how did Liza get involved?"

"She must have sensed something. She never joined us. Wyatt said she was on the roof before he was. If it weren't for Liza's sacrifice, Misha would be dead."

Joe swallowed. "Is she...?"

"She's in labor, and at the hospital."

"I meant Liza." Was she injured? Dead? "Do you have any idea where they took her?"

Parker's silence was louder than any words, and when he eventually spoke, Joe's resilience was at breaking point.

"Liza got knocked out cold. We don't know anything beyond that. I planted a tracker in Daisy's tattoo ink, but the technology is paired with AIMI. The same goes for the tracker in Liza's suit. Until I get the system up and running, we don't know where they've gone."

Joe's fist clenched around the cell. "That's not good enough. We need to find her."

"We're trying. But in the meantime, we've got two injured parents. A woman in labor. And a dead computer to fix. We'll be in touch."

The call cut.

Joe blinked at the dead receiver. The bastard had hung up on him. *We'll be in touch?* Hell, no.

"I'm keeping this," Joe said to Lilo.

It had Parker's number in it, or someone's.

She nodded. "I'm sorry. They do that to me sometimes too. They forget we normal people can help. We might not be special, like them, but we have old ways of doing things that have worked for centuries. Every bit counts, right?"

His gaze landed on the woman with respect. "You're right. We do have old ways of doing things."

He was an investigator, so he'd find out where Liza was taken his own way. And that started back at the precinct, and with the man who'd caused her suspension.

"Get your footage on the air—"

"Already done."

"Good. I'm going to see the captain." He would need backup.

JOE BURST through the Cardinal City precinct doors and made a beeline for the captain's office. Even with the hour being past eight, he knew the man would be there. He may have the personality of a shark, but Morais also never stopped swimming. If shit went down, he was here.

"We need to talk," he said as he let himself in the office.

In his dress uniform, the captain looked up from his computer screen, sat back, and steepled his fingers.

"Shut the door," he said. "I've been waiting for you."

This could go two ways, but Joe plowed onward. He shut the door and sat down.

"I need access to the person who raised charges against Liza."

Annoyance flashed in Morais' eyes. "I just got off a call with your director."

Fuck.

Joe rested back in the uncomfortable wooden chair. Already steeling himself against the admonishment he expected, he was surprised when Morais spoke.

"That bastard has the gall to tell me how to run my precinct." Morais' desk phone rang. He picked up the receiver, then slammed it down again.

"What did he say?" Joe ventured.

Morais studied him. "He said you were acting out of orders. Is that true?"

"I have reason to believe the man who pressed charges against Liza is tied to the terrorists, and to the Ripper killings."

"The terrorists haven't claimed affinity to a known terrorist cell."

"I can tell you what they call themselves. The Syndicate. They're all over the world, they have ties in law enforcement from the

Pentagon down. Let's just say there's a reason why they haven't been investigated yet. The white-robed lackeys are called the Faithful. They do the Syndicate's grunt work and sow chaos."

"Your boss says he's got it under control."

"If that were true, then why haven't there been other Feds on the scene? Or Homeland. Anyone?"

Morais knew it was true. Joe could see it in his eyes. He also had the notion the man was not happy with the state of his city. He'd worked hard at reducing crime, with and without the Deadly Seven involved. So Joe took a stab. "I think you see what's happening, and you hate it just as much as me."

"What do you want?"

"The name and address of the man who pressed charges against Liza."

"Why?"

"She's missing."

Morais' eyes flashed. "You're telling me this now? What happened?"

"That, I can't reveal."

A heavy sigh from the portly man. "Then, on the record, I can't help you. Wait the allocated time and lodge a missing person's report."

Meaning off the record he had another option?

"She's one of us," Joe chided.

Morais paused, then unlocked his desk drawer before standing up. "I need a coffee. Be gone when I get back."

Joe watched the man leave, and then quickly opened the drawer to look inside. As expected, there was the case file. He'd also left his laptop unlocked. Joe rifled through reports until he found what he needed. A statement, and an address.

When he left the office, he almost ran into Briggs.

"We heard what you said."

Joe looked around the big man's body and found they weren't alone. Many of the local cops and detectives stood by.

"Liza's missing?" Briggs asked.

Joe gave a curt nod.

Houlahan stepped forward. "What do you need, G-man?"

Joe felt a rush of warm relief and held up the name he'd scribbled down. "I need everything we can find on this man. Geoff has started, but I want to dig deeper. Add a man called Julius Allcott to the list. While you're doing that, I'm going to pay Mr. Smith a visit."

TWO HOURS LATER, Joe walked away from Gareth Smith's place with blood on his hands. Unfortunately, the man was unprepared to give up any information, which, in itself, was a certain admission of guilt. Joe had tried everything he could to get the man to speak. He had beat him bloody, broke his fingers, and threatened him with psychological manipulation—but he seemed prepared to die for his cause, and Joe wasn't prepared to be a murderer. The only thing he squeezed out of Gareth was that he preferred to be called Quarry.

With no leads, Joe returned home alone. He considered visiting the hospital to check on Misha's condition, but without Liza, it all seemed empty, just like his apartment as he crossed the threshold. Dark, open, and full of ghosts from the evening before. Breakfast dishes. Case files, reports, and pictures on the floor. His bed sheets would smell like her.

There was no way he'd sleep tonight.

Scrubbing his hand through his hair, he went to the case files on the floor and stared at them. What use were psychic sketches if they

couldn't tell him where Liza had been taken? He dashed his hand through the pile, spraying the leaflets over the floor. Then he sat down hard and put his head in his hands.

He couldn't imagine a world without Liza. Just when he was getting used to her being infallible, this happened. Those people would use her as a lab rat. They'd drain her dry, or worse, turn her into the same sort of brainwashed killing machine as those Faithful who'd attacked in the street. And she'd given herself up to save Misha's baby.

He'd have done the same thing. With nothing left to do, he collected the sketches on the floor and stacked them one on top of another. Some had shifted beneath the couch. He speared his arm beneath and fished around for the missing leaflets, but his fingers hit something glossy and hard. Like a box.

Frowning, he pulled it out.

It was a gift.

He turned the box over in his hands. How long had that been under there? Curious, he tore the paper off. He stopped breathing. It was their baseball mounted on an official stand, displayed in a glass memorabilia case. Liza had scrawled on the only remaining white patch of space *I love you.*

He wasn't sure how long he stared at it. Long enough to cramp. Long enough for the coldness of night to seep into his bones. He wiped his eyes, cleared his throat, and placed it gently to the side before collecting the last of the sketches.

I'm coming for you, Liza.

Turning his attention to the sketches, he noticed they featured women in pain. Faces. Beds. Pipes. Angry charcoal strokes. He squinted at a page, then stood, flicked on the light, and held it to see better. Was that... a conveyor belt in the background? Hooks on the wall? Cautious hope hit him. He rifled through other sketches and found more of the same.

He redialed Parker's number on Lilo's cell. He answered in two rings.

"*Joe,*" Parker said. "*You have something?*"

"Maybe. I need to speak with Evan. Does he have more of those sketches?"

A shuffling sound came down the line, and then Evan spoke. "*My man, what do you need?*"

"I'm looking at these drawings Liza brought over. The ones with the women. I'm noticing the hooks and something like a conveyor belt in the background. Liza said you dreamed these scenes, is that right?"

"*Yes, I dream of them, but I don't remember everything. Keep talking, maybe you'll jog my memory.*"

"It seems like an industrial place. Metal?"

Evan made a sound, something like a thoughtful grunt. "*Yeah... sharp curved hooks were dangling from the ceiling... big metal corridors... plastic strips hanging from a ceiling.*"

"Shit," Joe murmured. "I think I know where it is."

He shuffled reports until he found two things. One was Geoff's and Brigg's notes from interviewing the crazy woman at the shelter. She'd said she escaped from aliens who wanted to impregnate her, but... what if they weren't aliens, but the Syndicate scientists?

He found the paragraph he needed. She'd said she come from the industrial area where they'd found the dead body. Joe quickly searched through the papers for the second thing. Gareth Smith's rap sheet. His father had pressed charges because he'd lost his livelihood —a meatpacking plant.

"*Joe?*" Evan asked. "*You got something?*"

"Yeah. A meatpacking plant." What's the likelihood of a Smith family-owned and abandoned meatpacking plant in the industrial area? "Give me a few, and I might have an address."

He cut the call and went to his room to find his laptop, but the room was still a mess of tangled sheets and Liza's sweet scent. He ignored the pinch in his heart, got to his knees, and searched beneath the bed. There were vague memories of kicking it last night. He found his laptop and pulled it out when Lilo's cell phone pinged.

Odd.

He checked the incoming message. It was from Sloan with two addresses of meatpacking plants in the city, and one out of town. Only one plant was abandoned. That had to be it. He let her know.

By the time he received a reply he was in his car, and on the road.

twenty-six

LIZA LAZARUS

THE SOUND of a helicopter woke Liza. Wind buffeted her face from the open cabin. She hadn't been out for long. Across from her, Daisy's empty gaze aimed outside, watching the lights of Cardinal City get smaller. Next to Liza, two black-clad soldiers held automatic rifles. A test on her hands revealed they were secured. From the feel of the tie, it ran up her entire forearm and cut into her skin at intervals... almost like they'd... she tested it gently but didn't want to look over her shoulder. It would alert them to her wakefulness.

Her bindings felt like thin strips of plastic. Must be cable ties. Liza was strong. She could break out of a few, but not the amount they'd used. She would have to find a way to cut them.

Without moving her head, she inspected the length of her body. Her belt was still on, but the only weapons she had synced to her outfit were a grappling hook and two shuriken throwing stars at her hip. Both were most likely left on her because of the same reason she'd had trouble detaching her karambits. If she could get her wrists around to the shuriken without being noticed, she could set herself free.

If only she had Wyatt's ability, she could smash through the ties... or Tony's fire to melt the plastic, but she had poison. Her facemask was still stuffed into her mouth like a gag, and her new battle gloves covered her hands. Since Liza's suit was non-responsive, she wasn't sure if the intuitive valves would work. Her best bet was to get the ties cut, and the gloves off. If she tried to release poison now, it might get trapped, and Liza didn't want to test whether her own body could take a concentrated dose of tetrodotoxin.

She kept a wary eye on Daisy and tried to wriggle her fingers out of the gloves, but they fit snugly. She shifted her hands to the side of her back and started to rub the cable ties against the shuriken, but when the helicopter descended she knew time was running out.

They lowered into a big agricultural type yard. Fenced pens and runways led to industrial sheds and multiple giant two-story warehouses. The old stench of death filled the air, and since Liza could only breathe through her nose, it was sickening.

From the look of the rusty and old metal equipment sitting outside the warehouses and empty yards, the place was an abandoned abattoir and meatpacking plant.

Daisy took one of Liza's elbows, and another soldier—the female —took Liza's other. Once the chopper's landing skids hit the ground, they dragged her out. The male soldier took up the rear, his rifle at the ready.

These weren't untrained Faithful. They were seasoned soldiers, ex-military. Liza could tell by the way their eyes scoped for danger, even in their home territory. The woman had a hard face and piercing eyes. Her jaw remained stoically clenched. She would be of no help.

Two shadowed figures waited for them near one of the warehouse buildings. Light from a door cast a halo around their figures, but they were no angels. One, a scientist in a lab coat. The other, Julius Allcott. A devil's castoff. Liza may not have met him before, but his features were recognizable. Handsome face, obstinate jaw, wide lips. He had all the Lazarus traits. Dressed in a designer suit, the man looked ridiculous in the dirty industrial setting. A silver chain twinkled around his neck, and a watch glinted at his wrist.

She wanted to punch the entitlement from his face.

A shove to Liza's back knocked her to her knees.

"Where's the pregnant one?" Julius demanded from Daisy.

"I couldn't get her. This is the next best thing. Her DNA is unlocked."

"You couldn't what?" he roared, then threw up his hands and paced. "You're useless. Fucking useless."

Liza met her father's eyes and mumbled loudly through her gag. He frowned and then flicked his finger at Daisy, who tugged the mask out of Liza's mouth. She choked and gasped in air, then smirked.

"What's up, Dad?"

"Lust," he sneered.

"What's the matter, no hello kiss?" She gave him her cheek.

Julius' pale eyebrow arched. "I'm not stupid."

She shrugged. It was worth a try. Besides, the shrug helped her move her bound hands closer to the shuriken. The cable tie touched the sharp, short blade.

She opened her mouth, already tasting the bitterness of her poison preparing. Daisy stuffed the mask back in Liza's mouth and then the two soldiers gathered Liza under her arms and picked her up. She refused to walk, so her feet dragged behind them as they headed for the warehouse. It was better for them to be occupied and not notice that every jostle and bump cut more into her restraints. A couple more ties fell to the ground.

Inside the warehouse, stainless steel conveyors and machinery filled the room. No products or packing supplies, just old equipment.

With a hard grip, they wrenched her arms back and lifted her

deadweight with a grunt of effort. She wasn't going to make it easy on them. They dragged her beyond the rusty equipment and through a small corridor with cattle hooks on a ceiling railing and u-bars that were once filled with 400 volts of electricity.

In the next room, Liza couldn't hide her astonishment and disgust. Hanging from the hooks on the ceiling conveyor weren't animal carcasses, but human, covered in plastic, dead faces squished against the clear wrap like sausages. Her stomach revolted, her vision blurred, and it took all her resolve to hide her reaction. She refused to admit weakness.

Julius and his scientist companion stopped.

In the absence of footsteps, disturbing sounds filtered from somewhere. Two doors led from the room. One was solid metal with frost edging along the seam. Must be a refrigerated room. The other door was plain and filtered soft moans of people in pain. Julius studied Liza, pausing to contemplate.

"I think we'll show her," he said, almost jauntily, and then opened the cooler door.

He's insane.

Inside, rows of halogen lights clicked on, illuminating the large room. They dragged Liza inside and dropped her to the cold concrete floor. She sagged the moment she hit the ground.

Replicate tanks filled with grown specimens filled the room. There had to be at least fifty.

Catching the astonishment on Liza's face, Julius said, "These are only our test subjects. We have facilities around the globe storing more. With the stem cells we harvest from you, we'll be able to finalize our designs and release the replicates. Our new world is imminent."

He gestured at his scientist companion, who handed him a touch-screen device. Julius tapped his finger on the screen and activated something. He slid his eyes to Liza, like a child waiting for praise.

He sickened her. She looked through him.

When he received no validation, he gestured at the tanks. "We don't need anything from you to start our war. We don't care if these replicates live past a few months, or a few weeks. All they're good for is destroying. Once they've fulfilled their duty, it is to our advantage that they die. They're full of sin. We want a perfect world. I'm telling you this because I want you to see that your fight is futile. We only need you to solve the expiration problem—"

"And we get the data for her poison mechanism, ja?" the scientist reminded Julius.

"Sure. Whatever," Julius replied, irritated to be interrupted, and then tapped another finger on the device as the scientist came over to Liza and jabbed a needle into her arm.

She jerked, using the action to hide another attempt at cutting her bindings. When the scientist was done, he retreated to stand next to Julius.

Lights in the front row of replicate tanks brightened, illuminating the contents. Inside, grown muscular men twitched as electronic jolts fed into them, working the muscles, preparing them for birth. Her eyes landed on the tanks closest, and to her revulsion, their eyes were open, watching her.

They're alive.

"You see, Lust. We have our army. If we wanted, we could release them tomorrow." He crouched down to her level and leaned forward. "You're the icing on the cake. With your stem cells, we'll turn *ourselves* into gods."

Her gaze darted to the tanks, then back to Julius. A silver chain holding a locket had fallen loose from his collar when he'd leaned forward. It now dangled heavily against his chest.

Liza shifted her gaze to Daisy. Her eyes were glued to that locket. Something she'd said came back to Liza.

He'll throw away my hair follicle from his locket, and then that will be it.

He'd been lying to everyone. The Faithful had been promised to be reborn perfect in a world free from sin, but he wasn't bringing them back. He was turning them into mindless replicates, disposable soldiers for his war. And if he lied about that, then surely he lied to the woman he'd just dubbed as being useless to him.

The only person he was going to turn into a perfect, powered, and immortal replicate was himself... and whoever was in that locket. He wanted to rule the world as a god. Daisy was a fool if she believed he'd bring her with him.

A plan started to form in Liza's head. If she could get to that locket, open it and prove no silver hair was inside, then she could turn Daisy once and for all.

A renewed sense of purpose energized Liza. She pumped her muscles full of tension and wrenched her hands apart. Multiple cable ties snapped loose. She focused on Julius's neck.

The snarl of a wildcat curdled in her throat as she launched, hit, and sent them both tumbling to the cold concrete floor. With lightning-quick reflexes, Liza pilfered the locket, hiding her action with her attack. Someone jerked her away so hard she got whiplash.

A hit to her face sent black spots into her vision. Daisy backhanded her, again. And again. It wasn't like a hit from a normal person, Daisy was one of them. She was strong. Contact floored Liza.

She tried to tell her sister what she'd done, but the gag was still in her mouth. Daisy was furious. If not in her facial expression, in the way she attacked Liza. This man, this cretin of a being, had brainwashed her so thoroughly that she couldn't see the truth.

He cared nothing for Daisy.

"Get her out of here," Julius barked, wiping a small drop of blood from where he'd been caught on the mouth.

Daisy gripped Liza's collar and dragged her single-handedly through the cooler door and back into the main packing room where she dumped her on a long, still conveyer.

Liza ripped her gag out and shoved the locket at Daisy.

"Just check it," she whispered hoarsely. "Check inside."

Daisy startled. She frowned down at the locket in her hand.

Liza urged, "If he's telling the truth, you'll find your hair in there, right?"

Daisy checked over her shoulder to the cooler door.

"Do it, Daisy. We're the ones on your team. Not them. *We're* your family."

To prove it, Liza held her palms up. She wasn't going to fight.

It took all of two seconds for Liza's world to end. Daisy unclipped the locket. Stared. Snapped it shut, and then her eyes turned a shade of violet so dark, they became black. Daisy had lost all hope.

She shut down.

Blacked out.

Because what happened next could only be described as something no sane person would do. Daisy shoved Liza to the ground, lifted her boot, and stomped on Liza's hands, crushing them.

Liza screamed in eye-watering agony.

"Why?" she cried.

"To stop you from coming after me." Daisy stuffed the gag back into Liza's mouth. "You'll thank me one day."

When Daisy straightened, the light had completely left her eyes. Liza had her answer. There had been no silver hair in the locket. Daisy's hope was extinguished.

Maybe it had been stupid of Liza to hope that Daisy would see how much she meant to them, that Liza could reach her. But some people can't be reached.

All Liza could do was squeeze her eyes shut, embrace the pain, and pray that she wasn't despairing, because if she was, then Daisy would attack her, not the enemy. And she couldn't protect herself. When silence answered her prayer, Liza opened her eyes and found the room empty, the cooler door closing with a thunderous *click*.

twenty-seven

JOE LUCIANO

JOE WAS the first to arrive at the abandoned meat packing plant. He parked his car down the street, filled his pockets with ammunition, and put his Kevlar vest on. He didn't expect the Deadly Seven to wait for him, so he wasn't going to wait for them.

With his gun in hand, he jogged through the darkness to get to the old shrubbery-covered stockyards. Dried weeds crunched underfoot. The entire compound was enormous. Multiple buildings, warehouses, and animal-holding facilities. As he drew near the buildings, he noted a light in the windows and smoke spewing from chimneys. Not abandoned as it should be.

This is it.

He found a spot near the fence on the outskirts of the property and hid behind a bush. Fifty feet of weeds separated him from the main buildings. The silhouette of a dormant helicopter looked out of place against the backdrop of the black buildings.

It was dark. Joe looked up. No stars. No moon. He smelled wet earth as it started to rain. It would get heavier soon, maybe storm. That could be a good thing for him. It could be bad.

Soldiers swarmed everywhere, black helmeted wraiths patrolling the perimeter with rifles and night-vision goggles. *Damn it.* If Liza was inside, he'd need an army to get to her.

He considered calling it in but knew he'd need the okay from the captain or the director for SWAT backup. And even then, he'd need a warrant. The building may be abandoned, but it was still registered to Gareth Smith's family.

The cops at the station had wanted to help. He considered the risks. They might find out about Liza's identity if they came, but they also knew she was one of them. They might turn a blind eye.

He rolled back to face away from the plant and contemplated the darkness of the field surrounding him. His priority was saving Liza. But he couldn't do it alone, which meant that if he didn't call for backup, he'd have to wait for the Lazarus family.

Minutes ticked by.

Thunder rolled. Lightning flashed. Giant drops of rain splatted the ground around him as he contemplated, torn. It was bad enough he was breaking the law, but to involve the others?

He'd give the Deadly crew five more minutes, and then he was calling it in. Briggs and Houlahan would come, regardless of a warrant being issued. He was sure of it.

Movement in the field caught his eye. He strained to see through the dark. Was it them?

Two dark figures moved so softly and swiftly that he wasn't sure if they were there at all. They drew closer, one of them spotted him and broke away from the other.

Joe tensed, his hand gripping his gun. He lifted it and aimed through the white cloud of his breath. The figure paused, looked up.

Two eyes glinted in the low light.

That wasn't one of the Deadly Seven.

Black clothing and a cowl covered the head. A dark red face mask covered the nose and mouth. Painted in the middle of the chest was a large crucifix. The figure tiptoed closer. He steadied his aim to prove he was serious.

The figure, now ten feet away, held up their palms, and then slowly reached for the mask. He narrowed his eyes but allowed it.

Slowly the mask came down.

It was a young woman. Freckles across her small nose made her look innocent and like your childhood next-door neighbor playing dress-up. But there was caution in her eyes, and when he looked deeper, a monster that crept in the darkness.

Alarm skated down his spine.

"I'm not your enemy," she said, voice deep and low.

"Who are you?"

No longer satisfied with intermittent drops, the rain became a steady light stream, pitter-pattering faster than the beat of Joe's heart.

Her lips flattened into a hard line.

"Friends of the Lazarus family," she said.

The tip of his gun lowered on instinct. She became a blur of action. He blinked, the rain poured, and then he was on the ground disarmed with a forearm held against his throat, cutting his air. A forked *sai* dangled from her hand, perilously close to his face. He hadn't even seen her draw the weapon. If she wanted him dead, the point would be in his throat, and his next of kin would be getting a visit from a uniformed officer.

He held his palms up in surrender. She eased the pressure.

"You're no friend," he accused.

A slight curve tilted her lips. "They just don't know it yet."

And then she was gone.

Fuck.

He scrambled around for his gun. Found it. Got to his knees and scoured his surroundings, blinking through the downpour. Gone. The ninja with the crucifix and red face mask was gone.

Jesus Christ. What the hell was going on?

He pulled out his cell, intending to call the number he'd taken from Lilo, but before he'd had a chance to dial, the phone was knocked from his hand. Twisting around, he lifted his gun, then lowered it.

One of the Seven loomed over him, virtually twice the size of the ninja, in a Deadly suit, but not the same one they'd worn before. This looked like beaten up leather. Strapped to his chest was a weapon's brace. A sword hilt and the handles of some other stick weapon peeked over his broad, muscular shoulders. Not Sloan, then. Purple face mask. From the scowl of disapproval in his eyes, Joe guessed it was Parker.

"Are you insane?" Voice modification failed to hide the note of derision in his tone. "The light from your cell marked your position. You're lucky it was me."

Fuck off danced on Joe's tongue, but there was no time for tempers.

"A woman in a ninja outfit," he said, pointing to the plant. "There was a crucifix on the front of her clothes."

Parker cursed loudly. "*Sinner.* They're here." He whipped his gaze back to Joe. "You see any more of us, warn them the Hildegard Sisterhood is here."

"She said she was—"

Parker ran off.

"—your friend," he finished to the air.

Goddammit.

These assholes had no idea how to work as a cohesive unit. Communication was key, yet they all worked on their own prerogative. They would fail if they couldn't trust each other.

If two had already gone, the chances he'd get through unseen were getting better by the second. Joe trusted the guards had been taken out. He wasn't waiting anymore.

He jogged closer to the plant. Halfway to the outbuildings, he heard a sound he'd never forget. Liza's blood-curdling scream.

Joe *ran*.

Gunshots started firing. *Pop. Pop. Pop.*

He kept running. Only a few more feet to the safety of the buildings.

The roar of a motorcycle grew louder behind him. His heart leaped into his throat. He was surrounded. The silhouette of a soldier above the warehouse spotted him. Raised his rifle. And fired.

Crack!

Joe shut his eyes. Nothing. He should be dead. In pain. He patted down his front, wet from the rain, and frowned. Even with kevlar, he'd feel the hit. The motorcycle roared past. Joe glimpsed two dark-clad riders, the one at the rear stared intensely at Joe, his hand out and making a fist. Blue face mask. Joe looked back to his front with a gasp, hardly able to believe his own eyes. Suspended before his face, catching drops of rain, was a spinning bullet halted by an unseen force—Greed.

The bullet dropped impotently to the dirt. *Holy shit.*

The bike sped toward the plant. Another engine roared in the distance, perhaps on the other side. Above the warehouse, beneath the light of a cloud-covered moon, two figures encroached upon the soldier who'd fired at Joe. They dispatched the guard together and then faced each other, both in an attack-ready stance. One big Deadly Seven warrior, and one smaller Sinner. They launched at each other. The chink of clashing metal echoed across the night.

They weren't his problem. Joe ducked and dashed for the ware-house where he'd heard Liza's scream.

twenty-eight

LIZA LAZARUS

THE AGONY in Liza's hands radiated through her body. Why, Daisy? She rolled into a fetal position, cradling her hands. Her tormented head spun, but she'd handled pain before. They'd trained by smashing shins and knuckles into hardwood trees. They'd hung suspended from nooses to toughen their necks. They'd smashed their hands against stone walls to condition for pain.

She blinked with understanding.

Her hands were tougher than her mind led her to believe. Taking a breath through her nose, she steeled herself and forced her fingers to uncurl, wincing at the scraping of agony radiating up her arms. Her fingers had moved. Good. They weren't broken. The kevlar-type fabric of the gloves perhaps had saved her. Pushing the tip of her tongue against the gag, she used her damaged fingers to tug it out, gasping with relief when the mask tumbled to the ground.

Another few calming breaths and she used her teeth to tug the fingertips of her gloves, inching them off until her hands were bare. She held her trembling fingers before her face. They were red, sore, but in one piece. Already tingling as they healed.

A single gunshot fired outside. Something had a guard spooked. Probably her family. If they were here, then shit was about to get messy. Multiple gunshots went off behind the cooler door, and then it went silent. What was Daisy thinking? Whose side was she on?

If there were gunshots in there, Daisy had attacked.

Sounds of battle increased. She was running out of time. Her only weapons were the shuriken still attached to her belt, but she had no hand power to remove them by force. She'd have to use other parts of her body then, feet, head, elbows. Poison.

Liza jogged to the refrigerator door but heard wails coming from deeper in the plant. People were injured.

"Liza."

She turned, eyes wide. Joe darted in and out of machinery to get to her. Dressed in tactical attire, he had his firearm at the ready, and eyes stuck on her. Her stomach flipped at the sight of him.

"What are you doing here?" she hissed. "Goddammit. It's dangerous."

"Don't fucking ask me to leave," he replied.

She ground her teeth, part furious that he'd risked himself, part ecstatic that he loved her enough to find her. She kissed him quickly, but then pulled back with a wince.

"What happened?" he asked.

"Daisy crushed my hands." She held them up. "But I'm good."

Crashes, bangs, and gunfire reverberated through the building.

"Your family is here," Joe explained.

Liza looked at the cooler door. Whether Daisy was on their side, or she'd escaped, Liza had to take care of the replicate tanks. And Julius. That fucker won't see her coming.

She moved. Joe followed, but she stopped him.

"I'm coming with you," he insisted.

She pointed toward the other room where she'd heard the pained

groans. "Remember those sketches of pregnant women and people in pain? I need you to check in there."

His brows lifted. "You want me to go through the room with meat hooks dangling body bags?"

"Yes. I'm going to the cooler. There are replicate tanks in there. And Julius with armed guards. Please, Joe. Save the people."

"You're hurt."

She forced herself to flex her fingers and kept the wince from her eyes. "I'm good."

He gave one last lingering look and then dashed away. Her love for him rushed to the surface as she watched him go. He was a good man. Whatever happened next, she was happy that she'd had the chance to love him.

Hardening her resolve, she shouldered the cooler door open. What she found made her stomach revolt. The replicate tanks had burst. Water, slime, and bodies were on the floor. Some replicates twitched and convulsed. Some were still. Some climbed onto all fours, testing the mobility of their limbs, about to get up.

Liza scanned the room and found two dead soldiers by the door, each bleeding from a throat wound, their rifles two feet away from them.

Standing in the middle of it all was Daisy with a knife to Julius's throat. She hadn't blacked out as Liza had thought. No, she was in her right mind as she threatened the man who'd ruined her life.

His touch-screen device blinked in his hand, as though he'd activated something—the release of the replicates. The scientist was gone, and the back door was open.

Julius stood stoically, calmly, and hadn't flinched when Liza had entered. As far as those two were concerned, no one else existed.

"If you kill me, it won't change a thing," Julius snarled at Daisy.

"I won't kill you, just your precious family." Daisy held up the locket.

Julius's hand went to his throat, realized it had been removed, and then glared at Daisy. With one hand still holding the knife to his throat, she thumbed open the locket with the other. Julius jerked, attempting to escape, but he nicked his neck and stilled. He eyed the locket as though there was still hope. Two strands of hair poked out from the metal rim. Daisy's nostrils flared, and then she tipped her head back and swallowed the strands, never once shifting her raging eyes from their father.

"You fucking bitch," Julius growled, but she held the knife firm.

"I'm not a bitch. I'm the killer you made me."

His face contorted with rage. "I'll kill you for this. I'll make you suffer."

Desperation was a wonderful thing. It could turn men into gods, if only for a minute. Julius somehow twisted in Daisy's grip, used his device to block her slice at his neck, and attacked his eldest daughter. Her knife glanced off the hard, robust screen.

A slurping sound stole Liza's attention. Two replicates were now standing, testing and flexing their muscles. Ignoring the battle, Liza crept toward the discarded rifles on the floor.

"You kill me," Julius snarled, "and others will come. You know the data exists around the world in labs just like these. I'm the only thing holding the Syndicate at bay. If it were up to them, the war would have started years ago. You *know* I kept you safe from them."

Daisy hesitated. Julius used the opportunity to tap something into his device, somehow still functional. The two replicates that had awoken straightened their spines as though receiving a jolt of electricity, or an electrical command.

For fuck's sake.

Liza aimed her rifles, one in each hand. If they healed like the

Seven, then a bullet might not kill them. But it would slow them the fuck down. Just like her poison.

"Call your dogs off," she warned. "Or I kill them."

Julius laughed. He hit more keys on the device. More replicate tanks exploded, more bodies spilled out.

"Take her," he barked at the two sentient clones. He pointed at Liza. "Secure her and bring her to me."

Liza fired, shooting straight into a clone. He jerked. Then kept coming.

Daisy glanced at Liza and a pained look ghosted her expression.

"Whatever you're thinking, Daisy, no," she shouted.

But her sister refused to listen. Daisy muttered something to Julius just as a loud crash shook the foundations and everyone stumbled. Her family was coming. Liza had to hold on a little longer.

She shut her eyes and let in every iota of panic she'd been holding at bay. All the fear, pain, hurt, and confusion that swamped her when her family was threatened, and welcomed it. Because it triggered her ability. Yellow mist oozed from her mouth. Her aching hands heated, ready to disperse the poison stored beneath her skin.

She inched toward Julius, but his eyes darted between Liza and Daisy, contemplating, and then he nodded as though reaching a decision.

Time seemed to stand still. Horror filled Liza. Daisy had done something. Offered him something.

"Daisy!" Liza shouted.

Daisy let go of her knife. Resigned misty eyes met Liza's and with the drop of her beating heart, Liza *knew*. Her plan to turn Daisy had worked... too well. Daisy had flipped sides. She was making the sacrifice play.

"No." Liza's throat clogged up. *No!*

Daisy whispered, "This is me catching you."

And then she allowed herself to be hustled toward the exit. Replicates blocked the way, hiding them from view as they left the building. The first replicate's veins flashed blue. He had Tony's firepower. *Shit.* They were powered, just like the Seven.

A scream of frustration tore from Liza. She pressed the triggers, a spray of bullets released, catching replicate bodies everywhere. When magazines clicked empty, she dropped the rifles, ran, and picked up Daisy's fallen knife. She whirled into a twister of yellow and red. Poison and blood.

Toxic projectiles hissed like missiles from her left palm into faces, making them flinch, and then she struck with the knife, severing tendons, slicing arteries. Liza screamed through it all, pushing as much toxin as she could from her throat. If she got close enough, she spat into their eyes. They might have recovered if given the time, but she didn't let them.

Time belonged to her, at least for a few moments. It wasn't until she slipped on a long puddle of liquid and almost flipped onto her back, that backup arrived.

"Greed," she rasped and pointed at the exit. "He took her. He took our sister."

Griffin's eyes bore into her as he flourished his long metal bo staff and then stopped to take in the scene. "The fight is still going on outside. There are soldiers everywhere." He pointed at the fallen. "There are more of these things out there. There were other warehouses."

Shit.

Liza's energy waned. Despair trickled in. "You should get out. There's a lot of toxin in this room."

He gave her a last look and left. When Liza turned to survey her devastation, there was nothing but blood and death.

twenty-nine

PARKER LAZARUS

THE SINNER HAD Parker by the throat. His rain battered head hung precariously over the edge of the warehouse roof as the battle raged below them. Every so often, shots were fired. Blue fire flashed on the horizon. Electricity crackled. Metal flew through the air. None of it was directly below, but everywhere at the same time. There were explosions, crashes, and fire. Chaos reigned. He ignored it all to face the threat on top of him.

One enemy at a time. He urged himself to focus on the Sinner.

She was an assassin for the Hildegard Sisterhood, a secret female-only faction of the church. The same organization had wanted Mary to kill seven innocent children born in a lab many decades ago. They weren't comfortable with the fifty-fifty chance of Parker and his siblings turning evil.

He snarled at the woman trying to strangle him, using her sharpened sai in a maneuver that made his brute strength useless. One twitch and he'd take a puncture to the jugular. She was frustratingly dexterous and strong for someone much smaller than him. She was the deadliest person he'd seen in battle since Mary and had drawn shallow blood with her sai, darted out of his reach, and kept it up like an annoying fly. The stamina it took to meet someone like him was remarkable, but he'd not gone without his own wins. She favored one leg, which meant he must have hit her. All he needed to do was exploit her weakness.

He glanced over the edge of the roof. Machinery and meat grinding equipment lay in piles beneath. A gun fired, its bullet ricocheted off equipment. Going down wasn't an option. He wouldn't concede, anyway. He would take this Sinner into custody if it was the last thing he did. Then he would torture her for information.

If he failed, Mary's life would be at risk.

She'd gone against orders, saved Parker and his siblings, and taken them on the run. It might have been thirty-or-so years, but the Sisterhood had found them. Mary always said if they did, then all of their lives were at risk. No one walked away from the Sisterhood.

"We don't have time for this!" the Sinner snarled. Two fierce eyes sparkled over her blood-red face mask. That was all he could see of her face. Even her hair was obscured by the black hood.

The Sinner uniform was similar to the Seven's because Parker had based the design on Mary's original gear. Since AIMI was down, today they were all in their old fighting leathers. A pang of irritation hit him. It was his fault the suits had failed them. He should have come up with a manual override plan in case the computer went down. He knew better.

It was unacceptable.

Parker sucked in his throat, giving himself some slack, and then kneed the Sinner, aiming for her bad leg. He sent her reeling back across the roof, skidding in the rain. Back on his feet, he resumed a standoff with the woman. They circled each other, neither willing to make the next move.

Her sai was now gone, making both their weapons lost some-where over the side of the building. All they had left was their bodies.

That's all he needed. He was stronger, and he had no handicaps. Not like her, with her limp and weak leg. That sai had been her saving grace, and he'd been holding back because he wanted to bring her back to HQ functional.

"I'm here to help," she said.

"Sure you are." He booted her weak knee.

But it was as though she expected it. Her weakness became a strength. She dodged, ducked, flipped back on one hand, used it to support her weight before kicking out with her other leg. He jerked back, missing the sole of her boot by a hair's breadth. They danced *around* each other, *with* each other, and if Parker didn't know she was a liar and killer without compunction, he might have enjoyed himself. But she was right, they didn't have time for this. He had to get down to his family.

What were the Sisterhood doing here?

Maybe they were in on it.

An explosion shook the foundations of the warehouse. He stum-bled. The Sinner used the shift in equilibrium to slam her foot into his sternum. He went back. Back. The horizon tipped, rain pelted his face, and he went over the edge. He scrambled for purchase, his hand gripped the gutter. Slipped. Held. He winced as the metal cut through his old leather gloves and into his palms. Gravity took hold, jerked him down, and his arm almost ripped from his socket.

The fall wasn't far. Two-stories. It was the equipment beneath that worried him. If he fell the wrong way, he'd injure himself. He'd survive, but recovery would be a bitch. Breathing hard, he looked up.

The Sinner's masked face dipped over the roof. Rain pattered her head, leaving a halo of mist that glowed under the faint moonlight.

"You stubborn mule," she chided. "Take my hand."

She reached down.

"Fuck you," he growled, and looked down to calculate the best way to drop.

If he pushed against the wall with his foot, he could get clearance.

At the ground, a dark figure walked into his scope. Another Sinner. She tilted her face up, eyes crinkling. She moved around the equipment and found something.

"What the fuck is she doing?" he mumbled.

The woman pulled a long power cord from beneath the equipment, made a show of searching, and then plugged it into an external socket. She looked up, saluted her friend on the roof, and then pulled a lever on the grinder. The rotating blades started turning.

"Crazy bitch," he snarled.

"Parker," the Sinner shouted above him. Her halo disappeared as a spray of cold rain buffeted the side of her head. "Don't let your pride get in the way."

She did *not* just say that.

She reached again.

He glanced down. *Fucking meat grinder.* Heat rose up his neck and slammed into his face. He would *not* give her the satisfaction. He couldn't. He was better.

"*Parker*," she urged.

The sound of a helicopter gearing up filtered through the din. Someone was getting away. The Deadly Seven were winning, and the bastards that ran this place were fleeing for their lives. *Damn it.* There was no time for pride. He swung his dangling hand up and latched onto the Sinner. She gripped his bare wrist as he gripped hers.

An almighty spark zipped up his arm, sending power soaring through his body. *No!* He knew what this was. This feeling of strength, roaring through him like a wild beast. His bones started to crack. His blood started to boil. He locked eyes with the Sinner.

She seemed to sense something was wrong. Very wrong, and it was. This woman was his mate.

Over his dead body.

He fell.

thirty

JOE LUCIANO

"WHAT IS the meaning of this, Special Agent Luciano?" Director Dixon asked as he strode through the crowded lot of the meatpacking plant. First responders were everywhere, from the Fire Department, to paramedics, to the Feds, SWAT and the local police. Dixon wasn't happy to be one of the last on the scene. "I told you to investigate the Deadly Seven, not..." He surveyed the devastation, illuminated by the blue and red of law enforcement. "Whatever hell hole this is."

Joe cast his eye over the mess, trying to be patient and to see what his director saw. Yes, there were mercenary bodies, slimy replicate bodies, and blood sprayed on walls. A meat grinder had remnants of Parker's body matter. The warehouse was riddled with bullet holes. Not to mention the dead bodies hanging from meat hooks, the broken replicate tanks, and evidence of more blood thirsty battle. Forensics were having a field day. The Deadly Seven had truly come in, decimated, and conquered. But if they hadn't arrived in time to catch the clones while they were fresh and still learning how to use their limbs, the body count might tell a different story.

Joe was grateful Briggs, Houlahan and the rest of the CCPD

arrived when he'd eventually called it in. They were first on the scene which meant the director couldn't sweep this under the rug.

"With all due respect, sir, I did. That investigation led me here."

"So they're responsible for this mess?"

Joe jerked back, incredulous. "No. Well, sort of. They stopped these clones from wreaking too much havoc, but they had nothing to do with the experiments."

"Destruction of property isn't exactly the charge we were hoping to bring against the vigilantes."

Captain Morais arrived and cleared his throat. He settled his shark eyes on the director. "You should be commending your agent, director, not chastising him. What he's done tonight is a win for our side of the law. Any fool can see that."

Dixon's eyebrows raised so high, they almost disappeared into his hairline. But the captain didn't back down.

"In fact," Morais continued. "If you're unhappy with Luciano, then we'll take him back. With a raise." He faced Joe. "Your work has been stellar. Not only did you capture the Ripper killer, but you saved one of our own, and uncovered this shit show at the same time. We would be lucky to have you back. You're a credit to our team. What do you say, Luciano?"

Joe didn't have the heart to tell him that much of what had happened was circumstance, but then again, a lot wasn't. Captain Morais was right, he'd successfully juggled three incidents, all with optimal outcomes, all finished on the right side of the law. Maybe he was better off working in this city. He was reaching the age of retirement for a Fed. Only a few more years and guys like Geoff would be in their prime at the agency.

Joe turned in the direction Liza had left in the back of an ambulance. She'd surreptitiously removed her Deadly Seven outfit, handed it to her family, and then stayed in her underwear until backup arrived. It made her look like one of the kidnapping victims they'd rescued, who were also at the hospital receiving care. A part of him still felt wrong about keeping these secrets, but he knew now that, in doing so, he was making the world a better place. He also knew the lie wasn't the first step to becoming like his father. He would never be like that man, no matter what. And he also knew he didn't need to strive to be better, to impress Parker, or gain his respect.

He may not fly from building to building, or have any superpowers, but Joe respected himself. He was where he needed to be, with Liza—helping her and her family. He'd found where he belonged.

He smiled at the captain. "This city has a piece of my heart. I'd love to stay, sir. Whether that's with the Feds, or with you, remains to be seen. One thing I know for sure is that this investigation is only beginning, but I'm going to see it through to the end."

Joe glanced at the director, hoping he got the message. Joe would investigate the Syndicate, hopefully with the FBI's blessing, but if he was road blocked, he'd find a way to continue elsewhere. Nothing would stop him now.

thirty-one

LIZA LAZARUS

THE WAILS of a baby filtered into the waiting room of the maternity ward in Cardinal City General Hospital. Like the rest of her family, Liza had come straight here after they'd returned home and cleaned up. She'd double scrubbed in the shower to remove any toxin from herself. Joe stayed at the packing plant. She'd wanted to stay with him, but knew it wasn't possible.

There would be more instances like this where she had to leave him to do his job. But on the upside, she had more freedom to live her life. Like now. At least until her suspension was over, and then she was returning to work. She would find a way to balance her two lives eventually, and if she had to take some time off while things heated with the Syndicate, then that's what she'd do. But her blood would always be blue.

A newborn baby cried.

"Was that us?" she asked Lilo, also pacing in the waiting room.

"I don't know. Griff, go ask someone." She patted her husband on the chest. He flinched at the sudden contact, but then softened his gaze on his wife.

"I'll be back," he said.

Tony and Bailey were there too, snuggled into a corner seat, preferring to wait virtually attached to each other. Sloan and Max were somewhere walking the halls. Mary and Flint remained at home. Mary had been injured more than she admitted, and moving was causing her pain, but she refused to send herself to the hospital. Not when there were so many of them here already.

Parker was in surgery, a floor down, being operated on by a colleague of Grace's. Sometimes they could triage in the medical room in the basement headquarters, but Parker was usually the one performing any emergency care. Grace was already at the hospital, so Evan had brought Parker straight here through a back entrance. "Grace will make sure he's patched up." His faith in his mate was echoed by the whole family.

Liza checked her cell for the ten millionth time. Nothing from Evan, but Joe was parking and on his way up. Her stomach did a flip flop, and she felt an emotional burn at the back of her throat. God, she couldn't wait to put her arms around him.

Misha had been in labor for hours. When Daisy had pushed her, Liza had been so frightened, but the long labor wasn't because of that. The baby was fine. Misha's waters broke because of the fall, sending her into premature labor. Apparently, they'd arrived and her labor stopped. Just like that. They induced it again, only for it to stop. Again.

From what Liza had learned from Lilo, Misha had gone through a few rounds of oxytocin to keep the labor progressing.

"No update on Parks?" Sloan asked, coming from the hallway that stocked a vending machine. She ripped open a candy bar and shoved it in her mouth.

Liza shook her head.

"He'll be fine," Sloan said. "He always is."

"It will grow back, right?" Max murmured, putting his arm around Sloan.

Both Liza and Sloan sent him a grim look. The truth was, they didn't know. Wyatt's voice box had grown back, and all of Gloria's notes said they could regenerate. But an entire arm?

"What did I miss?"

Liza twirled at Joe's deep voice, and she ran into his arms like a little girl, only wincing slightly at the residual pain in her hands.

"Hey," he murmured and took her into an embrace. "I missed you too."

He kissed her hair softly, and Liza melted into him.

"I'm so glad you're here," she whispered and buried her face into his chest. She inhaled his masculine, sweaty smell. It was heaven, and she couldn't wait to fall asleep next to him tonight. And every night.

He grinned down at her.

"Did everything go fine?" she asked.

"As expected. Oh, I just remembered." He patted his suit pocket and brought a tall, thin box out. "I got you a gift."

Liza's mouth parted. "What?"

"Probably not the right time, but I figure if we're waiting, you can open it. It's silly, really."

Warmth bloomed in her chest. She glanced at the box, then met his eyes. "I had a present for you too, but... I lost it."

"Was it the baseball?" he asked. "Because I found that."

Relief washed over her. "You did? Where was it?"

"Under my couch."

"Oh." She had fond memories of his kitchen floor. Perhaps she'd knocked it from the boxes she'd brought in the previous night.

"Open it," Joe said, looking at the package.

She ripped it open. Inside was a small packet of reusable metal straws. She laughed. "Okay. Straws."

His eyes lit up. "Perfect, right?"

They locked eyes. "Yep. Perfect."

Double doors to the birthing suite opened, and Wyatt stalked out, his face a mixture of exhaustion and astonishment. He wore one of those disposable hospital gowns and had smears of pink over his chest.

Shit.

Liza's heart thudded a million miles an hour. She couldn't take any more bad news. Not tonight. Not when there had been so much already.

He looked around, dazed.

"Wyatt?" She stepped forward.

Tony and Bailey slowly got to their feet. Everyone inched closer, holding their breaths.

Wyatt blinked. "It's a girl."

A unanimous roar burst out. The men clapped Wyatt on the back. The women hugged him. Liza was smiling so hard, her cheeks hurt.

"Misha?" Lilo asked in the sudden silence.

Wyatt nodded. "She's okay. The baby was strong. Misha needed stitches and was taken to the operating room."

"She's okay, though?" Lilo asked.

He nodded. "She's doing great."

"And the baby?" Liza asked.

He grinned. Liza had never seen him so happy. Tears glistened in his eyes.

"She's with the nurses getting checked. I just wanted to come out quickly and—"

The double doors opened again, but this time a nurse came out. In her arms was a swaddled baby girl, all wrinkled and sleeping. She handed the precious cargo to Wyatt, who froze, petrified.

"You want me to take her?"

"You're the father, right?" The nurse smirked.

He nodded.

"Then she's all yours." The nurse handed her over.

"Misha?" he asked. "Is she out?"

"Doc said she's fine. They had to put her under, so she's in recovery. She'll want to see you both when she's out."

He nodded, then turned to everyone. "I better get back."

But no one was looking at him. They all had eyes for the wondrous new life in his arms.

"What's her name?" Liza asked.

"Amari," he replied. "It means a miracle."

As they all watched Wyatt disappear into the maternity ward, silence descended. Liza pondered the little miracle of life and was grateful that even in the darkest times, something wonderful could exist. That little girl would grow to be loved. She would have a full life, protected by so many loyal uncles and aunties. She was hard evidence that miracles were possible, and the battle they fought had something worth it at the end. She was proof that sometimes the long road was worth it. They would need the reminder in times to come because Liza had a feeling life was about to get darker.

"Who needs a fucking drink?" she asked.

Around the room, voices raised in agreement. But it was another voice that grabbed her attention.

"I'm down for that," Evan said as he strolled in, Grace on his arm.

Surgery must be over. They both looked shattered but in good spirits.

"How is he?" Liza asked.

Grace smiled gently. "He's recovering as expected for an amputee."

"He doesn't want to speak to anyone," Evan said, heading off any further questions. "The baby?"

Liza grinned. "It's a girl."

"Shit." Evan groaned and then dipped his hand into his pocket to pull out two twenty-dollar bills. He handed one to each, Liza and Sloan. "You win. It was a girl."

"Thank you, very much." Sloan pocketed both bills.

"Hey!" Liza tried to snatch her cut.

"What?" Sloan shrugged innocently. "I'll buy the first round."

They laughed, and one by one, each couple filtered out of the room. Liza and Joe were the last to leave. She hesitated at the threshold, looking back in the direction of the maternity ward.

"You think they'll be okay?" she asked.

"Nope," Joe laughed. "Wyatt's not going to know what hit him. A girl." He whistled through his teeth. "She's going to have him wrapped around her little fingers."

Liza smiled but thwacked Joe on the chest. "I meant... you know, will they be safe here?"

Joe schooled his expression to serious. "Yeah. We did everything right this time. We called it in. The Feds and local law enforcement were all over it, and you're not even a suspect. You're a law-abiding officer who got the wrong end of the stick. Smith is in jail, waiting on sentencing. We're all good."

"Well, not all of us."

Daisy's last words had tattooed on Liza's heart.

"This is me catching you."

Her sister hadn't known what Liza was capable of. Hell, Liza hadn't been sure herself. But ripping through fifty-odd replicates was a surprise to her too. Maybe if Daisy had trusted her more, she wouldn't have sacrificed herself. Maybe if she'd waited just a little longer, Liza could have caught *her* as she'd promised.

"Come on," Joe said, giving Liza a gentle tug. "Let's go get that drink. Take that straw for a test drive."

She forced herself to relax and give a smile because a drink did sound nice. For once she'd be able to go out to a bar and not feel the slimy sense of lust oozing off the walls. As long as she had Joe, she had a future. A long one.

And as long as they had each other, anything was possible.

Even saving Daisy.

epilogue

THE PASSAGE of time had become irrelevant to Despair as she huddled in a fetal position on a medical gurney in some dank, dark place. Something inside her had broken. Snapped. She was no longer Despair. She was no longer Daisy. She had no name, no past, no present, no future. She floated in a sea of emptiness, a vast expanse of existence.

All she had was never ending pain and small moments of reprieve between scientific procedures.

The door opened behind her. Light washed the filthy wall ahead and brightened the small green stain that had become her only companion. She clutched her fists to her chest. She rolled in on herself—he liked it better that way, so her spine was open. The scientist said nothing as he brushed aside the opening of her medical gown to press something cold between her vertebrae.

She tensed in preparation for what inevitably came next, for what always came next. They wanted her to scream, to cry, to shudder. But she gave them nothing. They'd taken everything... except... she glanced down, opened her trembling fist—just a little, a crack—and locked eyes on the crushed daisy bud she'd picked from the bonsai plant.

When the needle pierced her spine, agony paralyzed her. Just as well, because if she blinked, then the daisy would disappear and take with it the last of her hope.

Thank you for reading Liza's and Joe's story.
If you loved reading their story, please consider leaving a review on Amazon. Other readers will thank you, and the author will be eternally grateful.
Review on Amazon.

characters &
glossary

THE DEADLY SEVEN

(Appearance in order of age from youngest to eldest)

ENVY: Evan Lazarus
SLOTH: Sloan Lazarus
GLUTTONY: Tony Lazarus
GREED: Griffin Lazarus
LUST: Liza Lazarus
WRATH: Wyatt Lazarus
PRIDE: Parker Lazarus
DESPAIR: Daisy Lazarus

Mary Lazarus: Adoptive Mother of the Deadly Seven and ex assassin for the Hildegard Sisterhood
Flint Lazarus: Adoptive Father of the Deadly Seven

OTHER CHARACTERS:

Dr. Grace Go: Surgeon at Cardinal City General Hospital. Mate to Evan Lazarus.

Lilo Likeke: Investigative reporter at the Cardinal Copy. Mate to Griffin Lazarus.

Misha Minski: Yoga instructor, exotic dancer and Mate to Wyatt Lazarus.

Maximillian Johnson: Sloan's mate and owner of the Nightingale Securities firm.

Bailey Haze: Tony's mate and ex CIA operative.

Joe Luciano: Liza Lazarus's mate and FBI Special Agent

THE SYNDICATE

The Syndicate is a secret organization who believe the only way to save the world from its own harmful self is to eradicate all sinners, even if that means destroying half the world.

THE BOSS: Julius Allcott

SARA MADDEN: Ex-girlfriend of Wyatt Lazarus

FALCON/DESPAIR/DAISY: Enforcer for the Syndicate and lost eldest sister to the Deadly Seven.

BARRY PINKERTON: Old friend of Flint's and ex employee of the Syndicate. He's now in hiding with his daughter.

LEVI VAN JANSEN: Evil Syndicate geneticist.

THE HILDEGARD SISTERHOOD

The Hildegard Sisterhood are nuns with a history reaching back to medieval times when the original Sister Hildegard struggled against a male dominated clergy. Now the world know her as the founder of scientific history in Germany, but back then, her opinions were disregarded until she claimed to have visions from God himself. Belittling herself as a woman in order to be heard was only the beginning of the humiliation the woman faced.

So she started her own abbey filled with women. That same abbey exists today and is a place where women are celebrated and their education encouraged—minus the male influence. Records at the Sisterhood archives reveal they had a hand in the rise of many women over history from *Joan of Arc* to *Indira Gandhi*. From *Catherine the Great* to *Margaret Thatcher*.

Under the surface of the auspicious abbey lays the secret mission that no woman will ever suffer the same struggle as Hildegard and they condition a select few "Sinners" to enforce this mission. These Sinners are trained as assassins for the cause: Sinners like Mary Lazarus. A necessary evil.

In the prequel novella, *Sinner*, Mary Lazarus escaped the Sisterhood who wanted to use the children for their own gain, much like the Syndicate who created them. To this day, she is still on the run.

join lana's vips

Subscribe to Lana's newsletter and receive a free box set, first dibs on giveaways, special printable freebies and more. You won't want to miss out.

subscribe.lanapecherczyk.com

On Facebook? Join Lana's Angels Reader Group https://www.facebook.com/groups/lanasangels

about the author

OMG! How do you say my name?

Lana (straight forward enough - Lah-nah) **Pecherczyk** (this is where it gets tricky - Pe-her-chick).

I've been called Lana Price-Check, Lana Pera-Chickywack, Lana Pressed-Chicken, Lana Pech...*that girl!* You name it, they said it. So if it's so hard to spell, why on earth would I use this name instead of an easy pen name?

To put it simply, it belonged to my mother. And she was my dream champion. For most of my life, I've been good at one thing – art. The world around me saw my work, and said I should do more of it, so I did. But, when at the age of eight, I said I wanted to write stories, and even though we were poor, my mother came home with a blank notebook and a pencil saying I should follow my dreams, no matter where they take me for they will make me happy. I wasn't very good at it, but it didn't matter because I had her support and I liked it.

She died when I was thirteen, and left her four daughters orphaned. Suddenly, I had lost my dream champion, I was split from my youngest two sisters and had no one to talk to about the challenge of life.

So, I wrote in secret. I poured my heart out daily to a diary and sometimes imagined that she would listen. At the end of the day, even if she couldn't hear, writing kept that dream alive.

Eventually, after having my own children (two firecrackers in the guise of little boys) and ignoring my inner voice for too long, I decided to lead by example. How could I teach my children to follow their dreams if I wasn't? I became my own dream champion and the rest is history, here I am.

When I'm not writing the next great action-packed romantic novel, or wrangling the rug rats, or rescuing GI Joe from the jaws of my Kelpie, I fight evil by moonlight, win love by daylight and never run from a real fight. I live in Australia, but I'm up for a chat anytime online. Come and find me.

Subscribe & Follow
subscribe.lanapecherczyk.com
lp@lanapecherczyk.com

facebook.com/lanapecherczykauthor

instagram.com/lana_p_author

amazon.com/-/e/B00V2TP0HG

bookbub.com/profile/lana-pecherczyk

tiktok.com/@lanapauthor

goodreads.com/lana_p_author

www.ingramcontent.com/pod-product-compliance
Lightning Source LLC
Chambersburg PA
CBHW030420120726
47904CB00007B/2356